FIRE AND FURY

WILLIAM A. DUCK

I DEDICATE THIS TO MY FAMILY

I want to thank my wife, without her encouragement, I would not
have written this book.
My sons for cheering me on.
To my brother and sister for being you.
To my late Mom and Dad, who were always there to listen.
To my family, I thank you. Without you, I am nothing.

Contents

Chapter 1 The Beginning 1

Chapter 2 Growing Up 15

Chapter 3 Good to be Home. 21

Chapter 4 Captain James D. Thomas 30

Chapter 5 Eyes for each other 40

Chapter 6 The Next Day 47

Chapter 7 Europe's Messes..54

Chapter 8 Back in time 60

Chapter 9 Shoot, don't Shoot..68

Chapter 10 Your Delicate Mission 78

Chapter 11 Long Flights 85

Chapter 12 Safe House 93

Chapter 13 Intel gathering 99

Chapter 14 Target 108

Chapter 15 After Math..114

Chapter 16 Kwajalein Missile Range 125

Chapter 17 The Visit...131

Chapter 18 Training and Recon 139

Chapter 19 Training in the Desert..148

Chapter 20 Prepping for Beirut..157

Chapter 21 Beirut...165

Chapter 22 Threat in Beirut 171

Chapter 23 Fury 183

Chapter 24 Holiday and Marriage 189

Chapter 25 Bad Guy 197

Chapter 26 No matter how long it takes. 206

Chapter 27 Back to the Farm and another Tour 212

Chapter 28 Vengeance and the Trigger 218

Chapter 29 Target 223

Chapter 30 Team Up 231

Chapter 31 Three months later. 244

Chapter 32 Tradition 261

EPILOGUE 268

Chapter 1

The Beginning

Elizabeth Allen was born the only child of Mr. and Mrs. Joseph and Isabella Allen at Womack Army Medical Center at Fort Bragg, North Carolina, at 7 pounds and two oz. They were typical parents doting on their daughter and how lucky they were to have her. Joseph was a Green Beret Captain in the 3Rd SF Group (Airborne) at Fort Bragg, North Carolina, who had a solid Army military career going for him after he had graduated at the top of his West Point class. Being at the top of your class is a big mark in his military folder and is a guaranteed general if you do an excellent job or stay out of trouble. Everyone knew Joseph was highly intelligent, and Joseph seemed to keep his cards extremely close to him. His friends always said it was hard to read him at times, and he admitted they were right, but he knew it was always to his advantage if people could not read him.

Joseph married Isabella, and he would always brag she was smarter than him by miles and she had a bigger heart. Isabella was a registered nurse and worked at the Dukes Children's Specialty Services, helping children with disabilities. She loved the work and challenge of helping these children, helping them recover from their medical problems or adapt to get through their lives with the problems they were born with.

Isabella was the sister of Robert Sturgill, Joseph's classmate. He introduced Joseph to Isabella while they were at the West Point Academy dance during Joseph's 3rd year at the Army military academy. Robert Sturgill was a good friend at the academy and throughout their long careers in the army. Robert Sturgill went in a different direction in the army than Joseph. He went into the intelligence community because he was the brainy type and loved the mental challenge it would have for him.

Joseph and Isabella dated for a few years, and Joseph finally proposed to her before he went off to train to be a Green Beret. Once he completed his training, he married Isabella after he received his Green Beret. Isabella later gave up her career as a nurse to be a full-time mother of their child, who was named Elizabeth after Isabella's sister.

Mr. and Mrs. Allen were living the military life when she delivered Elizabeth. Everything was going fine during their marriage except for the parts where Captain Allen had to leave for his combat tours or training exercises. The good thing was that he only received minor injuries during any of his tours compared to other soldiers. They lived at his parent's farm due to his parents insisting on them living with them.

The Allen family was well-liked in the Green Beret community and were invited to all the military get-togethers. Captain Allen had many friends and was well-respected in the SF community. This all changed in a blink of an eye on a sunny Tuesday afternoon. The accident rocked the Green Beret community due to the tragedy of the young wife of an up-and-coming soldier and officer.

Captain Allen would end up being a widower with a little girl to raise upon Isabella's death in a traffic accident in Fayetteville, North Carolina, outside Fort Bragg. Isabella was killed by a drunk civilian driver, Herbert Clinton. He left a small local bar celebrating winning a thousand dollars from a lotto ticket. He never won anything during his life and was celebrating hard due to his luck turning around.

The bartender at the club, whose name was Lewis told the investigators when he was interviewed about the car wreck and said Mr. Clinton brought rounds for everyone and had several for himself. The bartender also mentioned that Herbert ended up buying another bottle and walked out before Herbert realized that the person had left with the bottle. The bartender told the investigator he did not permit people to leave with a bottle knowing he could lose his license and be prosecuted and held liable for the accident. Lewis said he was aware nobody is supposed to walk out with a bottle at any time.

Isabella and Elizabeth were heading to the Cross Creek Mall, which is close to Fort Bragg, to shop for some new clothes and shoes. Elizabeth was barely two years old when she lost her mom. When she got older, she would say she remembers a little about her mom but not a lot. Elizabeth would always say she was incredibly lucky not to have been killed by the drunk driver. She always felt the child seat had saved her life, and being in the back seat was a lifesaver. Elizabeth would always push child seats to everyone and use her story as an example of the importance of child seats and how they save lives.

The drunk driver was driving in the wrong way, and it was a head-on collision. The drunk driver ignored all the swerving vehicles believing they were driving the wrong way. Herbert crossed the intersection and turned onto another road when the car in front of Isabella survived to the right to avoid the oncoming car. Isabella did not have any time to swerve out of the way of the oncoming car. Both cars collided, and the large vehicular impact killed both drivers immediately. The other vehicles behind her were able to stop in time to prevent multiple cars from being involved.

Herbert Clinton had a record of eight drunk driving arrests and four different accidents where people were injured, all caused by him. Herbert never served anytime due to smart lawyers and weak prosecution laws. This time, he had not only killed himself; he had also killed an innocent person and ruined a family's life forever. Herbert Clinton's license had been suspended many times, and the fines were not enough to hinder his behavior. An alcoholic is not concerned with driving rules or laws that forbid drinking and driving. Herbert ignored, as usual, the no-license decision and still drove whenever he decided to. As Captain Allen told his friends, "Pathetic judicial loopholes and weak judges continue to force many victim families to have to deal with a system that allows this behavior to continue and ruin lives."

As soon as the accident happened, people stopped their cars, and several men jumped out of their vehicles to attempt to help the victims. The drunk driver was pulled out of his car, but he was already dead. People attempted to get Isabella out of the car, but it was severely damaged, and they were unable to do anything to help her. They could tell she was dead, but they kept trying to get the smashed door open until the fire department arrived.

When the rescue Firefighter crew arrived at the incident scene, it took almost an hour to get her body out of the front seat. At first, the firefighters thought there was no one else in Isabella's car due to the damage to the car. The vehicle was all twisted up. When a firefighter walked by gathering up their tools and equipment, he heard whimpering from the back seat. He realized there was a child in the twisted back seat, and he yelled for more help.

The Firefighters had to use the jaws of life to get both the mother's corpse and little Elizabeth, who was in the baby seat, out of the vehicle. When they got Elizabeth out of the back seat, little Elizabeth was taken and placed on a stretcher and taken to the nearest hospital. She was frightened and shaking and saying over and over again through her tears, "Where is my mommy? I want my mommy."

When little Elizabeth arrived at the hospital by ambulance, they completed a full examination on her with no major injuries, just some scratches and a few small bruises. One of the firefighters who got her out of the vehicle stayed with her the whole time. He was a father and had a couple of children himself. The Firefighter who held her little left hand in the ambulance also told the Doctor her name was Elizabeth when they first arrived at the hospital. Elizabeth had whispered it to him in the ambulance when he asked her what her name was. She was scared and kept asking, "Where is my mommy, and where is my daddy?"

The Firefighter could not answer her, and he knew it was not up to him to tell this frightened, scared little girl about her mom being killed in the car wreck. He did ask, "Where is your daddy?" Elizabeth smiled and said, "He is in the army."

A few minutes later, a police officer arrived and gave the last name of the child as Allen. The police had run the plates to find out who owned the vehicle and who the victim was. The driver's license found in the victim's purse also helped.

The emergency room Head Nurse walked by and saw several cops and firefighters surrounding a bed, looking at someone. She walked over to see what was going on and told them to step back, to which they complied. The Head Nurse, Shirley, was stunned when she saw Elizabeth. Shirley asked the men what had happened, and the police traffic investigator told her about the unfortunate accident.

 Shirley started to get teary-eyed and covered her mouth. Shirley then told the officer she knew the family. Shirley told the officer that Elizabeth's dad was in the army with her husband. She then stepped away from everyone with tears coming from her eyes and, using her cell phone, called her husband. Her husband, Walter Gear, was the First Sargent in the same SF group, but he was in a meeting on base.

Shirley Gear, with tears in her eyes, kept calling her husband and leaving messages on his blackberry cell phone. She kept leaving the same message for her husband to call her back because it was an emergency.

Shirley called his unit. Specialist Davidson, a unit clerk, answered the phone with, "How can I help you, Sir or Madam?" She told Specialist Davidson who she was, and he immediately said, "Yes, ma'am. What can I do for you?"

"I need to speak with my husband. It is an emergency." Shirley stated.

"Your husband is in a meeting. Do you want me to interrupt it?" Specialist Davidson further said.

"Yes, please. Write on a piece of paper, Car wreck, CPT Allen's wife killed. Hurry, please call me."

He told her he would notify him immediately. Still crying, she thanked him.

Specialist Davidson hung up the phone and ran out of the building to the Group Battalion Headquarters in a full sprint. He ran up the stairs and into the building. Specialist Davidson ran to the room where the meeting was and knocked hard on the door. There was no answer, but he knew they were in there. He knocked on the door again, and this time louder. Seconds later, he heard a loud voice say, "Enter."

Specialist Davidson opened the door and saluted Lieutenant Colonel Milusnic, who was near the door. Lieutenant Colonel Milusnic saluted back and said in a strong tone of voice, "Why in the hell, Specialist, are you interrupting my meeting?" Specialist Davidson answered, "Sir, I have an important message for 1SGT Gear." 1SGT Gear stood up and waved the Specialist over. Once the Specialist handed the note over, 1SGT Gear looked at the message, and his mouth opened in shock. His face showed concern, and he said the word, "Damn it."

Lieutenant Colonel Milusnic, seeing the expression on 1SGT Gears' face, knew something bad had happened. He asked 1SGT

Gear, "Is everything all right?" 1SGT Gear answered back, "No, Sir." 1SGT Gear stepped up to the Lieutenant colonel (BC) and showed him the piece of paper. Lieutenant Colonel Milusnic stated, "Damn." He then turned to everyone and stated, "Captain Allen's wife was killed in a car wreck."

Everyone was shocked. Some cussed in anger about the bad news. Everyone liked Allen; he was loyal, hardworking, and always willing to help anyone whenever they needed help or advice. Lieutenant Colonel Milusnic then yelled, "Meeting is over," and turned to the battalion Sargent Major Robertson and told him to "find Allen and get his ass here right now." The Battalion Sargent Major stated back, "Absolutely, Sir, he is in the field with his Company."

Captain Allen was in the field at the time, observing his company's teams during the field exercises. It took about two hours to locate him due to his location deep in the backwoods of Fort Bragg. His communication system was turned off so he could properly monitor the exercise with which his teams were involved. While standing on top of a MOUNT site building, Captain Allen's XO Lieutenant Keller came running through the woods at a full sprint, sweating profusely due to the heat and humanity. He ran up to one of the observers and asked where Captain Allen was. The observer then pointed in his direction. Once Lieutenant Keller climbed the stairs, he ran to Captain Allen and tried to catch his breath; he finally told Captain Allen "he needed to call the BC immediately."

Captain Allen thanked Lieutenant Keller and turned his communication system back on, and he called the Battalion Commander on the radio. The Battalion Commander answered and told him "to report back to his unit asap with no delay and Grab a chopper and get here asap." Captain Allen then asked, "what is going on?" The BC told him that there was a family emergency and he needed to get to his unit immediately. The BC said he wanted to tell him, but he did not want to discuss it on the radio with everyone listening. Besides that, he wanted to do it the right way, face to face.

Captain Allen commandeered a Humvee and drove to the location where the Blackhawks were staged in the field. He told the pilots to "get the bird up and get me back to my Company Headquarters at all speed." Captain Talt, who was nearby, asked Captain Allen if everything was alright. Captain Allen said, "no." They were friends, and the chopper Pilot Captain Talt was one class behind him at the academy. Captain Talt, seeing the concern on Captain Allen's face, patted Captain Allen on the shoulder and said, "Get in. I will get you there as fast as I can push this bird." They took off and headed back to the company area.

While sitting in the Black Hawk, wondering what was going on and why he needed to report back to his company, Joseph knew Captain Talt had the bird heading back to the company area at max speed. Captain Allen sat in his seat, looking out the side window and rubbing his hands nervously.

Captain Allen was feeling nauseous during the flight back because not knowing what had happened was driving him nuts. He knew something bad had happened, and he thought something must have happened to his mom or dad because of their age. It never even crossed his mind about what he was getting ready to be told by his superiors.

After about 35 minutes, the Black Hawk landed outside the company area in a field that was not authorized for choppers. A First Lieutenant came running up, yelling about the chopper illegally landing here. Captain Allen jumped out and told the Lieutenant to "shut the hell up" and ran to his company headquarters. The Lieutenant immediately complied and saluted.

Captain Allen ran as fast as he could move. Captain Talt saw Captain Allen have words with a Lieutenant and then began running to his company, so he shut the bird down and got out to find out what was going on. He looked at the Lieutenant, who saluted him, and Captain Talt returned the salute and told the Lieutenant the "best thing he can do is let it go." The Lieutenant said, "Yes, sir," and headed back to his company. Captain Talt then headed to Captain Allen's company area to see what happened.

When Captain Allen entered the company building, he observed the Battalion Commander LTC Milusnic with the Sargent Major outside his office. Captain Allen saluted his Battalion Commander, who returned the salute. All of them entered his office, and the Battalion Commander told Captain Allen to "please sit down." Captain Allen drenched in sweat, stated, "No disrespect, sir, I would rather stand and say what is the emergency, sir?"

Captain Allen then looked around and saw the Chaplin walk in, and then Captain Allen, in a firm but angry tone, asked, "What the hell is going on, Sir?" The Chaplin stepped up to him and told him, "Son, I am so sorry, but your wife died four hours ago."

Jospeh was stunned and, after a minute of quiet, got teary-eyed. In a choked-up voice, he asked, "how?" He felt his legs weaken, so he sat down. The Chaplin told him what had happened and "how his wife was killed immediately in the car accident." The Chaplin also told him the "other driver was also killed." The police said "he was drunk." The firefighters smelled alcohol coming from his body, and there was a half-drunken bottle of rum in the car. The bottle was discovered on the floor of the passenger seat, and it was not even broken.

After a few minutes of trying to sort it out in his head, Captain Allen looked up and asked, "Where is my daughter?" The Chaplin told him, "She is doing fine and was saved by being in the back seat strapped in her car seat." The Chaplin started to ask a question when the Battalion Commander cut in and looked at the Sargent Major and stated, "take Captain Allen wherever he needs to go, and

Chappy go with them." The Chaplin responded, "Yes, sir." The BC was fond of Captain Allen because he reminded him a lot of himself when he was a younger soldier. They always got along, and he saw things in Captain Allen on the possibilities of how far he could go in his career. He helped mentor Captain Allen and was amazed at how quickly he picked things up and took care of business, and was very respected by everyone.

Before they left the Company area, the Lieutenant Colonel's Vehicle drove up. Lieutenant Colonel Milusnic stepped out and up to Captain Allen, stating, "Son, if you need anything, and I mean anything, you call anytime. My thoughts and prayers for your wife and family." Then the Group Command, a vehicle drove up, and Colonel Antonelli stepped out and approached Lieutenant Colonel Milusnic and Captain Allen, who were saluting him. Colonel Antonelli saluted back and then said, "Captain Allen, my condolences." Captain Allen said, "Thank you, sir." Colonel Antonelli then asked, "How was his daughter?" Captain Allen said, "His daughter is fine," and shook the Colonel's hand and stated, "Thank you, sir, for your support." Colonel Antonelli looked at the BC and said, "He is being taken care of, right?" The BC said, "Absolutely, boss." Everyone saluted the Colonel, and he stepped back in his vehicle and drove away.

Once he arrived at the morgue, Captain Allen, the Sargent Major, and the Chaplin walked into the building. Captain Allen was taken to a room where he had to identify his wife. The Morgue staff pulled the sheet back, and Captain Allen was still stunned, even knowing his wife was dead before he got to the morgue. His eyes began to water when he caught himself and wiped his eyes. The Sargent Major stepped over to him and said, "Son, let's go." The morgue staff apologized and recovered her up, and stepped back. Captain Allen then signed some paperwork that was required to sign for the body to be released to the funeral parlor.

Captain Allen was taken back to the Company parking lot where his car was, and the Sargent Major asked Captain Allen if he was going to be okay. Captain Allen said, "No, but I guess I must step up for my daughter's sake." The Chaplin gave Captain Allen his number to call if he needed to talk. He said, "Thanks, Chappy. I will call you tomorrow."

Captain Allen went to his car and got in. He sat there for a few minutes looking at his steering wheel, trying not to lose his composure, but he couldn't. It started to rain, and he started to cry, not for himself but for losing the woman he loved. Then after about ten minutes, he wiped his eyes and drove to pick up his daughter from the hospital. Once he arrived at the hospital emergency room, he was taken to the room where his daughter was.

Captain Allen recognized Shirley and her husband, who was watching his daughter. There was also the same firefighter who pulled Elizabeth out of the car and rode to the hospital in the ambulance. Captain Allen shook the firefighters' hand and said," Thank you for everything you've done." The firefighter stated, "No problem." He continued saying he had a daughter about her age, and he just couldn't leave her alone.

Captain Allen then gave Shirley and her husband a hug and said, "Thank you for everything. I could never repay you." They told Captain Allen, "Don't worry about it." He then shook 1SGT Gear's hand and said, "Thanks, I owe you and Shirley so much." 1SGT Gear then said, "Boss, we are here for you, and Shirley said if you ever need someone to watch her, call me." Captain Allen said, "Thank you," and again gave them hugs. He signed his daughter out, carried her to their car, and then they went to his parent's farm.

Both of his parents knew what had happened and were outside on the porch waiting on him and Elizabeth. Friends of Captain Allen's have been calling the house all day since Captain Allen was not answering his cell phone.

Captain Allen saw his mom crying and his dad with a sad expression on his face. When he and Elizabeth walked up onto the porch, his parents hugged him and little Elizabeth. He asked his mom if she could put Elizabeth to bed after she ate, and his mom nodded her head. Elizabeth turned to her dad and asked, "Where is mommy?" Everyone got quiet. He picked her up and walked inside the house, where she ate dinner. He decided to tell her after he took his daughter to her room and put her to bed. While being tucked in, she asked again, "Where is mommy?" He looked at his daughter and whispered, "Mommy is in heaven, and she is watching you." Elizabeth smiled, "When will I see her?" she asked.

"I don't know, but she loves you, and she will be with you."

With a simple *okay*, she closed her eyes to sleep. Joseph then stepped out of the room and went downstairs.

His parents were waiting for him. His mom was all crying out and hugged her son again and said, "I am so sorry, Joseph."

"I know. It's going to be all right," he replied.

Joseph stepped over to his dad and hugged him. He walked to the living room and sat down. He was exhausted, dirty, and tired. Joseph looked at his parents as they sat down, and he scratched his head. He looked down and then looked up and said, "Mom, Dad…. I will need help raising her." His parents said, "Do not worry about her, son, she is our granddaughter, and we will help raise her as if she was our daughter."

"Thanks. I love you both."

"We love you, and we are proud of you, son."

Joseph closed his eyes and fell asleep in the chair. His parents got up, and his mom leaned over and kissed him on his head, saying, "I love you, son." His parents went upstairs to their room. When they passed by Elizabeth's room, they opened the bedroom to check on Elizabeth. She was sleeping. They closed the door and went to their room.

The battalion Chapel organized the funeral at the Green Beret Chapel on Fort Bragg. The funeral was conducted a week later, and the Chapel was full of Green Berets who were there to support Captain Allen. Others went to school with Captain Allen, and they flew in from other bases. They all were there because they respected Captain Allen, and his friendship was important. Many soldiers were standing outside who could not get in. He was a great leader of men who would help any one of them, and they were there to show their support.

It seemed like the entire Fort Bragg Brass showed up, with all of Captain Allen's Chain of Command. Captain Allen's family was there, and his wife's family. Little Elizabeth sat between her dad and his dad. The service was conducted militarily. Officers from his unit carried the coffin to the hearse, and everyone headed to the cemetery where Elizabeth was buried. The weather was clear and warm. He held his daughters' hands during the whole funeral process. Elizabeth cried when she placed dirt on the coffin. Captain Allen also placed dirt on the coffin. His parents stood on each side of Elizabeth, holding her hands. He was able to keep his composure as he watched his wife's coffin lowered into the ground.

Once the funeral was over, he shook hands with many people. Some people he knew, and others he did not. He was very appreciative of the turnout and the support from the military community. Captain Allen worried about how he was going to take care of his daughter, but he knew his parents and his wife's parents, who showed up, would help raise his little girl when he was out of town, either because of missions or field exercises. He promised himself he would do whatever was necessary to make sure his daughter grew up happy and content with life. Joseph knew it would be tough being a single father, but he was glad his family was always close and tight.

Chapter 2

Growing Up

As time went by and Elizabeth Allen grew up, she was supported by both sides of the family, and there was no shortage of love between the families and her. While her dad was overseas, training or running missions, young Elizabeth rotated, living with both grandparents. However, most of the time, she lived on her dad's parents' farm.

The farm, as it was called, was about 25 miles outside Fort Bragg, North Carolina. She loved the farm and the freedom it brought. Elizabeth grew up riding horses, helping with the cattle and chickens, and helping her grandparents around the farm. She enjoyed farm life. It was fun and relaxing.

When her dad was home, he would teach her how to shoot so she could protect herself. They also went hunting and camping when the opportunity came around. By the time she was 18, her dad had taught her to shoot just as good, or better, than any boy of her age group. He also taught her to be self-reliant and survive in the woods. She was also taught the importance of helping people like her mom did, being caring and understanding, and not judging people prior to knowing all facts.

When Elizabeth entered high School, she worked hard and kept straight A's. She also joined the 4H club; since she grew up on a farm, it was something she could relate to and understand. She dated a little in high school, but nothing serious. She was more focused on her schoolwork and things around the farm.

Elizabeth had a few good friends, but she always remembered what her dad said. Most people who have a lot of friends always find out only a few are solid. Most are into themselves and go in whatever direction the wind blows. Another reason for limited dating in High School was the boys in her school feared her dad. A Green Beret dad was the best protection for keeping any teenage boy from doing something stupid with his daughter. Fear is a big weapon a father can use against young men who are looking at their daughters as an item to be conquered. A man who is highly trained to kill will destroy any threat to his loved ones and especially his child.

She would always laugh when the boys would always quickly speed away when her dad came outside when they were dropping her off at their house. There were a few times Joseph sat on his porch cleaning his shotgun or handgun when she drove up with her date. Sometimes her date would not even try and kiss her. He would hop out and open her door, close it, then run to his side and jump in and drive away fast, causing her to be extremely upset, but when she saw her dad's grin, she would calm down and start laughing, and then she would hug him. Her dates always took her home exactly at the time he told them she better be back.

She loved the farm, but as she grew older, she realized she wanted to see more of the world. So, when she graduated high school, she went off to the University of North Carolina to get a medical degree in therapy for kids. She wanted to do something worthwhile and help kids with disabilities. Her dad was supportive of her goals and her career plans. He was also glad she did not go out of state for her college degree.

At the end of her third year in college, she graduated early with a B.S. in Child Therapy. She had taken full loads of classes, including during the summer, and finished one year early. During her college years, she dated here and there, but none of the men could be taken seriously. They were more into themselves than being serious with any college girl, including her.

Her nickname at the University was the ICE Queen, and she was proud of the nickname. She would tell her dad the things people said, and he would tell her to stay focused, and they would have a good laugh about things. The college boys all seemed fake or clueless about how the real world was, and they came across as quite foolish. They came across as entitled and spoiled. Elizabeth also stayed out of the college political scene, taking her dad's advice. When she graduated, she felt worn out and run down. It was a tough non-stop three years.

When it was time for the graduation ceremony, she was thrilled her dad was coming out of his way to see her graduation. Lieutenant General Allen put on hold some major problems occurring to go and see his daughter's graduation. This was important to them both. She knew he would not come all dressed up in his uniform. Her dad was a Lieutenant General and had to sneak in dressed as an average parent due to the radical students who always protested and blamed the military for every world ill. Lieutenant General Allen had nothing but contempt for these spoiled radical hypocrites but understood the importance of freedom of speech and views in this country. Lieutenant General Allen respected the freedom that allowed them to have their views.

Lieutenant General Allen did what he could to not bring any attention to himself during the ceremony. He sat in the back quietly with his bodyguards spread out within a few feet away from him. When she finally saw him, she smiled and waved. He also smiled and waved back at her. She knew he could not stay long because he might be recognized by some of the more radical students and college instructors who don't like the military and what it stands for.

Lieutenant General Allen was becoming famous, and he had been on the news more than he liked. His superiors have been pushing him out in the limelight more than he chose to be, but he understood the politics that come with his job. He watched the ceremonies and looked around to see other parents' reactions. They were like his, full of smiles and cheering and clapping.

Lieutenant General Allen earlier briefed his bodyguards on how to act, and he also told them to stay far away from him as they could. He took some pictures of Elizabeth when she received her diploma. She stopped and waved and threw a kiss toward him and waved back at her. Once she walked off the stage, Elizabeth went and sat down. His bodyguards approached him and told him he needed to leave, and he was escorted out of there by his bodyguards because some people started pointing at him.

He told his bodyguards earlier if he started to get too much attention, let him know so they could leave. He left with no disruption. While in his vehicle, he just sat there and smiled. No one talked, then his bodyguard driver said, "Congratulations, sir." Lieutenant General Allen replied with a thank you and "Let's get back to Fort Bragg." He was extremely proud of his daughter.

He was a proud father, like all fathers whose kid(s) graduate or succeed. The plane ride was quick, and when they landed at Fort Pope, his escort to his office was waiting. Fort Pope is one of the staging Air Force Bases for the Army units at Fort Bragg. Once the plane landed, he was escorted to his vehicle by his bodyguards and driven to his headquarters.

After he arrived back at his Fort Bragg Headquarters, his driver opened his door, and he stepped out of his vehicle. He walked up the stairs and entered the Headquarters building, and he went to his office. When he entered his office, he closed his door and turned his light off. He sat in his chair at his desk and looked at the last photo of his wife. His eyes began to water as he kept staring. "Our daughter did it," he said. "I miss you, honey," he whispered. His telephone began ringing, so he wiped his eyes, cleared his throat, and answered. It was the Army Chief of Staff who was wanting some information on some issues in the Special force's community.

Elizabeth observed her father leave, and even though she understood, she felt sad. Her dad promised her he would not cause any problem, and if something did happen, he would attempt not to cause a major incident if it could be avoided. She was very proud of him and the work he does to protect this nation against our enemies. Occasionally she wished her dad was like anyone else's, but she knew she was lucky to have a dad who would risk it all for her and this country.

Once the graduation was over, she went to a graduation party with a couple of her friends and had a good time. She danced with some of the men there but did not take any of them seriously. When the party was over, Elizabeth, and her friends took an Uber back to their assigned student building. They entered the building, showed their IDs, and took the elevator up to their floor. Once the door opened, they saw a hallway full of people celebrating graduation. They hung around the hallway for about 30 minutes and then went to their rooms.

Elizabeth called her dad and knew he would answer his phone because she knew he always had two cell phones on him. One for work and the other one for family and friends. When Lieutenant General Allen answered, he knew who it was.

"Congratulations, kiddo."

"Thanks, dad. How are you doing?"

"Fine, and how did the party go?"

Surprised he knew, Elizabeth asked him, "How did you know about that?"

"If it was me, I would have gone and partied also."

She laughed and said, "It was fun, but my friends and I are back in our rooms getting ready to hit the sack."

"Good. I'm crashing here on my office couch for the night."

"You should go to the farm to get a good night's sleep." He said, "I should, but I sent the driver home." The conversation prolonged for a few more minutes prior to them both hanging up. Elizabeth then went up and crashed in her bed.

Lieutenant General Allen lay on the couch as he went over the last couple of days. He thought about his kid's graduation and how pleasant it was. He was happy there were no issues with him being in the crowd at the university. It was unfortunate he could not hang around, but the universities have gone too far in one political direction. College life has changed in many ways over time, but it is usually the few that initiate the biggest problems at colleges. Soon, he closed his eyes and fell asleep.

Chapter 3

Good to be Home.

Instead of starting her master's degree during the summer, the next phase of her education, Elizabeth decided to go home and take the summer off. She called her dad and again, thanked him for coming; they spoke for a little while. Elizabeth finally got to the point and told her dad she needed a good break from school, and that she was wanting to go home for the summer. Her dad told Elizabeth "Well, come home and enjoy the summer and just relax."

Before he hung up, he said "call your grandparents and let them know you are coming. Let them know we talked about it." Once she finished talking with her dad, she called her grandparents and let them know she is coming for the summer. After she was done talking with her thrilled grandparents, she was coming, she packed her stuff and loaded up her car. Elizabeth then hit the road and drove home to the family farm to relax and have a nice summer vacation.

Elizabeth's dad was a three-star general and responsible for all Army Special Forces units and he was projected to be in the running as a future Army Chief of Staff. Lieutenant General Allen turned down his 4th star to do one more tour in this position, knowing he could not turn down the promotion next time. If he did his career would probably be over. The Pentagon does not like to be told "No" by any officer or soldier. But he did such a fantastic job in his position they allowed it but dropped hints of it being only a one-time thing.

Staying in the Special Forces throughout his career had slowed his career down a little, but he was not worried about it. He enjoyed what he was doing, and he was very well respected in the United States Defense community and had lots of support in the political arena due to some extreme risks he took when he was younger in the Special Forces community. Lieutenant General Allen also did a young United States Senator out of Florida, a big favor that could have been a catastrophe if it went wrong; politically and militarily.

Lieutenant General Allen never remarried after losing his wife in a car accident, and he stayed focused on his career, looking out for his daughter. He dated here and there, and almost remarried once, with a successful woman who ran her own business, but the woman wanted him to retire. He made the decision to break it off. He was happy about his career and she was unwilling to give up her career which helped make her wealthy but expected him to give up his career. He never had any regrets about breaking it off because still enjoyed his job.

When Elizabeth arrived home on the farm, she found out from her grandparents her dad had been called back to Washington D.C for a meeting at the pentagon and would not be home for a couple of days. They had dinner and they all walked around the farm with her grandpa pointing things out. She felt so good being home, with no schoolbooks, no classes, and no tests. It was a big farm; about 70 acres being passed down from one generation of Allens to another. Elizabeth went out to the garden with her grandpa to see what he was growing, and she saw lots of watermelons and cantaloupes getting close to being ready to be picked. She also saw cucumbers, onions, carrots, and other vegetables.

After spending a few hours visiting with her grandparents, she decided to go out to a club and relax and listen to some good music. Once she got cleaned up, she left the farm around 7:30 PM and drove to a dance club outside Fayetteville, North Carolina. Elizabeth had read in the entertainment section of the local paper that they played rock music. She enjoyed the rock music from her dad's generation. As she was driving to the club, her entire future was now being rewritten in a major way; something she would never have foreseen.

Once Elizabeth arrived and paid her five dollars to get in, she worked her way through the crowd and went to the back bar, and sat on a bar stool which can be turned around to face the stage. The club was packed with at least 250-300 people. She ordered a rum and coke and sipped it and then spent the next couple of hours telling soldiers and civilians no thank you politely when they asked her to dance or if they could buy her a drink.

Elizabeth was simply listening to the rock band happily while sipping her drink. During the breaks for the band, the DJ played 1970s dance music and the floor was packed. She kept on refusing men's advances and men who wanted to dance with her. She just sipped her drink and watched the band and people dancing.

 Around 10:00 pm, during the band's second break she was thinking about leaving when suddenly, she heard a bunch of people in the front of the club started yelling loudly and cheering. She stood up to see what the yelling was about. She saw this tall, blonde, handsome guy who wore a tight blue shirt entering the club. He was getting patted on the back and he was shaking people's hands.

 She turned around and with a grin asked one of the bartenders, "who is that?" and "why is he so popular?" The guy smiled and told her "That's James D. Thomas." She asked, "what does the D stand for" and he answered back, "I do not know but he is one of the best Green Berets in the army." The bartender hesitated and continued saying "he is a Captain, and extremely popular with his men, doing whatever he does." The bartender went on and mentioned, "he is a chick magnet, and all the guys respect him." Elizabeth took a sip of her drink and the bartender finished up and said, "The thing is he is for real and he is not fake, and he would give his last drop of blood to help his soldiers, and they would do the same."

As James worked his way through the crowd heading to the back of the club Elizabeth saw several women trying to get his attention but he politely told them later. As he was getting closer to the back of the club he looked up and made eye contact with Elizabeth and grinned. He walked up and stood next to her with a smile and said "hi." She said nothing to him. James then turned around and ordered a couple of shots of bourbon and shook hands with the bartender whose name was Bob.

They started talking and he never looked at Elizabeth once in 30 minutes, as the bartender and James talked sports and the bartender served other drinks to the people coming up to the bar. Men continue to approach her about dancing or wanting to buy her a drink, but she kept saying no thanks.

After 30 minutes James turned around and sat down on a barstool to watch the band and everyone else having a fun time. Several women came up to him and asked him to dance with them and he accepted. Elizabeth noticed he never told one no and even danced with the fat and ugly women. After the last dance with an unknown woman, James sat back on the stool he had been sitting on and ordered another bourbon which Bob put in front of him.

James took another shot of Bourbon and turned to Elizabeth and said "I noticed since I walked in, you do not dance with anyone and you do not talk to anyone. Do you dance?" Elizabeth looked at him and said, "yes, but not with you." James looked at Elizabeth with a grin and said, "may I ask why?" She said, "you think you're god's gift to all women." He turned and looked at Bob the bartender and said, "did you hear that Bob?" Bob shook his head and they both laughed loudly.

James turned back around and told her "do I know I am a good-looking lady?" "You better believe it." Her jaw opened in shock and she said, "wow what an ego." He smiled and laughed again at her. Elizabeth had never met any guy in college or high school who would have said that. James also said, "I am a beast and Yes, I am egotistic at times." "But no, I am not god's gift to women." He looked around for a moment and continued saying "I treat all women with respect including the fat and ugly ones." She had a puzzled look on her face when he said, "what man does that?" James turned around and looked at Bob who was listening, continued talking, and said, "I treat people the way I would want to be treated, and if I want to have a good time, I do." James turned back towards Elizabeth and said, "you see, lady, I could be dead tomorrow or next week, or next year for something you know nothing about." Elizabeth then said, "you are nothing but an asshole." James laughed and said, "wow big words, lady, I am impressed- NOT" as he laughed he then said, "what a spoiled bitch you are."

In a sarcastic tone of voice, he said "what have you done lady?" He looked at her hand seeing a college ring. James again chuckled and said, "I see your fancy college ring, whoopee" as he added, "It does not mean squat if you do not do something good with it." He looked down at her with an irked look on his face and said, "by the way, bitch, who the hell are you to judge me? I grew up poor and worked my ass off in school to get into West Point." James downed his drink and continued talking and said, "I have seen things you will never see or understand, I bet your daddy is some high and mighty dickhead who thinks he is better than everyone else." Elizabeth was in shock at how this guy was talking to her because no one has ever talked to her that way.

Once Elizabeth stopped shaking in anger, she took a sip of her drink, stood up, and slapped him. Bob who was watching and listening to both, yelled out "WOW that took guts. Lady, he put people in the hospital for less." James stood up and said with a smile as he looked into her eyes "you were scared and shaking because I didn't back down, what a snot-nose daddy's little spoiled brat."

Elizabeth tried to slap him again, but he grabbed her hand and said "is that all you got" as he looked into her eyes. He saw fear in her eyes, and he let go and said, "spoiled little bitch." James then asked, "who is your daddy sarcastically?" She said, "he is important and a good man." He said in a sarcastic tone of voice "what about your mommy?" She then became teary-eyed and said, with emotion, "she is dead, asshole" and started crying.

James got quiet and looked down at the floor and shuffled his feet for a moment because he was feeling bad about what he said to this woman. He looked up at her and realized he went too far. He took a deep breath and in a sincere tone of voice said," I am so sorry you lost your mom and I do understand how you feel." Elizabeth looked up with tears coming out of her eyes and said, "how would you know what it's like?" James in a lower tone of voice said, "I also lost my mom." She looked up at him and he got very quiet and was looking down with a sad look on his face, which surprised her. James then looked up and with a straight face asked her "how did her mom die?" Elizabeth stopped crying as he handed her a napkin. She wiped her eyes and explained the story to him of how she died.

Elizabeth left nothing out and told James what her dad told her when she was old enough. With a serious look, James said, "I am truly so sorry" and he again said, "I apologize for what I said." Elizabeth said, "I am sorry too." She said, "Bob, the bartender said your name is James" and he responded and said, "yes, it is, what is yours?" She told him "Elizabeth." He said, "how about we start over?" He put his hand out and she shook his hand and smiled and said, "I agree let's start over."

Elizabeth asked, "James how did your mom die?" He told her "she died during my delivery." He then got very quiet and took a big gulp of his refilled drink. She could see how painful it was to him, talking about it and it seemed to her he blamed himself for his mom's death. She looked into his eyes and James stuttered and said, "he caused her to have massive bleeding because he was so big, and she hemorrhaged to death before the ambulance could get there."

She could see the guilt written on his face as he looked down at his feet again and said "maybe we do have something in common losing our moms." James grabbed a napkin and reached over and dried her eyes. Elizabeth was surprised and said, "thank you." Bob who was listening said, "dam lady you got him to talk like no one I know."

Elizabeth looked James in the eyes and said, "I am sorry too." They sat there talking with each other for the next two hours when Elizabeth said, "I need to go." She turned around and asked Bob to call a taxi for her. Once Bob called for one James told her "I could drive you home." Elizabeth smiled and said, "no, and thanks anyway." James laughed and stated, "yea, maybe I should not drive." He then said, "can we share a taxi since I have been drinking." She looked at him and smiled and said "sure."

James held Elizabeth's hand as he escorted her through the crowd, and they exited the club and stood out front. He asked her "what did you study in college?" Elizabeth told him and she talked and talked, and he listened. For some strange reason, she felt comfortable with him. James did not criticize her and smiled when she looked into his eyes. James' blue eyes showed something other men she met did not have. He came across as caring and compassionate, but she knew he was a man whose job was to kill America's enemies and break things. He seemed to show two important traits she cared about, Caring and compassion which she felt were extremely important in a man.

They continued to talk while they waited for the taxi and they talked like they have known each other their whole life. They both talked about their college time, and how she wanted to help kids, and they also talked about how they wished they knew their moms and how it bothered them. James then turned around and asked one of the bouncers, he knew to call for a taxi again. One of them stepped inside and made the call for them. The bouncer came back out and told James "they should be here any minute." James shook the guy's hand and said "thanks, I appreciate it."

Elizabeth asked James "why did he join the army instead of working in the civilian world?" James said, "he wanted to serve his country, and this was the best way of doing it as he earned a degree in Mechanical engineering which will always help him."

Elizabeth smiled and asked him "what was his ranking in class?" James tried to change the subject and she smiled and said, "what are you embarrassed about?" James said, "I'm not embarrassed." She said, "don't avoid the question." He looked down and answered, "first." She said, "first? you should be proud of that." James said, "I am, but I do not like to brag about it." She thought, "wow a smart guy who does not brag about it." That is a rarity because most men would brag about that.

When the taxi arrived, he opened the door for Elizabeth, and she stepped in with James sitting next to her. She gave the driver her address and the taxi headed to her home. They talked till they got to the farm, laughing over how they first met. Once they arrived at the farm, James jumped out and opened the wooden gate. He jumped back into the vehicle and the taxi drove up to her grandparents' house. As he jumped out again and opened the door for her she said, "I will pay my half." He said, "no, I got it." She began to argue as he bent his head down and kissed her on her forehead. It surprised her. He then turned to the driver and gave him a look, and the driver said, "lady, please let him pay for it." The taxi driver gulped and said, "he looks like he can rip my head off." Elizabeth smiled and laughed and said "ok."

James was still looking at the driver when she stood on her toes and kissed him on his lips. This time he had a surprised look on his face and laughed, and she also laughed. He walked her to the door and told her "I hope I can see you again?" She smiled and said it was possible, as he turned around and walked back to the taxi.

While he was walking back to the cab, she watched him and saw the confidence he had, that men at the university did not have. They had an entitlement mentality. James did not. When he opened the taxi door, he turned around and asked her with a big smile. "Do you like seafood?" Elizabeth smiled and laughed and said "yes." He said," it's a date, not tomorrow but Saturday." She said you do not have my number, and he responded I know where you are staying." He smiled and waved goodbye. The taxi door closed, and the taxi drove away.

Elizabeth sat on the swing for a few minutes, looking around the yard. She then went inside and went to bed, thinking about this guy she met at the club. He seemed not to be like anyone she ever met. He could be hard when challenged but he could be caring, and he seemed to have a big heart. She went over the evening in her head and thought this might be an interesting summer, staying with her family. Elizabeth was glad she was taking time off from her schoolwork as she needed a break. She went over everything that happen during the evening and how different this guy was. One thing which made her smile as he did not ask her for her phone number or give her his. She was surprised by that and then she finally drifted off to sleep, with a smile on her face.

Chapter 4

Captain James D. Thomas

James D. Thomas was born in a poor family in Newton County, Arkansas. The town is located in the hills of the Ozarks Mountains in the Northwest part of Arkansas. The people there are hardworking; farmers and blue-collar people. Flag-waving and hard-core Christians of many faiths. Football and baseball are the big sports in that area and hunting and fishing are a big part of most people's lives.

James' dad David did not take education seriously when he was young, and it hurt him financially during his life. He did graduate from Newton County High School but barely. He hated school and was more of a goof-off than a kid wanting to better himself. The further lack of any further education caused him to end up working tough laboring-type jobs throughout most of his life.

David married a local girl he went to school with, named Alice Bradley, who also worked odd jobs to help with the family. Losing his wife during the delivery of his son also affected him throughout his life. He ended up relying too much on booze to numb his guilt over the death of his wife as he felt some blame. He felt that if he had a better job and lived closer to town, it might have made a difference in her living or dying.

David always knew the importance of raising a son the right way and promised his wife on her deathbed that he would do whatever was needed for their son as he kissed her lips on her last breath. Her death beat him down and he thought he could never get over the pain he felt, for her loss.

David worked many jobs and sometimes two jobs together, with no days off to give his son what he needed. David would always make sure his son would not feel embarrassed wearing worn-out clothes in school. David's new kids could be cruel to other kids because they may look different or not fit their little click, especially bullies. So, he would make sure James' clothes were always good. Not fancy but nice. Sometimes he would repatch his own pants and spend the money on getting his kid what he needed. David did not care what people thought about how he looked in patched-up pants. Sometimes, he would skip meals so his son would always sleep with a full belly. People told him about getting food stamps and assistance, but he was too proud to go down that road. He saw too many lazy people use it as an excuse not to work and get free food.

David pushed schooling and sports on his son to help him stay focused in the right direction. James loved his dad and always wanted to make his dad proud by maintaining straight A's through school and excelling in football and wrestling. Football taught James teamwork and wrestling taught him how to defend himself. James' dad would take him to a gym on the old main street to learn boxing and self-defense. Once a week David would take James up to Springfield Missouri which was about two hours on Highway 65 to learn Brazilian Jiu-jitsu.

As James got older and into his teens, he learned the difference between being poor and everyone else. James never felt out of place or angry about the situation he was in. He always worried about his dad who was doing whatever it took to earn extra money. He loved his dad and promised him he would make it. James' dad installed into him to treat everyone the same and never bully anyone, and defend the kids who were the weak ones.

As James got bigger, students respected him because he treated everyone the same even the nerd kids who he defended several times in fights after school. James never lost and only a fool would challenge him and usually suffered serious consequences after that.

When he entered High school, he tried to get his dad to let him help him get a part-time, but his dad said no. Focus on school. James was disappointed every time he brought it up, but he knew his dad felt school was more important and it could define you once you become an adult.

James would always step up and defend the kids who were being bullied by the cruel kids whose parents spoiled them into thinking they were better than everyone else. The bullies would learn it the hard way and have an extremely bad day. James would correct their actions by slamming them against the hall locker and telling them off in front of everyone, including the teachers. The teachers would turn around and act like they did not see anything. But they were glad that Mr. Thomas would stop the big kids from picking on the smaller students.

By the time James was a senior in high school, he was the most popular and respected kid in school. Even James' enemies, over time, respected him and put aside their animosity of getting their asses kicked. One kid later said that James kicked his ass but he never held that against him. James dated a lot, but he refused to get serious like some High School kids who get the words love and lust mixed up. James had a goal, and he did not want anyone or anything to interfere with it. The goal was the one he promised his dad. He would go to college and would make his dad proud of him.

He also made a promise to himself that he would help his dad in any way possible when he made it. Because he was a great student and athlete, he received a nomination to the Army and Air Force Military academies. James asked for his dad's advice and they both agreed that West Point was the path he should follow. He signed the paperwork and went through the process. He even got the instructors to notice him when he had to go through the West Point introduction period for a couple of weeks during the summer and he dominated the PT test and all physical testing.

The four college years at West Point went by faster than James thought it would. While he was there, he started on the wrestling team and took other self-defense training opportunities when they popped up. The college tried to get him to play on the Army football team, but he did not want anything to risk the career he was shooting for, in the army. One major injury would ruin his goals for his future.

James kept focused and became popular and gained his fellow student's respect. One thing he would always try to do was when he dropped an underclassman for pushups no matter where the location was, he would knock them out with the underclassman. This behavior also helped him stay in great shape. This was noticed by everyone including the instructors and this made him very respected among his peers.

When James finally completed his last year, His dad showed up at James' graduation and ceremony. David has been sober for almost four years and he kept the promise he made to his son that he would stop drinking before James left for college. When they saw each other, they hugged each other and congratulated each other on their success, in doing what they promised each other. David was proud when James was called up to give the class speech as the number one rated student at West Point. David was amazed at how professional all the students looked, during the entire ceremony.

When it was time for James to pick his job skill in the army, he chose Special Forces because they were the best in the army. Once James made it through his Green Beret training as a Second Lieutenant, his dad was authorized to give him his Green Beret. When James ended up going overseas to Europe, he was assigned to an SF unit in Stuttgart, Germany. While in Stuttgart, he lived in the officer's barracks. Every month he sent his dad half of his paycheck. He also helped his dad get a place in Fayetteville, North Carolina so he could be close to him. He knew how much his dad hated to be by himself.

As time went by, his dad got a good job working at Fort Bragg and David sent back most of the money he owed James back to him, and he wrote he is doing good. James was always proud of his dad and just wanted him to be happy. When his dad told him, he met a woman who lost her husband in Iraq for the first time, James was thrilled, and happy, and told him so. James felt great that his dad was finally, after so many tough years, happy. James felt things were coming together for his dad and him.

After spending some time in Germany, James received his promotion to First Lieutenant. Later, he ended up doing multiple tours to Iraq, Syria, and Afghanistan. He earned a great reputation for taking the most dangerous missions and completing them. His reputation in the Green Beret community began to spread. Every time he earned a medal, he proudly sent it to his dad. When he had to dress up, he showed his modesty and would only have a minimal number of medals on his class A uniform. His fellow soldiers and his commanders noticed how down-to-earth Lieutenant James Thomas was.

On his second mission in Syria, James was shot in the left shoulder, by a jihadi soldier who was hiding out in a pile of rocks and debris. His team took out the shooter with a 203 round. Since he lost a lot of blood and his wounds were serious, he was flown to Israel. They had no time to fly him to Bagdad, Iraq for medical treatment. The hospitals in Israel were much closer, and the seriousness of his wounds forced him to be medevacked to Tela Aviv, Israel where he was treated. The Israeli hospitals are some of the best in the entire world and he knew his medical treatment would be second to none.

After the emergency surgery, and once James came and got his brain working, he was able to call his dad. During the call, he told him that he was alright. His dad got upset on the phone, but James calmed him down and told him, "it's ok." His dad gathered his composure and they talked for a little while about other things. When they were done talking, they said goodbye to each other.

David told James that he loved him and told James to be safe and careful. James knew his dad was stressed but David told him he was ok. He said, "dad I have to get some other minor surgeries, but I will be alright, and I love you too", and then he hung up.

Once all the other surgeries were done, and after a couple of weeks in the hospital, he was medevacked to Ramstein A.F.B in Germany where he recovered and began his physical therapy. Once he was done recuperating and getting back into shape, he was given orders to go to Fort Bragg North Carolina. Before he left Germany, he was promoted to Captain and given a few more medals including the Purple Hearts. James was happy to get his promotion and to head back to the states and his new assignment at Fort Bragg, North Carolina which is an Army base and has a key SF program.

While stationed at Fort Bragg his reputation continued to grow, due to him never refusing any type of mission, no matter how tough it was. While he was at Fort Bragg, he dated a lot there, but none of the women could be taken seriously. They were either bossy, nagging, entitled, wanting, or just plain selfish. Then there were the ones who were just worse. The ones who were always doing selfies. James stopped dating, and he would often go fishing or hunt with his dad. His friends or soldiers in the unit would try and set him up with their sisters or cousins, but he would politely turn them down.

Things were going well with his career and when he was not in the field or running overseas operations, he spent his free time with his dad. One day they were on the lake, fishing, when David looked at his son and said well are you seeing anyone? James laughed and said no. It is hard to find the right one. His dad said I understand. Give it time son, when you are not looking for it, that's when you find that one special person. James laughed again as he threw his fishing line into lake Surf. This lake is about ten miles northwest of Fort Bragg.

One day James decided to go to the Rock Club he usually went to, so he could relax and have a good time. He hadn't been there in a long time so when he drove up and got out of his black Mustang, he saw a long line, mostly of women and he smiled then laughed. He then grinned and thought this may be an interesting night. He stood in line and some of the women would turn around and look at him and smile. Once he paid the entrance fee, he walked in and shook the hands of the bouncers he knew. After he entered the club, he could see people dancing to rock music being played by the band. He saw some men from the teams under his command and other soldiers that started yelling and went up, shook his hand, and patted him on the back. James stopped and talked a minute with a couple of them and then worked his way through the crowd.

When he was almost to the back, he looked up and saw this attractive woman sitting at the bar, watching him work his way through the crowd, sipping a drink. He approached her and said hi. He then turned away from her and started talking with Bob the bartender. He knew Bob for a while, and they became friends as they enjoyed sports and hunting. James was a Raider fan and Bob was a San Francisco 49er fan.

James ordered a couple of shots of Bourbon and continued to talk to him about sports. Football, and Baseball. He never looked at the attractive women next to him. James, while talking with Bob, noticed that she turned down every guy who wanted to dance with her or buy her a drink. This lady seemed only interested in listening to the music. She did not come across as bitchy or stuck up when she was turning the other men down. She seemed like she was just trying to enjoy the vibe and wanted to be left alone.

James was just tired of dealing with women who were full of issues. However, there was something different about this one. She seemed to be more down-to-earth, but he was wrong before. Women are always hard to figure out. Any man who says he has figured them out is full of crap. After dancing with some other women, He then began talking with her.

It turned out to be an interesting evening. James was not expecting to meet anyone of interest at the club. James smiled. He got slapped in the face, got choked up a little bit, talked about his mom, and had a good time talking with the girl, scaring the hell out of the taxi driver. The good thing was he knew where she was staying for the summer. Before he closed his eyes for the night, he smiled and said while slurring his speech, one hell of a Friday night. Who would have thought?

It was Saturday morning and James woke up around 11 am. He got out of bed and ate lunch, a large salad with veggies and strips of grilled chicken that he already had prepared the day before. After he was done eating, he sat down and read for a while. Once he was done reading a couple of chapters from his book, he went and changed into sweats to go and work out. After a few phone calls, he went to the nearest base gym and worked out for a couple of hours, and then he went for a five-mile run. James needed to sweat out the booze from the night before, so he pushed himself and finished it in about 32 minutes. He puked a couple of times when he finished his run. Some other soldiers who were running yelled out "way to go." He waved back and went to his car. As they say "if you ain't puking you are not trying."

James went home to shower and prepare for the evening. It was the Green Beet Ball, and everyone was going to be there. This included many of the base brass and noncoms. He expected a dull night with a lot more boozing and talk. He made a promise to himself that he would only drink two bottles of beer then he was sneaking out, after the big wig's speeches. He first had to get his uniform ready. He was ordered to wear all his medals or expect a kick in the ass, by his commander.

James decided to go see his dad first before he got dressed up in his uniform. He remembered his dad had most of his medals. When he arrived at his dad's place, he knocked on the door and walked in. His dad walked up to him with a smile and they hugged each other, and he said, "dad, I need my medals." After being told where they were, his dad asked, "what's up?" James told him "he was ordered by the BC to wear all his medals or he would get his ass kicked for not wearing all of them." So, "he promised his boss he would." After visiting with his dad, he went back to his room in the officer quarters to get ready for the big night.

The ball started at 6 pm, and it was just 4 30 pm. So, James took a quick nap on his couch and woke up at 5 35 pm and jumped in the shower, and got dressed. At about 6 15 pm James hung his dress jacket out in the back of the vehicle so it would not wrinkle and headed to the ball. James wanted to look good because of all the brass who would be there including the top SF general. This was the guy who could help or hurt your career with one snap of his finger or one phone call. He also knew through rumors he was projected to be the Army Chief of Staff down the road.

While driving to the base, he was pulled over by the Military Police. He did a California stop and was pulled over. Two Military policemen stepped out of the vehicle and approached his jeep from both sides. The driver came upon Captain Thomas's left side and said, "good evening sir." Captain Thomas smiled and said, "good evening Sargent." The Sargent said, "Sir, do you know why you were pulled over?" Captain Thomas realized he coasted through the stop sign while shifting gears. He said, "yes, I coasted through the stop sign and I just realized it. I guess I am in too much of a hurry."

Sargent Fremont responded by asking "Sir, where are you heading?" Captain Thomas responded and said, "the Ball." Sargent Fremont had a what the hell look on his face. Captain Thomas said the "SF Ball." Sargent Fremont said, "oh ok, I get It." Then he asked for Captain Thomas's ID, Driver's license, insurance, and vehicle registration. He handed everything to the Sargent, and the two MPs went back to their vehicle.

While in their patrol car, they ran a check on Captain Allen and wrote him a ticket. Once they were done writing the ticket, they got out of the patrol car and walked back to Captain Thomas who was sitting patiently in his vehicle. Captain Thomas was handed back his information and his ticket. Sargent Fremont said, "Sir please be a little careful next time. The ball is not going anywhere, and getting hurt in a stupid car wreck is one way of screwing up the evening." James smiled and said, "it's on me, and by the way, you guys have a good and safe night." Sargent Fremont said, "thank you sir" and the two MPS returned to their vehicle.

James started the jeep and headed to the ball, and made sure he followed the driving laws as he was listening to Def Leopards High and Dry; one of his favorite albums or in this case, disk. He saw them in concert a few years ago and enjoyed the show and their music. Some of his other favorites were Skillet, AC/DC, Led Zeppelin, and of course the Beatles. Another singer he liked was Daughtry, who he always thought, deserved more respect. James usually liked old music and straight rock and roll. Most of the music nowadays was cheap crap with most of them being similar in many ways. People lip-singing and dancing around the stage seemed silly to him.

Chapter 5

Eyes for each other

James arrived at the ball at 6:30 pm, and he drove around the parking lot until he found a spot and pulled in. After he walked in, he saw a few friends, and they shook hands and patted each other on the shoulders, as friends do. They talked and joked around for a few minutes and stayed out of the way of people coming in and out of the building. When they were done talking, they went to find their assigned table. When the Brigade Sergeant Major stepped to the microphone and asked everyone to go to their assigned tables, so they could get this thing started, James located his assigned seat and introduced himself to the other men at the table. The table was full of bachelors, and they had all heard of each other and had some good discussions about issues going on in the community.

Three-star General Joseph Allen had his daughter Elizabeth as his escort to the ball, and she was very happy and proud to go. She had always wondered what it would be like and was very interested in seeing a Green Berets Ball in person. They were picked up by Lieutenant General Allen's driver and taken to the ball.

When the car drove up and stopped, the driver jumped out and immediately opened the door so Elizabeth could get out first. Then the Lieutenant General stepped out. Everyone who was walking towards the entrance stopped and saluted the General, who immediately saluted back. With Elizabeth at his side, they walked into the ballroom when someone loudly yelled "ATTENTION." That startled Elizabeth as her dad squeezed her hand to let her know it's okay.

Lieutenant General Allen with Elizabeth at his side walked into a large room with eating tables lined up, and people were either sitting or standing, talking with each other. He then said, "Carry on." Everyone followed his instructions and went back to what they were doing. The food was going to be brought out at 7 pm. The main table was in front. All the Officers and senior Noncoms then headed to the front and lined up to shake hands and meet Lieutenant General Allen and his daughter.

James never looked to see who the General was, and he really didn't care. He jumped to attention with everyone else, and then when he heard "carry on," he went to line up with everyone else. He always called these types of gatherings a dog and pony show. He hated this stuff, but he understood it was all part of the Military tradition.

While waiting in line to step up and introduce himself to the General, he started to think about the girl he met last night. He was irked with himself for not asking for her number. One thing he was sure of, he knew where she was staying at. James was planning on going there tomorrow and doing a proper introduction. He could hear people behind him talking about the General and how they worked with him in the past. They said he was a hard charger and he expected his officers to be leaders, not followers, and once they made a decision, they stood by it. He heard he hated cowards who made decisions but tried to blame others for their decisions.

When it was his turn, James stepped up and put his hand out and shook the General's hand and said, "Sir, I am Captain James D. Thomas." Lieutenant General Allen stated, "It's nice to meet you, Captain, and I hear good things about you." He looked at Captain Thomas's chest with his medals and saw some good medals and knew this young man took care of business. He knew of Captain Thomas by reading his record before he transferred in. He always read all the new Captain's records coming into Fort Bragg. Lieutenant General Allen turned towards his daughter and said, "By the way, let me introduce you to my daughter, Elizabeth." Both James and Elizabeth turned to each other and immediately recognized each other. They both smiled and shook hands.

Elizabeth smiled and said, "Good evening, Captain." James smiled and stated, "Good evening, Ma'am."

Everyone was watching as they still held each other's hands and smiled. The general looked at Captain Thomas and his daughter, then looked back at Captain Thomas. Both James and Elizabeth asked how each was doing, still holding the other's hand in a handshake. James realized people, including the General, had a puzzled expression on their faces. James let go of Elizabeth's hand, slightly bowed, smiled, stepped away, and went back to his table with a grin on his face.

James ate his dinner while talking shop with the others at his table, but he would occasionally try to see where Elizabeth was. If someone was watching both James and Elizabeth, they would have seen both trying to locate and look around to see if they could see each other. They finally made eye contact a couple of times and smiled at each other. Lieutenant General Allen noticed his daughter looking around and smiling while she was eating and kept trying to look for someone. It was not hard to figure out who she was trying to see.

He asked his daughter if "she was enjoying herself." Elizabeth smiled and said, "Yes, Dad, I am enjoying myself, and the food is good." He asked with a grin, "I hope you have a good time tonight." She looked back at her father and said, "I will, Dad," with a smile on her face as he went back to eating and talking with the other generals at the table. Occasionally, he would look back to see if she was not bored. If Elizabeth had that look, he decided he would call it an evening and take her home.

Once the dinner portion was over and the speeches were given by the brass, including Lieutenant General Allen, everyone left the dining room and entered the ballroom. Music began playing, and people began dancing. After about 20 minutes, James was done talking with some of his friends, and he slowly worked his way to where Elizabeth was. James noticed Elizabeth had been dancing with several of the other officers after she danced with her father to open the dance. When James finally was able to get to her, he asked Elizabeth, "Would you like to dance?" She looked at him and said with a smile, "What took you so long?" James shrugged his shoulders and said, "Sorry."

They spent the rest of the night dancing and talking only with each other. Both enjoyed dancing with each other and spending the evening together. Elizabeth refused other officers' requests who wanted to dance with her, and this did not go unnoticed by the General. He asked his aide, Major Johnson, "I want to know more about this young Captain who has my daughter's interest." Major Johnson smiled and said, "Absolutely." The General said, "By 9 am Monday." Major Johnson said, "Yes, sir." The General then told Major Johnson, "Go and have some fun." Major Johnson smiled, stated "Yes, sir," and went to his wife, who was waiting, and escorted her to the dance floor. At around 11 pm, the General believed he had met everyone he needed to and started to feel the drag of the long day. He felt worn out and was ready to sneak out. So, he finally approached his daughter and the young Captain Thomas and asked, "How are you doing?" James immediately stood up and said, "Good, sir." Lieutenant General Allen said, "Relax, Captain." Captain Thomas then sat back down as the General turned to his daughter and asked, "How are you doing?" Elizabeth smiled, looked at Captain Thomas and said, "I am having a great time." James smiled back at her and said, "I'm glad."

Lieutenant General Allen smiled at her, then looked at Captain Thomas and asked, "How has the night been going for you?" Captain Thomas said, "He was having a good time with great company," and both Elizabeth and James smiled at each other again. The General asked if they wanted anything to drink, and James said, "No thanks, we have just been drinking lemonade all evening." The General chuckled. He had not seen his daughter this happy in many years. He then asked Captain Thomas, "Well, young man, why did you choose the Green Berets?" James got serious and looked at the General and stood up, telling him, "My dad always told me to be the best in everything I do, and this job allows me to push the envelope in everything I do." He looked at Elizabeth and continued by saying, "I also have the best company full of men who are the best in the entire army, and I enjoy working with all of them."

The General asked Captain Thomas, "How did you do at the Academy?" James looked at Elizabeth and felt proud. It was not considered bragging when he said, "First in my class, sir." The General then said, "Good, me too." The General turned to his daughter and asked her if she was ready to go. She hesitated but saw how tired her father was, so she said, "Yes."

James looked at the General and respectfully asked Would you mind if I escort Elizabeth to the car. The General turned to his daughter and asked if that was fine. Elizabeth smiled, seeing how James gave her dad the courtesy of asking him, and said, "Definitely." They exited the building, and the General's car drove up. The driver opened the door, and the General turned to Captain Thomas, who saluted him. The General saluted back, shook Captain Thomas's hand, and said, "I hope you have her number?" He stepped into the back seat and slid over so his daughter could get in, then pulled out his cell phone to see who had been calling him during the evening and decide which phone calls he would return.

James and Elizabeth looked at each other and held each other's hands. Neither noticed people standing around watching what was going on. He wanted to kiss her, but he did not want to disrespect the General. So, he started to shake her hand when she reached up and grabbed his tie and pulled him down and kissed him on the lips, which surprised James. Then Elizabeth told him to pick her up for dinner tomorrow at 6 pm. James smiled and told her he would be there. She then handed James a piece of paper with her number on it, and she stepped inside the car, and James shut the door. The driver drove off with the General and Elizabeth, and James could see her turn and look at him through the back window. He smiled and gave a slight wave, and then she waved back. Then the vehicle was gone.

James headed to his car when a couple of officers walked by and said, "What the hell does she see in you?" James laughed and said, "I do not know, but whatever it is, I hope it keeps working," as he got in his car and headed to the officer barracks. When he got back to his room, he crashed and realized he did not have one drink all night. It was a good night, and he finally learned her name and who her father was, but he did feel bad for calling her dad a dick at the club. He knew her father was important and would not allow anyone to hurt his daughter, and he realized she was different than any woman he had ever met. He told himself not to screw this up and fell asleep.

While heading to the farm, the General sat quietly for a while in the car, looking out the window. Then Lieutenant General Allen finally asked, "So where did she meet the young Captain before tonight?" She looked at her father and told him everything that happened the night before. The General smiled and laughed at the end of the story. Lieutenant General Allen grinned and said, "So he called me a dick head." He chuckled.

He then asked her, "Does she like him?" Elizabeth said, "I believe so," and her dad said, "Why?" She told him, "Because he seems real, and not fake." Elizabeth also told her dad, "James grew up poor, and he pulled himself up by his bootstraps, and most college boys are full of themselves." She then looked at her dad and told him, "I feel safe when I am around him because he seems different." She said, "It feels like he would do whatever it took to make me happy and protect me." The General understood. He said, "Honey, I just want you to be happy." Elizabeth leaned over to her dad, kissed his cheek, and told him, "I know, Dad."

Once they made it to the farm, they hugged, and she said, "Dad, thanks for taking me. I had a great time." The driver opened the door, and Elizabeth stepped out of the vehicle, followed by the General. The driver saluted and asked, "If the General needed anything else?" The General answered back, "No, go home and pick me up at 6 am." The driver said, "Yes, sir" and got back in his vehicle and left.

The General opened the front door to the house as they walked in. They said goodnight to each other, and Elizabeth hugged her dad and kissed him on the cheek, and said, "I had a great time," and he responded by saying, "Good." Once they went to their rooms, she fell asleep quickly, and he had to return a few important phone calls before he went to bed. He was very curious about this young Captain who had an interest in his daughter. She seemed extremely happy with this young man.

However, he had more important things to worry about, and he had to go back to Washington in the morning, with many issues popping up that needed immediate attention. They usually involved elected officials who believed they knew everything but were dumber than a box of rocks. Some are highly intelligent and quick to respond with facts, but most are stupid. These people usually had someone or people who had them dance around like a marionette on strings.

Chapter 6

The Next Day

The next morning Elizabeth got up and found out her dad had already left early in the morning for Washington. She went to church with her grandparents, and when they got back, they ate lunch. Elizabeth helped around doing chores and then laid around the rest of the day. James slept in, got up around 10 am, went for a run, showered, and went to his dad's to have lunch and meet his girlfriend. Once he arrived at his dad's place, he was introduced to his girlfriend, Ann, and they all had a good lunch.

James' dad asked him, "How the ball went last night?" He said, "he had a good time, and it was fun, and it was better than he thought it would be." David asked him, "Did he meet anyone?" James replied, "He did, and she is a smart girl, and she really impressed the hell out of me." David asked, "What is her name?" James responded, "Elizabeth Allen," and "Her dad is a Three-star general." David was surprised and smiled. Ann looked at David and said, "That's impressive." James said, "I met her the other night, but I did not know who her dad was until last night." David chuckled and said, "Well, son, when is the next time you get to see her?" James smiled and answered, "Tonight, we have a date for dinner." David smiled again and asked, "Do you like her kiddo?" James replied, "I believe so, Dad." After which, everyone stopped talking.

David grinned and said, "Son, whatever you do, just be a little careful and remember someone with that power; you must be extremely careful." He looked serious and said, "Son, just one phone from her to her dad and your career is done with." James smiled and said, "He is not worried, and it is all good." He continued to have other discussions, including how his dad and Ann met and how things were going with them. Ann asked a few questions, but she mostly sat and listened to David and his son talk. Ann knew David loved and cared for his son and always worried about him. She understood because of her own experience.

James hugged Ann and his dad after they were finished talking and left to head back to the base. While driving back to his place, he realized how happy his father was having someone in his life. James has never seen his dad that happy, ever. His dad was always happy about James, but never for himself, and his dad never smiled or felt good about his personal life.

When James made it back to his room, he took another shower and got all cleaned up. James sat down and read a book for a few hours. He enjoyed reading about history, the good and the bad. James was reading about Julius Caesar and his life. He always had an interest in Caesar, both Julius and Augustus. James was also interested in Washington, Alexander, and any books on guerrilla Warfighting. He honestly believed that history can always help make people better if they understand it and learn from it.

James was also taking the Rosetta stone to improve his Arabic, and he was also interested in Latin. Besides English, he spoke Spanish and German fluently. James was trying hard to learn Arabic and Hebrew due to his multiple tours in the Middle East. The Rosetta stone helped in many ways in speeding up his learning of the language and understanding of their culture.

James left for his date around 5:00 pm because he had to stop and pick up two sets of roses, one for Elizabeth and one for her Grandma. Once he was done picking them up, he headed to her house to pick her up for dinner. While heading down the road to the farm to pick Elizabeth up, his government cell phone went off.

James pulled over and called Lieutenant Deaton, his XO, who told him over the phone, "They were going to get a warning order, and it will be coming in around Midnight." He knew it had to be important because his XO Lieutenant Deaton had a lot of friends in high places. Lieutenant Deaton is also a fourth-generation Army Officer with fourth generations of all West Point Graduates. All his relatives ended up being generals in the army and served in every major military war in the twentieth century. All retired three-or four-star Generals. He was projected to carry on the tradition of Army success and duty to the nation.

James told Lieutenant Deaton, "He will be back in his office at 11:30 pm and make sure all his officers are there at the same time and don't forget to call the 1st SGT to tell him to be there also." James disconnected the cell phone and got back on the road.

James arrived at the farm at about 5:55 pm and walked up to the front door of the house. He knocked on the door, and Elizabeth answered the door with a smile on her face. He smiled back and presented her with a dozen roses, and when he saw her grandma, Mary, he handed the other dozen to her. She was surprised and said, "Thank you very much; it's been a while since I got any," She elbowed her husband, who just walked up. Joseph, Elizabeth's Grandfather, walked up and smiled when he saw all the flowers. He then said, "What? None for me." James smiled and said, "No sir, just a handshake." Joseph and James shook hands and introduced each other.

Elizabeth then introduced his grandma Mary. James and Mary shook hands. She said, "My father had to fly back urgently to Washington early this morning." James grinned and said, "That is why he is a general." He realized that might be the reason for a possible alert at midnight. James turned around to Elizabeth and asked her if she was ready. She said, "Instead of going out tonight, how about having dinner here?" James smiled and looked at Elizabeth's grandparents and said, "I do not want to impose on anyone." Joseph said, "Not at all, son. Besides, we have extra food because my son had to leave." Joseph and James went and sat down at the kitchen table.

The evening went great, with everyone talking like they had known James for years, and James realized why Elizabeth wanted to eat at home. Joseph let it out when the ladies went to get the desert. James smiled and said, "I hope I did not disappoint anyone." Joseph smiled and said, "Young man, the only one you will have to prove yourself to is my son." James smiled with a serious expression and said, "I would be very protective also if I had a daughter." He felt that is what fathers are supposed to do. Joseph said, "I am glad you understand, and Elizabeth is my only grandchild, so you know we are very protective of her and are also scouting for her dad." James smiled and said, "I have had no doubt I would be too."

When the ladies returned, they brought small plates with homemade apple pie and a cool whip. James said, "Thank you," and slowly ate his piece of the pie. He realized it was homemade and said, "This is the best apple pie I have ever had." Mary said, "Thank you," and when James was done, she asked him, "If he would like another piece," and he said, "Absolutely." He mentioned, "It has been a long time since he has had a homemade dinner and dessert-like he had eaten tonight."

After the dessert was eaten, James and Elizabeth went outside and sat on the swing, and she reached for his hand. James smiled and said, "It has been a nice evening, and you have a good family." He added, "He was sorry he called her dad a dickhead." She chuckled and said, "I told my dad what you said, and he laughed out loud in the car." James smiled and said, "He knew he had to prove himself to be worthy to date the General's daughter." Elizabeth asked, "What?" James got quiet. She asked again, "You are not intimidated by his rank?" James grinned and said, "Not the General part, just the dad part." He looked at her and added, "Generals are easy to please. It is the dad looking out for his little girl, which is a big part of everything." He thought to himself he understood how it works.

They continued to talk about their dads and how their lives were when they were growing up. Elizabeth could see how he loved his dad and how difficult life was growing up, and how James needed to succeed in the things he had done. She talked about growing up with her dad and her life on the farm. James said, "You have nice grandparents," and added, "He never knew his." James continued by saying, "His mom's family broke ties with his dad when James was one, and his parents disowned his dad and James when he was little." James got quiet and said, "They just cut ties." Elizabeth was amazed at how James turned out because life made it so hard for him. But he kept fighting. Most people would grow up angry at life and everyone. She knew James was not fake and he was a caring person, and she was impressed with him because he never once talked about himself in an egotistic or narcissistic way. James was humble about his achievements and the things he had done.

At about 9 pm, James told Elizabeth, "He had to go because he got a call on the way here, and he had to be back at his company HQ at 11:30 pm." James added, "He needed time to ensure his gear was ready for a possible field exercise or actual mission." She understood and walked him to his car while they were still holding hands. Joseph and Mary were looking out the window smiling. James saw them from the corner of his right eye. He smiled and waved, and they waved back.

He then turned back to Elizabeth with a serious look on his face and told her, "I had a great time, and please tell your grandparents thanks for a great home-cooked meal." He added, "They are nice and good people." She looked into James' blue eyes and said, "Thank you for not getting upset about not going out." She also said, "My grandparents wanted to meet you, and I am sure they will scout you out in front of my dad." He smiled, saying, "I know," as he leaned down and kissed Elizabeth. She pulled him closer, and they held each other kissing for a minute when he stepped back and said, "Wow." She smiled and also said, "Wow," as they kissed each other again and held onto each other.

51

James then said, "By the way, I need your number, and asked her where she was testing him?" She laughed and realized she had given him the wrong paper that was in her pocket. The number she gave him was to the Pentagon. She apologized and gave him the right number. Elizabeth then said, "Do I get yours?" James smiled and said, "Absolutely." He gave it to her and then kissed her again. She smiled, and he reached into his car, grabbed his phone, and tossed his Government phone in the passenger seat. He put the number on his regular phone. Once they exchanged numbers, they kissed again. He then got in his car and started it up. James rolled his window down and said, "I will call you when I get back, whenever that is." She said, "Please be careful." He said, "I will try to talk to you later."

James slowly headed away and drove home to grab his combat gear and head to his office on base. Elizabeth went back inside and called her dad. When she got hold of him, he asked her, "How was her date?" She said, "It was fine, and told him they ate at the house instead of going out." The General then asked Elizabeth, "Well,?" Elizabeth said, "Dad, I like him." The General said, "Elizabeth, you are an adult, and I just want you to be happy because that is important to me." He got quiet for a moment and said, "Your happiness has always been the most important thing to me." She said, "I know Dad, and Dad, I love you." The General smiled and said, "I love you too, and I will be home in a couple of days, and you want, we can go fish or hunt if you want to." Elizabeth said, "How about going to the shooting range on base when you get back?" The General said, "Absolutely, and why shooting?" She laughed and said, "Just in case James gets stupid." The General laughed and said, "Good night." Elizabeth said, "Good night," with a smiling face.

When he hung up, the general continued discussing what was needed to end the threat emerging in the Middle East and South America. It was a late-night briefing, but it was serious. The problem involved Hezbollah working with South American cartels smuggling narcotics in the western hemisphere. These funds were used to pay for terrorism and other criminal acts throughout the West and the world.

Intelligence agencies believe Hezbollah is attempting to gain possession of a nuclear bomb or plutonium to make a dirty bomb. One of the two used in a hot spot city or against a Middle Eastern country like Israel, or Saudi Arabia, would start a major war with dangerous consequences. For example, using it in Israel could cause a domino effect with an all-out war with Hezbollah, Iran, Palestinians, and other countries.

All the Arab countries would have to pick a side, and it's usually against Israel, which has been consistently repeated throughout history. Arab countries have made peace with Israel, but when it comes down to Arabs and Israel, there is no such thing in the Middle East as being neutral. When a middle eastern country has failed to line up against Israel with other Arab countries, there are usually economic repercussions and even assassination or assassination attempts by radicals who feel betrayed by their country's leadership. One good example is Anwar Sadat, the Egyptian leader who was killed by an Egyptian extremist called the Islamic Jihad during an Egyptian celebration. The Middle East has a consistent history of political leaders whose troops or political enemies were assassinated. The Middle East is a tough and dangerous world beneath the dunes of time.

Chapter 7

Europe's Messes

Most of the problems we have in the Middle East can go back to the end of World War One, and they continued after World War Two and how the Middle East was cut up by the west. The magic cards were oil and the East VS West Cold War after 1945.

In Palestine, there were going to be two lands cut up in Palestine. Israel was one, and they declared its Independence on May 14, 1948, and the Palestinian state was to come after that. But the Arab nations decided to destroy Israel and invaded with great loss to both sides, and Israel won again at a great loss.

Due to the first Israeli vs. Arabs war, the action of making the State of Palestine never happened. This was caused by Jordan refusing to give up the West Bank and Eastern Jerusalem. The British Government, which was aligned with and trained the Jordanians, refused to pressure Jordan into falling in line with the United Nations agreement for a Palestinian homeland. Egypt refused to give up the Gaza strip and ignored all UN agreements with this area.

This just furthered decades of Palestinian hatred in the wrong direction-straight at Israel instead of the United Nations and Western Europe, who failed in forcing a homeland in the late 1940s. Because of the failure of the United Nations, terrorism throughout Europe and the Middle East continues today with no end in sight due to the Palestinian Authority leadership and Hamas, who are corrupt and the rest of the world for not looking for an honest way of creating this second country.

In Post-World War 2 Europe, most of the countries would lean on NATO to help them protect themselves from any country which was a threat. Usually, that meant the Soviet Union and the Eastern Block. The National Atlantic Treaty Organization was originally set up to protect western Europe from the Soviet Union and its Eastern European allies.

As time went by, European countries got more dovish than having any interest in protecting themselves. No European country could fight back by itself against any threat. They relied on a joint defense, with the United States playing a major role. Everyone relied on the United States for everything.

Once the Cold War was over, Western European Nations neutered themselves. They then took the money they would use for their military and increased social programs thinking the billions spent in those areas would strengthen their nations. The opposite has happened. Terrorism and rogue nations began running amok, and Western European Nations only doubled down on spending in non-self-defense areas and running down their defense capabilities. They allowed terrorist groups knowingly into their countries and looked the other way. Some even made deals with them that if they left them alone, they would look the other way.

They began to act as Europe did before World War Two, allowing the Nazis to run freely. The primary countries of Germany, England, and France were the worse. It is true they not only looked the other way, but they also paid bribes to terrorists to leave them alone, which would only last a short period before a terrorist act would happen again. As they say, you can't fix stupid.

The seeds of giving up their self-reliance had been planted years before the cold war ended. The problem began with the seeds of complacent behavior started when the Treaty establishing the European Economic Community was signed in 1958. This later turned into the European Union in 1993. Most people do not know that some of its creators were former Nazis Soldiers like Walter Hallstein. Many supporters tried to distort his history to help push the European Union agenda. He served in France as a German Officer and was later captured after the Allied invasion. They stated that he had never joined the Nazi Party. What they left out was most German soldiers were not members. However, killing their enemies like Jews was alright to his defenders.

Under General Charles de Gaulle, France tried to be the big dog in European affairs for many years. However, when the Cold War was over, East and West Germany united. They began to become the bully of the European Union. They also cut defense spending and began pushing social programs, leaving them with a very weak military to use in anything involving a large NATO force. However, when it just involved France, they used the Famous French Legion and did not use troops inside France. The French leaders during certain periods looked the other way when it involved terrorism.

Once World War Two was over, the British went straight into a Socialist form of economics which helped weaken the English Lion even more after the bloody conflict. World War Two wrecked them economically almost as badly as other countries. England did not have the Nazis marching down Piccadilly. The sad thing was that they, with French help, removed Adolf Hitler when they had the chance. Millions of people would not have died in Europe, and countries would have been ruined. Europe would not have been wrecked with an estimated twenty million dead.

England smartly cut some of the militaries due to the declining Empire. However, instead of using it to strengthen the economy and fix the job market, they went into free-spending on social programs. In translation, they ran debt up so bad they almost bankrupted the country, making things worse. What do they do to fix the problem? Keep spending money. They have never recovered as an economic or military power. They cannot defend themselves unless they get help from America. The Falkland War was their last hurrah, even after winning the war with Argentina. They needed the United States' help.

England helped during the Wars in the Middle East with other NATO countries, but they kept cutting their military, going the "We will lean on NATO and the Americans." This thinking is not just for the British; it is all for Western Europe. The problem with this thinking is it has made these countries extremely weak and almost impotent in protecting themselves against enemies foreign and domestic. They have lowered the standards in many of their fighting units due to political correctness. The dangerous enemies of freedom have noticed this.

This political thinking has also affected the United States Military. The one thing which saves America is its technology---at the moment. Once the cold war ended, radical elements flooded into England and other countries. England's system refused to remove these radicals who encouraged destroying England.

These three major European nations countries are allowing terrorists into their countries. This is again due to political correctness. When they do something to kick them out of the country, Some Court Judge(s) overrides it. These radicals lived in what people call no-go zones, and some small towns were dominant and forced the town leadership to submit to what they wanted. Terrorists see this and know Western leaders are weak because of political correctness.

The problem with terrorists is they usually need funding. In the post-cold War period, most radical groups were funded by the Soviet Union through allies, dummy businesses, and leftist groups through university sympathizers. The Soviet Union used their KGB and the GRU to funnel these funds to the organizations they believed could help disrupt the west and their allies worldwide. When the Soviet Union collapsed, the number one supporter of terrorism became Iran. The next supporters were those lone wolves or organizations who sought out chaos for political differences, revenge or both. Revenge has been a huge motivator throughout time. Wars and the loss of loved ones have pushed people to do things they normally would not do.

The European countries have been leaning on America to defend against any threat from Russia since the end of World War Two. Lieutenant General Allen told his staff to put all the teams at Bragg and in Germany on standby and tell the unit in Germany to prepare to go to Poland. He added to notify NATO Command and prepare to fly them where needed.

He told his Chief of Staff, Colonel Ray, to get hold of the CIA liaison and to send the head of the DIA to his office in two hours. To which Colonel Ray agreed and exited the room. Colonel Ray made phone calls to these people and told them the General wanted all the information on Hezbollah and nukes and dirty bombs. He also wanted to know who their contacts were in South America. They each told him that they would be there in two hours.

Captain Thomas arrived in the company area and was met by his XO Lieutenant Deaton. They started discussing all the possibilities of an alert and went to Captain Thomas's office. He threw his equipment with the rest of his gear on his office corner floor. Lieutenant Deaton, who walked in after him, smiled and said, "Hey, boss, look in the mirror." He stepped over to the small mirror on the wall and looked. He had lipstick on his face. Captain Thomas grinned and turned to Lieutenant Deaton, and said, "Thanks." It would not have looked good going in front of the BC with lipstick on his face. They both laughed while Captain Thomas cleaned his face.

Captain Thomas asked Lieutenant Deaton, "How was he doing?" Lieutenant Deaton replied, "He is doing good," and stated, "I had a date tonight, but unfortunately, I had to cancel it." Captain Thomas smiled and said, "Sorry." Lieutenant Deaton said, "Oh well." Captain Thomas smacked LT Deaton on the back and said, "I owe you one." LT Deaton said, "Sounds good." Then they both returned back to their business.

While going over all the possibilities they could think of, they had the other officers step in with the top NCOs in the unit. They discussed how prepared the company is for any small or large activation in any part of the world. They continued to talk about the incidents happening throughout the world and if they could be heading to one of those hot spots. Captain Thomas went over the activation list as they had to make sure all equipment and staff were ready for whatever was thrown their way.

Chapter 8

Back in time

Lieutenant General Allen was a hard-charging officer when he was younger who always led from the front because he was taught that way. Joseph loved military history and knew the great leaders in history always, at one time or another, led from the front. Joseph pushed himself and was first in his class at West Point and was proud of his achievements. Like most hard-chargers looking for action, he hated the boredom of sitting at a desk from 8 am to 4 pm.

Joseph grew up on the farm with his parents and enjoyed working hard on the farm. He knew the farm would be his one day, and he was proud of his work to keep it going. Joseph understood the meaning of hard work. He was proud of planting seeds every year and watching his family's work grow to the full stage. Working in the garden was a stress release from work and life, and it was joyful to watch their hard work succeed.

Joseph had no siblings due to an injury his mom had working on the farm, and he was lucky to have all the attention from his parents focused on him. He just wished he had a brother or sister like other people Joseph knew, but he understood the injury to his mom prevented it, and it was one of those things life throws at people.

Joseph had a good upbringing and understood the values his parents stowed in him. He was usually up before dawn to help around the farm before going to school and even during the summers. He had many friends growing up and was well-respected among his friends and fellow students. Joseph played Baseball, and his dad taught him how to play golf. He did not play on the school golf team due to the schedule conflict with baseball, his favorite sport.

While on the West Point Baseball team, he was a pitcher who had success on the mound. He started to think during his junior year, after his mandatory time in the Army, he might be able to go pro. That all changed in one game. He threw a curveball, a large pop in his elbow, and damaged a tendon, and there went any chance of pitching in the pros.

Once he had surgery, he knew his baseball dream was over, and Joseph was at first angry, then realized while recovering he was lucky to be where he was and appreciated the opportunities most people would not have. So, he focused on his future military career and pushed himself in academics. Joseph finished first in class and chose the Green Berets as his career. He later married Isabella Sturgill, the sister of a fellow West Pointer David Sturgill. They would help each other during their careers as friends do.

He bounced first to Fort Campbell, Kentucky, then Fort Carson, Colorado, where he was well-liked and respected among the teams. Then one day, his Company Commander, Captain Charles, reported with him to meet Lieutenant General Scott. He was told "his team was selected for an extremely important mission in another country, and the odds were slim of success, but it must be done and attempted." Captain Charles further added, "Our intelligent agencies cannot get in, so I told my boss we will get it done somehow."

The General said, "I know you are married, so you could back out if you chose Lieutenant. He paused and continued, "I cannot tell you what it is unless you say yes, and by the way, you would be on standby and could not go home and make any phone calls." Captain Charles said I would take a note to your wife tonight if you accept it, and you have 5 minutes to think about it. Both the General and Captain stepped out of the room and shut the door.

First Lieutenant Joseph Allen was a twenty-four-year-old Team leader on the best team in the Special Forces. Lieutenant Allen was proud of his guys and knew they would be angry if he said no to his team. His team knows the dangers and hazards of their jobs and what type of risk they take wearing the uniform and the Beret. Joseph reached into his jacket, pulled out a pen and paper, and wrote, "Honey, I love you, but unfortunately, my team has been activated, and I promised to be safe. Love Joseph."

Lieutenant Allen went and opened the door and stepped back, and watched his bosses come in. When the door closed, and they both looked at him, he told his bosses his answer was "yes." Right after he said yes, General Scott signaled to some men on the outside of the room who were looking into the room, and these officers came in and shut the door. They were the General's aids carrying maps, video, and boxes of intelligence.

They began to brief him on the mission, and at first, he seemed a little overwhelmed. Then it all started to click in his brain. Lieutenant Allen asked questions that surprised everyone in the room about things they did not think about. Lieutenant General Scott said, "Lieutenant, you do what you think is necessary." Lieutenant Allen's Captain smiled, looked at the General, and said, "That's why he was picked." The General shook his head up and down, smiling, realizing this young Lieutenant was different than the usual team leader. He was impressed with how Lieutenant Allen carried himself and the questions he asked. Lieutenant Allen and Captain Charles reviewed a couple of items in the intelligence gathered and agreed to adapt on the ground if needed.

Once the briefing was completed, General Scott told his aid, "It was time to go," and turned to the Captain. "Good?" The Captain smiled and said, "We are good." General Scott whispered to one of his aids Captain Jones and asked, "What's the odds?" Captain Jones said, "65%." Lieutenant Allen heard that and stated in a strong voice, "80%." General Scott grinned and headed to the door. As he was leaving, someone yelled, "ATTENTION." Everyone stood at attention until General Scott left.

Captain Jones then turned back to Lieutenant Allen and said, "What do you need from us, Lieutenant?" Lieutenant Allen said, "Let's get my team here first, and then we can brief them and get the show going." The 1sgt then picked up the phone and told someone over the phone, "Activate Allen's team and get their asses in here now." Then Captain Jones said with a smile, "That was ballsy telling the General 80%." Lieutenant Allen laughed and replied, "I had to sound confident in case it goes bad." Captain Charles, who was watching and listening, started to laugh and said, "Smart thinking, Lieutenant."

When Lieutenant Allen's team arrived, they were separated from everyone and briefed. His team was a little surprised by the mission and where they were going. They all made sure their wills and other paperwork were up to date. They made sure all their equipment was good. They examined their equipment a couple of days earlier to ensure it was all combat-ready. Once your equipment is checked, it is doubled and tripled checked and a higher rank to ensure there is nothing that will fail during combat or a combat situation. Something could always go wrong.

They took apart their weapons to check the smallest piece to make sure it won't malfunction when it was getting used. They all got in a circle with a selected noncom to run it. He called out a list of things to make sure they had it. Once that was done. Each person stated what he was carrying and where it was. This included maps and other information. This was done in case someone was wounded or killed. Everyone knew where those needed items were.

The team loaded their equipment in the Humvees and headed to Butts Army Airfield. When they arrived, they loaded the C-130 with their equipment themselves. The Air Force staff assigned to the plane did not help because they knew and understood the SF team did not want anyone to touch their equipment. The Pilot came over to Lieutenant Allen, and both saluted each other, and the pilot identified himself as "Captain Franks." Lieutenant Allen did not identify himself due to the type of mission it was, and Captain Franks understood that. They shook hands and had a five-minute friendly conversation. Captain Franks said before he walked away, "He will try and give you a good ride." They shook hands, saluted each other, and the Captain went and started the plane.

Then before they loaded up, Captain Charles showed up, saluting and shaking hands with each team member. Captain Charles then patted Lieutenant Allen on the back, and they stepped away from everyone else. Captain Charles said, "Joseph, I gave the note to your wife," and Lieutenant Allen looked at his boss and said, "What did she say?" Captain Charles answered and said, "She loves you, and congratulations, you are going to be a father." Joseph smiled and shook hands with Captain Charles. He then turned to his team and yelled out over the plane engines, "I am going to be a father." They all yelled "congratulations" and came over, patted his back, and shook his hands. Then Lieutenant Allen got serious and told his team to "get on the bird." They smiled and walked and got on.

Lieutenant Allen then turned to Captain Charles and said, "If I bit it, please check in on my family." Captain Charles smiled and said, "It was going to be fine." Captain Charles said to Joseph with a serious expression on his face, "If it is going bad, get the hell out and protect our men." He looked around and said, "We can always try another time again." Lieutenant Allen saluted and smiled and said, "Yes, sir." They shook hands, and Lieutenant Allen added: "Sir, just make sure those boats are at their assigned spots." Captain Charles walked away and gave the thumbs up. They both knew that Two AWACS would be in the sky if one plane covering the area suffered any type of malfunction.

All branches were involved in this delicate mission, and only a couple in the army was aware of who the Top-Secret target was. Each branch had an area to cover in this mission, but due to its importance, everyone in the war room in the Pentagon was not allowed to leave or use the telephones. All communication to the outside was shut down except to the Whitehouse, and the Pentagon was locked down. The media was told they were conducting a security exercise.

All this was to protect the SF team from leaks to the media and foreign spy agencies. As everyone knows, the biggest mouths that always help our enemies are the American media and our politicians, who try to embarrass the other side and do not care about the results of their actions on the country. The press always considers ratings or papers sold instead of soldiers' lives. It has been that way since Vietnam War.

Once the C-130 was airborne, it headed east along the routes the airlines flew. Then when it made it to the Appalachians, it flew to Atlanta. The plane then turned and headed South toward Miami. Once the plane made it to Miami, it turned East again for the navy base on Andros Island in the Bahamas. At approximately 330PM, when the plane landed, it was parked on the far side of the runway. It was surrounded by Navy security forces for protection. All the men were taken to an empty building where they could shower, eat, and nap in a bed.

The next morning at 01:00 am., everyone was up and began preparing for the next seventy-two hours. This mission was to rescue a U.S. Senator's father who had been locked up in Cuban prisons for 20 years. The Senator's father snuck into Cuba to get some relatives out, but he was caught, beaten, and tortured. The U.S. government refused to do anything to get him out until now. Presidents have a habit of talking tough, but most are spineless and cowardly.

The target was El Pitirre Prison outside Havana, Cuba, guarded by the Avispas Negras. In English, it means Black Wasps. They are known as a Special Forces unit in the Revolutionary Armed Forces. They are guarding the VIP prisoners. These are and have been highly trained by enemy nations of the West. This prison is on the opposite side of the Cuban island from the American Military base at Guantanamo, Cuba. The Prison is just off the Autopista National Highway, Southeast of Havana.

One part of the plan was to increase flights into Guantanamo and conduct a larger exercise than normal on the eastern part of Guantanamo to make the Cubans nervous. This would pull troops and some security out of the city of Havana. The Cuban Government believes the Americans would not want to destroy Havana in an invasion. This would turn the Cuban people against the Americans for leveling their Capitol and causing a large loss of life. This exercise would involve the U.S. Navy, Marines, and the United States Air Force.

The C-130 left the Bahamas at 02:30 am. They flew the same routes as the other American military planes. All the Military planes were flying 15 miles off the Cuban coast, West to east. The Cubans who were monitoring the flights were puzzled. Why West to East? The American Base was in the Eastern part of Cuba. The C-130 back door opened at 03:55 am. While they were getting ready, Sargent Johnson turned to Lieutenant Allen and asked, "How come Delta is not doing this?." Lieutenant Allen smiled and said, "Buddy, they are already there." He looked around and stated, "A team is there in case we need help." Lieutenant Allen added, "They are all Cuban and speak the dialect." Both smiled and stepped up to the back of the plane. At 04:00 am, the light went green, and they jumped out of the plane into the night after two wet subs were dropped from the plane.

When they landed in the Caribbean, the water was warm. They unlatched their parachute and began swimming toward the wet subs. They disconnected the parachutes and loaded them up. Once both wet subs were loaded, they headed to Havana to the entrance of Havana Port when Lieutenant Allen saw a large fishing barge getting ready to enter the Port. This would provide a perfect cover to sneak into the Havana Port due to radar and any sensors the

Cuban country might have. If they had those, they would show just a large fishing barge. Anything monitoring the entrance would not show two wet subs right under the barge as it moved inside the Port.

When they made it into the Port, they slowly moved away from the fishing barge towards the entrance to the Martin Perez River opening. They put the subs on the bottom of the Port near the River entrance on the side. Once this was done, they would swim to the exit point. The weather in Havana was heavy rain and steady. They would stay at an empty, run-down building they saw in the photographs by the river entrance. The river was heavily polluted and smelled. The intelligence documented the river is used as a dumping point for all types of sludge, human waste, and toxic materials. They would follow the river up to the prison at night on the side of the river through the weeds, grass, and trees. While in the old building, they rotated to catch a little sleep.

Once everyone rested, they all stood by, watching the weather as it was still raining. This weather kept traffic down in the area. Once it started to get into the late afternoon, everyone checked and double-checked their equipment. They reviewed the plan, and everyone discussed their primary and secondary assignments. Then they went over the regress action and how they would work their way back down the river to the Wet Subs or if they had to use a vehicle to get back to the water. No matter what, it's approximately five miles in and five miles back.

During the day, they continued rotating, resting, and watching the area to ensure nobody would point them out. They checked in every two hours, and there was no recall coming from the Command Center, so all was good in being in a communist country with a government that would love to catch them dead or alive and show them off to the world. The best friend they had was the nonstop rain and darkness.

Chapter 9

Shoot, don't Shoot

Once night came, and with it still raining, they headed up the river with half the team on one side and the other half on the other. They slowly moved up the river watching in all directions. They started at 9:00 P.M. While moving up the river; they attempted to stay out of the river due to its contamination. Going in into the river was the last result. They saw some old boats by some docks going up the river but ignored them. If they took them, it could cause an alarm. So, they kept moving and used the terrain.

When they got about 4 miles up the river, they ran into two little kids, about 8 and 10 were fishing down by the river when they saw Lieutenant Allen and two other soldiers. The two kids must have snuck out to fish without the parents knowing. This is every Special Forces nightmare because it could blow a mission in a blink of an eye. Do you kill them to protect the team or mission? That is a tough decision to make over American lives. It's what every Special Operations prays that they do not have to make this serious decision. Adults are one thing when it comes to shooting, but teenagers are another and not something anyone would want to do unless they are using a weapon to kill an American.

Since they were not in American uniform, the kids had puzzled looks on their faces. Lieutenant Allen said under his breath, "Oh Shit." The young little boy said in Spanish. "Are you Russians?" Sargent Johnson, who spoke fluent Russian, stated in Spanish and Russian. "Yes, we are young men, and please do not tell anyone because we are playing soldier games and going against other Russian soldiers helping your great country of Cuba." The boys listened, and Johnson continued, saying, "We are acting like those stupid Americans sneaking around." Sargent Johnson whispered and said, "Shhhhhh, do not even tell your parents." The team watched Johnson talking with the two kids when he said, "If you promise, I will come and leave a gift for both of you by that bush tomorrow." The two little kids smiled and responded back with, "We promise."

Sargent Johnson then made them say, "In the name of Jesus, I swear not to say anything until we get our gift." They promised, and Sargent Johnson and the two kids shook hands and made a promise to God. He was well aware in Cuba, even though the government's atheistic view on religion is well aware the citizens believe in god. Then the young boy and girl waved by and returned home in the rain. Everyone was glad it did not turn into another direction none of them would want to go.

Lieutenant Allen stopped and looked around at his men because he knew the mission had just been compromised. He then turned to Sargent Johnson and asked him, "What do you think?" Sargent Johnson whispered, "I think we are good." And "We will need two things to leave behind on the way out." Johnson smiled and pointed at Lieutenant Allen's cross on a chain? Lieutenant Allen smiled and said, "Sounds good as he took off his necklace."

Joseph then broke the silence on the radio and notified Headquarters of what had happened. General Scott, who was in tactical command, told Lieutenant Allen "to return to the pickup site." Lieutenant Allen hesitated and looked at his men, and they all shook their heads no with pissed-off look on their faces. Lieutenant Allen responded on the com, "Negative, we are too close to turn back, and we are only a few clicks away, and we all believe we can keep going." General Scott looked around the command room with everyone either just shrugging their shoulders to others who said, "Don't stop," and then General Scott said, "You are green." Lieutenant Allen responded, "Get everything ready to come and get us if this fails or works."

They moved forward, climbed out of the river ditch, and approached the Prison. They were about 100 yards in the brush, watching the prison. This prison was extremely old; many political prisoners went through the Gates, and most were carried out. They had no idea how many other prisoners were there besides their target. If the opportunity arrived, he planned to free as many as possible, but only the Senator's dad will be leaving with them. With prisoners scattered around Havana, this could cause some disarray and help them escape.

While Lieutenant Allen was looking around, he realized what he was looking at was the Cuban Special Forces unit (Wasp) Barracks, not the prison section. He let everyone know that the pictures were wrong. The prison was on the other side, and the intelligence they received was all messed up and wrong.

So, Lieutenant Allen and his team worked their way around the left side and came around under the Autopista Nation Highway. When they came around, they saw one tower with two men looking inside the prison yard. They were smoking and leaning over the tower rail. The Tower roof was large enough to cover them. They all split up to check everything around the barracks and the prison. After one hour, they all returned and passed on their information to Lieutenant Allen. The only ones who appear to be awake are the two in the prison tower. There appeared to be a road that entered both facilities, and they were connected. They observed no movement anyplace inside the buildings or around them.

Lieutenant Allen was gathering all the information when he saw two Russian-made trucks about 20 yards behind the trees. He told Sargent Del Gardo to "go check and see if we can use both vehicles." Lieutenant Allen started to kick a couple of different options around in his head since the original plan was shot due to the prison almost inside the whole WASP compound. When Sargent Del Gardo returned, he smiled and said, "One was secure, but the second one, which is closer, has a full tank and no lock on the wheel." Everyone agreed there were no video cameras to be seen anyplace. Lieutenant Allen put out his plan of attack and how it needs to fall into place.

Sargent First Class Jackson, when given the signal using a silencer, shot both Tower guards, and they died immediately. Staff Sargent Shultz ran to the fence and cut through both fences. They all entered on a run. Each took turns covering for the other as they bounded up to the building. Lieutenant Allen had Staff Sargent Rodriquez provide cover on the outside to ensure no one came in behind the rest of the team.

He gave the signal, and they went to the nearest door and entered the prison building. Working their way down the corridor, they found it led to different cell areas. So, with one person guarding the corridor, the other four men split into two teams, and one group went and entered one cell area at a time on the left and the other on the right. Both teams found guards sleeping in their chairs and shot them quickly. The guards never knew what happened when the headshots occurred, and they fell to the floor dead.

Once it was safe, the team members opened the prison cells and noticed the cell conditions were horrible. The prisoners all looked like they had been physically tortured many times. The Cuban military had a reputation for torturing their prisoners and doing whatever was necessary to get what they wanted. During the Vietnam War, they tortured American POWs while in the Vietnam prisons.

Finally, halfway downrange, they found the prisoner they were sent in to get. The cell door was opened, with Lieutenant Allen going in first and helping the old prisoner up. The prisoner smiled and asked in Spanish, with a puzzled look on his face, "Who were they?" Lieutenant Allen said, "We cannot talk now just say we are friends of your sons." They told everyone in Spanish "to head out quietly through the first door and head down the range to the corridor." The prisoners could not move fast because of the physical torture they received from the Cuban military. They staggered and slowly walked as fast as they could.

They exited the building when they heard shouting from inside the building. One of the guards that did not get shot because he was in the restroom on the other side of the building began yelling and shooting. Everyone was running through the cut in the fences when Lieutenant Allen saw five guards running out of the building with AK-47s. He sprayed them down with help from Sargent Del Gardo. Four of them died before they hit the ground. The younger one was wounded but got back up and staggered to the cut in the fence. Lieutenant Allen stepped back toward this young soldier, and they made eye contact with each other. Lieutenant Allen then fired three shots into this Cuban soldier's chest. The young Cuban soldier looked down from where he was shot, looked up at LT Allen, and fell dead to the ground.

Then the alarms started going off all over the prison and the soldier's barracks. The Truck was started, and everyone, including some other prisoners, jumped on. The other prisoners decided to stagger off into the night. Sargent Johnson shifted the truck gears, drove off, and headed towards the highway. He was going as fast as he could. He believed no one saw what direction they went. But Sargent Johnson was not going to take any chances. He kept his foot down on the pedal. They needed to go five simple miles to get to the water.

Once they made it to where they started, they got out and could hear sirens way off in the direction they came. The remaining prisoners thanked them and took off in different directions. However, one stayed. He refused to go and said in Spanish, "Take me to America; my family is there." The Senator's father said in Spanish, "He speaks the truth, and he is also my dearest friend." Lieutenant Allen said no way but was told by the senator's dad, "He saved my life more than once." Lieutenant Allen shook his head again no, and said in a firm tone, "We do not have any room." Sargent Rodriquez, who was Cuban-American, said boss, "He can sit on my lap." Lieutenant Allen shook his head, smiled, and said, "What the hell, why not" and, "Let's get the hell out of here."

They walked into the water and crawled around till they found their equipment. They pulled their hidden equipment out of the water and put it on as they slowly went into the deeper section of water. Sargent Rodriquez shared his with the prisoner who he helped into the water. They swam down and went deep into the Wet subs and got in. There was extra breathing equipment, and the prisoner was helped to get it on. The Wet Subs engines were started and took off for the Caribbean. The tough part was getting outside the 12-mile zone so they did not get caught, knowing what could happen to all of them.

After a few minutes, they made it just outside the Port when they noticed boat activity behind them on the water. They radioed to the Command center, "They had the package plus one." The Command Center cheered, and some patted each other on the back. General Davis said, "Outstanding job, guys." Then suddenly, there were some explosions coming over the speakers as everyone got quiet.

Lieutenant Allen came over the loud static and stated, "They were being pursued by ships on top who were dropping explosives into the water." Everyone in the command Center got quiet as Lieutenant Allen came over the radio and said, "Someone must have seen us enter the water and reported us." Lieutenant General Davis then turned to Admire Johansson and said, "Get your navy to provide a roadblock for those guys." The Admiral stated, "It's done," as he began talking on his communication system. Lieutenant General Davis then turned to the Air Force General and said, "Cover the skies and protect them from the Cuban Air Force." Some of the brass stopped in place, knowing this could go bad and looked back at the General when he looked around and said all these orders are coming directly from the President of the United States gentlemen. He knew that would make everyone move a little quicker, knowing who was involved in the decision-making.

Air Force General Fox said, "It will happen," and called in his jets who were over Guantanamo waiting for the signal to provide cover in the air in case any Cuban planes became a threat. He had full confidence in his fighter pilots to knock out any threat involving the Cuban Air Force. They were the best in the world, and most had flown many combat missions in the past.

Lieutenant Allen told his men to keep the peddle down. He knew It was a race to the finish line. They went deeper as the boat traffic above them got louder, and some of the explosions were getting closer. He believed they were still shy of the 12-mile limit when suddenly everything above them got quiet, and the explosions stopped. They kept on going when they looked up and saw some large boats on top of the water in front and behind them. They went even deeper to avoid the boats in front and behind them, making it harder so the surface ships could not force them up. Suddenly, he looked up and saw some divers swimming toward them from the surface.

Then suddenly, Lieutenant Allen could hear General Scott come over his communication equipment. "Come up, son. It's us. You're safe." Lieutenant Allen gave the signal, and they headed up to the surface. He waved at the men coming towards him when he realized they were Navy Seals coming to escort them back to the surface. When they came up and looked around, they saw they were surrounded by American Navy ships and choppers flying over them. Then some American jets flew over. The mission was over, and it was a success. Lieutenant Allen was happy and relieved as he looked at the rest of the team and the two former Cuban prisoners, who were all smiling. The Senator's father started to cry, knowing he was free and he will get to see his family for the first time in twenty years.

Once they made it onto the Aircraft carrier, they were all debriefed. They were flown back to the Bahamas, where General Scott and other VIPs met them. They observed the U.S. Senator come running down the runway and grab his father in his arms, and both men began crying. Once they were done hugging each other, they turned to Lieutenant Allen and his team and said "thank you" in English and Spanish.

The Senator let go of his dad and stepped up to Lieutenant Allen, and they shook hands when the Senator told Lieutenant Allen, "You will always have a friend no matter what or where you are at." The Senator also said, "I will be watching your career, and if you have any problems, you can always call me, and I mean always." The Florida Senator got choked up and said, "What you and your men have done?" He stopped talking as he wiped tears from his eyes when Lieutenant Allen smiled and interrupted and said, "Sir, it's always good to have friends. Thank you." The senator smiled and said, "Thank you, Lieutenant." The senator turned around and hugged his dad, and they walked towards another building and went inside. The other prisoner walked behind them smiling, and then he turned around and went up to each person on Lieutenants Allen's' team and shook their hands, and said in Spanish, "Thank you." He then limped to the building where his friend and the senator entered.

General Scott told the team to step over, and they saluted, and he saluted them back and notified them, "It was a job well done, and you guys are officially promoted as of now one rank." He then turned to the newly promoted Captain Allen and said, "The Promotion comes from the order of the President of the United States, and he appreciates what you men did." General Scott was amazed it was successful and continued talking and told the men, "You men took a high-risk situation and made it work. General Scott looked around and told everyone, "The President and the U.S. Senator whose dad you rescued will be meeting with each one of you in the future, and from me, I want to say to you, soldiers, you make me proud."

Everyone laughed, shook each other's hands, and hugged each other. They all knew they were lucky in completing this mission with only minor scrapes and bruises and without any loss of life on their side. They each knew all hell was going to break loose in Cuba and the international arena.

Captain Allen said loudly, "Gather up." Everyone stopped and walked away from General Scott and everyone else. General Scott turned to another officer and said, "That's a hell of an officer." When Captain Allen and his men were about 20 yards away, they circled Captain Allen, and he looked down, choked up and, with a tear in his eye, said to his team. "Thank you for doing your duty and caring for each other." He said, "I owe each of you a thousand times over and no matter where you go in your career, please keep in contact." He shook their hands again and said, "Let's go home." They all yelled, "hell yes."

General Scott watched the men head to the C-130 and board it. He then headed to his private jet, and when he got inside his plane, he called the President and briefed him personally by order of the Secretary of Defense. He then requested "Captain Allen be transferred to the Pentagon to be on his staff." The President agreed and said, "We will make that happen." The President said, "Any Lieutenant who led a team deep into Cuba on a rescue mission and had to change the plan in mid-stride and had no causalities, those talents need to be used." After 30 days of leave, Captain and Mrs. Allen were transferred to Washington.

While working at the Pentagon, Captain Allen watched what and how things worked in and out of the Special Forces community. Not many people were aware of the mission he was involved with. However, others knew he did something big due to the way several three and four Generals dealt with Captain Allen. Both his wife and he got to go to many cocktails get, together and events with the Washington élite. He saw the narcist behavior of too many people and had nothing but contempt for many of them.

As time went by, he traveled with Lieutenant General Davis to Military Bases. He watched how the different bases were run, including the different types of troops. He felt the opportunities for some of the troops to get further training was hindered by too many stupid rules and regulations, and officers and Senior Non-Comms personally interfered with soldiers advancing in other skills. This has always been a problem in the army during post-World War Two. Captain Allen felt the more trained soldiers were, the more likely they would reenlist and stay in the Army. If people are bored with their job, why should they wait until they reenlist to move into another job field? Most soldiers will refuse to stay in their present job and leave the service. The Army is too rigid in its ways and always loses talented soldiers due to a rigid system.

Captain Allen tried to push some new rules through, but he could not get support from the higher-ups in anything he tried to do. When it came to the soldiers, he tried to explain to the Generals that if someone after their halfway point should have that option to better themselves for the service, it's also to the armies' advantage. He was shut down. Later, he tried to increase bonuses in more special units. One year later, he was transferred to Fort Bragg, North Carolina, upon his request. He was tired of the B.S. at the Pentagon. Too many people, including Generals, were just checking off their requirements to get their next promotion. He had enough of this and could get out of his tour at the Pentagon sooner. General Davis, who was promoted to his fourth star, apologized for how miserable things were at the Pentagon and told Captain Allen sometimes "the political appointees can make things good and sometimes bad, and this brings out the good and bad in Generals."

General Davis understood there were too many bootlickers, and some avoided tough decision-making by straddling the fence. He then told Captain Allen, "Remember, down the road, if you make it this far, remember what you saw so it can be fixed." Captain Allen shook the General's hand and said, "I will."

Chapter 10

Your Delicate Mission

Captain Thomas and his Officers met at the Battalion Headquarters at 01:30 am. As they walked through the Metal detector and emptied their pockets, their cell phones were confiscated. A Lieutenant said, "They would get them back when they returned from their mission." Captain Thomas and his men looked at each other with puzzled looks on their faces, and Captain Thomas shrugged his shoulders and said, "Alright."

Captain Thomas and his group entered the Battalion Commanders Command Center. They saluted the Battalion Commander and Lieutenant Colonel Roberts, returned the salute, shook each one's hands, and told them to sit in the chairs at the big table. The entrance door was closed. Two Armed soldiers stood on the outside to prevent any entrance.

The Battalion commander's assistant then walked over to turn on the large television, and he typed in a code. Lieutenant General Allen popped on the screen from the Pentagon War room in seconds. Everyone stood, and Lieutenant General Allen stated, "At ease, gentlemen, and please sit," and everyone sat back down. The General then asked, "Everyone to identify themselves." Each officer in the room stood up and identified themselves. Lieutenant General Allen said, "I am not going to state who is here with me," and then asked, "Colonel, are you ready?" Then Colonel Roberts stated, "Yes, sir, everyone is here, and there is no problem with the video feed."

Lieutenant General Allen's Chief of Staff, Colonel Hazelwood, began the briefing and a world map showing their target came on the screen. Colonel Hazelwood explained intelligence from several

European counties, including Israel's Mossad, believes a dirty bomb is being built at this location. The good thing is it is not 100% completed, or it is believed it would have been used already. The estimated completion is about 70%. All we can do is hope the intelligence community is right. The source has a good record of being factual and pretty dam consistent.

 The Captain and his officers looked at the screens on the desk in front of them to see where the target was. They got very quiet due to being surprised at the target's location. The mission involved three targets that were going to be hit, which were all vital. Captain Thomas was informed that your team would focus on one target in Germany.

Once the briefing was almost over, Colonel Hazelwood said, "The President attempted to get the Prime Minister of Germany to hit the target with either the Polizzei (Police) or use their military, but the German Prime Minister refused." Colonel Hazelwood looked around and continued talking. He said, "The Prime Minister said the intel is not 100%, and it could be a major threat to Germany and her allies." Everyone in the room shook their heads in disgust, and Colonel Hazelwood mentioned the Germans were concerned a raid could backfire and cause a political nightmare if the intel was not right."

Information was passed around to everyone, reviewed by everyone in the room, and then turned back in. Captain Thomas's Team would not know who else was involved and where the other targets were in case of capture. General Allen then asked, "Does anyone have any questions?" After about five minutes of answering questions, Captain Thomas and his officers talked for a few minutes.

Lieutenant General Allen told Colonel Hazelwood "to dismiss everyone except you and Captain Thomas." Once everyone else left the room, Lieutenant General Allen asked Captain Thomas, "How was his date?" Captain Thomas smiled and said, "It was good I had a good time General." Captain Thomas smiled and said, "General, you have a great daughter." General Allen smiled back and said, "I know I am very lucky to have a daughter like her." Colonel Hazelwood looked at Captain Thomas and smiled, and said, "She is the most important thing in my life. Nothing else matters to me. Do we understand each other, Captain?" Captain Thomas looked at the General and responded, "I would be the same way with my child General." Lieutenant General Allen grinned and said, "Well, that's out of the way and also, be extremely careful on your mission Captain Thomas." Captain Thomas said, "Yes, sir."

Captain Thomas then grinned, changed the subject, and asked, "Why are the Units in Germany not doing this raid?" The General looked at Captain Thomas, who continued talking, and asked, "Is it because they are being watched?" Lieutenant General Allen said, "Yes," and it's not just the bad guys." Captain Thomas learned Germany and other European intelligence units monitor us just like we monitor them, and this is going to be a quick sleight of hand movement, so if they are focused and watching us there, they will not be expecting a team coming in from Bragg.

Captain Thomas asked the General, "Why is Delta not doing this?" Lieutenant General Allen smiled, responding, "They are already there and your safety net in case it goes bad." LTG Allen hesitated and added, "The BC will give you the information you will need to get hold of them in case everything goes south, and by the way, you will jump into Germany. This is so no one has any record of you entering Germany."

Lieutenant General Allen added, "You will only use team members who speak German and Arabic and ask how many speak German or Arabic fluently in your Unit?" Captain Thomas said, "Half of my company speaks those languages fluently." Lieutenant General Allen stated, "The ones who don't are to be used as a decoy for a training exercise in Florida with the Seals who will be a practice run for future joint exercises or Missions."

LTG Allen handed Captain Thomas a sheet of paper to be released to the press about combined exercise information will be a diversion. He smiled and said, "Our enemies and friends will believe your whole Unit is training in Florida, and all of you leave tomorrow at 0600 am out of Pope AFB in C130s." Colonel Hazelwood jumped in and said, "They will meet up with Seal Teams in Pensacola, and also, You need to split everyone on who is staying in Florida and who is heading to Europe." LTG Allen said, "Make sure you do not brief the teams you are taking until you are flying over the Atlantic." And "Make it look like the Florida exercise is on the agenda."

Lieutenant General Allen said, "Battalion Commander will give you all the rest of the information you will need, and by the way, the number of sites has been built copying the whole block." The room got quiet then the General said, "You will practice for at least 4-5 days on it and also make sure you come up with a good plan, Captain." Captain Thomas asked what happens if we get confronted by the German Polizei?" The General explained, "By the way, in no circumstance will your men shoot any Polizei you run into as he looked at Captain Thomas. He continued, saying, "If this part of the Rules of engagement is violated. You, the officers, and the shooter(s) will be court-martialed and sent to Leavenworth for life. You will be court-martialed at Ramstein, and I will fly there and run it myself. That is all."

Captain Thomas and the LTC Roberts saluted Lieutenant General Allen and Lieutenant General Allen saluted back and said, "Son, whatever you do, don't fail me because when this happens, it's going to get very ugly here in Washington if there are any bumps or a disaster." While looking at both men, he said, "Once you get to Ramstein AFB after the mission is completed, your team is going to Kwajalein Missile Range in the Marshal Islands." Captain

Thomas looked surprised as the General continued, saying, "Your team will stay there for a couple of months and will be debriefed, and then you and your team can have a paid vacation." Captain Thomas smiled and said, "Basically, out of sight and out of mind." The General said, "Your team will return to Bragg when things cool off." Captain Thomas smiled and stated, "Copy, sir." The signal was disconnected from the Pentagon.

The Battalion Commander turned to Captain Thomas, smiled, and said, "So you are dating his daughter?" Captain Thomas smiled and said, "Yes, sir." Colonel Roberts then said, "Wow, dating his daughter and having a threat of a Court Marshal over your head- wow. By the way, good luck, Captain, and be safe." Captain Thomas laughed and said thanks, we will need it.

Captain Thomas said, "Well, Colonel, let's go over everything," so they discussed everything from beginning to end except for the assault. The BC said, "He will be watching it live. So make sure you guys do it right." Captain Thomas chuckled, and the BC added, "Whatever you do, make sure your guys don't shoot the wrong people. Got it?" Captain Thomas responded by saying, "Boss, we will be fine." They looked at pictures of the street and all the intelligence reports they had. Both men kicked around some ideas, and then the BC told Captain Allen, "I have no doubt you will put something good together."

Then suddenly, the huge television screen popped back on, and Lieutenant General Allen was standing there with a serious look on his face. He asked, "If was there anyone else in the room?" Colonel Roberts said, "Just us, sir." General Allen said, "I thought about something I did many years ago, and I learned never to rely on any photographs or video." Captain Thomas said, "Yes, sir." The General continued, saying, "Make sure you put your eyes on the target yourself, Captain, by scouting out everything yourself. Do not rely on any information you receive." He continued talking, saying, "When I was a young Lieutenant, the photographs and intel were pretty much wrong, and my team could have been wiped out, but we were lucky." Captain Thomas said, "Yes, sir."

Lieutenant General Allen then showed a black and white picture of a Hispanic Man. He said, "No one involved in this yet is privy to this besides you two, so I will tell them once you and your team enter Germany, "This is the person you are also hunting. His name is Roberto Gonzalez." The Colonel and Captain looked at each other as the Genera; continued talking. He said, "This man was in the Cuban Special Forces for most of his career and has been all over the world. He was a Colonel in this unit before he moved up into the top roles in the Cuban military."

Captain Thomas was getting ready to ask a question when the General raised his hand to say I am not done. He continued, saying, "General Gonzalez was as cold-blooded as you can get, and he showed no mercy to his targets or prisoners, including women and children. The General paused and continued saying, "That is why Fidel Castro loved him and supported him in all his missions." Both the Captain and the BC sat down as the General continued to explain more about this person the General wanted dead. He added, "Gonzalez has been trained worldwide, including in the old Soviet Union." General Allen mentioned, "Gonzalez was allowed by Castro to leave the Cuban military after doing Castro a big favor." General Allen said, "No one knows what it was, but he continued to do favors for the Castro brothers when needed."

Lieutenant General continued speaking, saying, "Intelligence gathered by the CIA says he has been putting something together to cause some type of disaster in the West for simple revenge." Captain Thomas asked, "What is it, sir?" Lieutenant General Allen said, "I believe it's because I shot and killed his 19-year-old son who was guarding some prisoners we helped rescue." The General looked at Captain Thomas and said, "You had a question?" Captain Thomas responded and said, "You answered it, sir." In a low tone of voice, General Allen said, "If you can't catch him, Captain, Take him out with extreme prejudice and do not ever mention this at any time because it is considered a need to know." Once he was done talking, the screen went black. Captain Thomas and the BC looked at each other but said nothing, and they both stood up from the table and exited the room. They went to the BC office and discussed things for a while. Then Captain Thomas stood up and saluted the BC and left.

Chapter 11

Long Flights

Captain Thomas's teams were in two separate C-130s, heading to Florida as he gave a briefing on the exercise to his teams over the Plane video system with the other C-130. Once, the briefing was completed and the questions answered, he recommended everyone get some needed rest. He went to his seat and closed his eyes to relax, and while he was relaxing, he thought about what the general said about the targets before he fell asleep.

About one hour out from MacDill A.F.B south of Tampa, Captain Thomas was nudged by the Senior Airman who said, "Hey Captain it's time we are almost there." James stood up and stretched and observed everybody was asleep. He yelled, "Get up let's get ready, goof-off time is over." Everyone started to wake up and stretch before starting to get their equipment on. A lot of joking and smack-talking was going on, and plenty of jokes went around.

Suddenly, Captain Thomas heard a beeping coming from the plane communication system phone on the emergency line from Washington. He answered it and identified himself. Colonel Hazelwood came over to the Mic and told him that He is to drop off his assigned team at MacDill AFB and then take his other half and bring them back to Pope AFB. Captain Thomas asked, "Boss, what's going on?" Colonel Hazelwood said, "We will brief you face to face, the mission is the same but there is a slight change."

Captain Thomas asked, "What happened?" It was finally explained to him the Germans somehow found out Special Force soldiers were coming in on an American or military flight. Their Prime Minister called the President and told him if we fly in any SF and drop them in for any reason out of the normal this could hurt their relationship

85

and affect NATO in major ways. The President after a heated conversation with Germany's Prime Minister promised he will not fly anyone into Germany without their permission. The Prime Minister excepted the President's word.

Captain Thomas said, "He understood, and we will see you when we get there." Once everyone stepped off the planes. Captain Thomas gathered his team and said to Lieutenant Carson "Take your group and good luck because the rest of us have to fly back to Bragg." Once the plane was refueled and a new flight crew came in, Captain Thomas and his group loaded back up onto the plane and headed back to Fort Bragg, North Carolina. None of the men were happy about having to do another long flight back to where they started but they knew it was important.

After the long flight back, they landed at Pope AFB, Captain Thomas and his group stepped off the plane first and he told his men to go stretch their legs. Captain Thomas approached Lieutenant General Allen and Colonel Hazelwood and he saluted as they returned his salute.

Colonel Hazelwood said, "Let's take a walk, Captain." All three men walked down the flight line as Colonel Hazelwood briefed Captain Thomas on the change of plans. He was told your men will be taking an Israel EL AL, flight and your men will be all dressed as civilians, and some of you will have wives. The women are Mossad agents. Everyone will be acting like they are heading to Israel for regular tours.

Once they made it down the flight line they turned around and headed back to the plane where Captain Thomas had his men standing by. Colonel Hazelwood continued speaking and said, "You will have the required weapons, communication equipment, and other items." Captain Thomas also found out the teams will jump outside the town and work their way to your safe house." Captain Thomas asked, "Where we will be flying out of?" Colonel

Hazelwood said, "Tomorrow everyone will load up on buses and be unofficially taken to New York City and fly out of La Guardia." Captain Thomas asked, "Why are the Israelis helping us?" Colonel Hazelwood said, "Somehow, they found out like the Germans, but they understood the importance of it and their Prime Minister called the President on the secured line and offered their assistance and the President immediately agreed."

After being briefed they shook hands and saluted each other. Lieutenant General Allen then said, "Son be careful I do not want to tell a certain person you will not be coming back because I would never hear the end of it." Captain Thomas smiled and said, "Thank you, sir." Lieutenant General Allen and Colonel Hazelwood walked away to Lieutenant General Allen's car. Lieutenant General Allen while in his car said to Colonel Hazelwood, "I like that kid take care of him." Colonel Hazelwood said, "Me too." Colonel Hazelwood said, "Does he remind you of someone?" Lieutenant General Allen laughed and said, "Only time will tell." General Allen looked out of the car window and then he turned back and looked at the Colonel and said "He shows a lot of positive leadership abilities and I hear people around him respect him."

Captain Thomas and his group were taken to a secured building where they were locked in for the night. Everyone was exhausted from the long flights. Each person walked by a stack of mattresses and grabbed one and threw them on the floor where they will plan to crash for the night.

Once all the men had a spot to crash Captain Thomas had everyone grab a chair so he could explain what happen and any other information he had. There were a few "What the hell, and did they catch the snitch?" Captain Thomas said, "Who knows so here is the plan about jumping into Germany." James told them to "behave on this flight because there will be Mossad agents who volunteered to help us." Captain Thomas looked around at his men to see if he had their full attention and he continued talking, saying "These agents are also putting their lives in danger because Israel is aware of the threat and how it can affect them so just be a professional gentleman and wake-up is at 6 am, get some sleep."

Ten minutes later everyone was asleep. At 6 AM, everyone got up took showers, and dressed in civilian clothes. Two officers came in with a box full of passports and IDs. They were all handed out to the appropriate person. They were told to memorize the information, and everyone was tested to make sure there would be no issues. Once that was done Captain Thomas briefed everyone again from the beginning of the operation and regressed back to the nearest U.S Air Force Base. During the briefing, it was made clear by saying no matter what happens you do not shoot any Polizei. He let it sink into their brains If you do, we will be getting Court Martialed. Once he was done he asked his men "Does everyone understand what I just said?" Everyone responded by answering with "Yes sir."

During the morning everyone was up getting dressed to make sure they look like civilians, including fake mustaches, and beards. Their new equipment had been sent up to La Guardia and stored on a secured sight, and heavily guarded. At about 9:00 A.M, they loaded up on a civilian Travel bus and when they stepped up on the bus they were surprised when they saw women on the bus. There was some hooting and hollering when Captain Thomas turned around and gave a serious look to his men. They immediately shut up and realized they needed to act professionally instead of a bunch of clowns on a three-day pass.

Captain Thomas said loudly," I will be calling out your names and you will go and sit next to the person you are assigned to and go over your background in case the TSA agents have any questions for you and the person you are assigned to." He paused for a moment and said, "I will check your fake passports and IDs when I call your name to make sure you have them."

Captain Thomas looked around and began going down the list and checking out the documents. Once everyone was on the bus he jumped on and sat by the person who was assigned to be his wife. Everyone was introduced to each other and went over their information with no problem. He told the bus driver who was in a Greyhound Uniform "Let's get the hell out of here" and the driver said, "Yes sir." The bus then headed to La Guardia Airport.

After going over the route with the boss driver making sure they were on the same page he turned to the woman playing his wife they each smiled and shook hands and went over their part. No one gave their real name and only their assigned name was used. They each asked each other any possible questions they might get asked, in case they are questioned at the airport. After an hour went by, Captain Thomas got up and asked each couple of questions that might get asked at the airport.

Only one time, did someone forget. This was easily corrected. He went back up the bus aisle asking questions again. Everyone knew their lines and possible questions the airline people might ask or the TSA or any Police and security at the airport.

Everyone on the bus knew one thing they must look relaxed, and the less said is best. The bus driver understood he could not make any stops unless it was an emergency. Captain Thomas knew they were being tracked by satellite for security reasons, and the bus had a tracker on it. There wase also DIA (Defense Intelligence Agency) following them from far off. The agents tracking them only knew to follow them and only assist if there were lives at risk. They were told nothing about what was actually going on. They were also miles ahead at several intersections waiting to follow in case needed. Vehicle problems could always happen. Small Drones also were used to follow the bus to make sure nothing would interfere with the mission in any way.

The Air Force drone operators were told it was an exercise to assist law enforcement. No one inside the CIA (Central Intelligence Agency) Or FBI was notified due to the risk of leaks to the press. Both agencies were well known to pass information around Washington D.C. over the last few years. They have gotten involved in the America Political Arena, causing mistrust in these once-proud agencies.

Lieutenant General Allen knew how Washington had kept everything a needed to know and nothing was put on paper or in a computer. Nothing was done by telephone or cell phone. No one in Washington would be told unless it was done face to face by the order of the president. No congressperson or senator, not even the Vice President was made aware due to risk to the operation. No one working for the President could be in the loop. No one could be trusted, and he would deal with the blowback when it happens. Tight lips were important. Most of the few people who were involved were told it was an exercise. Maybe twelve people not counting Captain Thomas's team knew this was for real.

Passports and driver's licenses were done using the real system through the back door that some Federal agencies have excess to. It is no different than all satellites which are in space. Certain agencies can get into them through the back door. Three individuals inside the National Security Agency who once worked years ago for Lieutenant General Allen entered the secured sights for Florida and put together the needed Drivers licenses. The Passport office's computer system was entered through the computer's back door and made with all the needed information. All this was done by one of Captain Thomas's college friends who left the Military due to being wounded in combat. He worked for the C.I.A. now, with a left leg that was barely usable. He had to use a cane to assist himself in walking. He gathered the information and made the needed passports, as a favor. The hologram in the passport and false information was the tough part but it got done.

When the bus arrived at La Guardia airport everyone piled out and went to retrieve their made-up luggage in the baggage section. The bus driver pulled out the bags and called out the names of each couple. The couples stepped up and grabbed their luggage. The baggage had actual clothes and hygiene items. Everyone had different types of luggage. It could have been suspicious with everyone had the same color and type of baggage. So, imagination was used for this mission. All clothes were used but nice. If they were inspected someone might think it was odd that everyone had brand new clothes.

Everyone entered the La Guardia airport and went to Israel's Ticket line. When each couple retrieved their tickets, they went through the security checkpoints and went to the gate where their flight was. They saw their plane being loaded with luggage. Captain Thomas watched as the baggage was being loaded. Then he saw another baggage Tran drive up and start to be unloaded what appear to be heavier baggage. He believed that is how they were loading their equipment. So far everything was going to plan. Then suddenly, a man came up to him and said, "Hey Thomas." James ignored him. Then he heard "Hey James." James felt a hand on his shoulder. He turned around and it was a friend of his Captain Shultz who was in the 5TH Special Forces.

James was irked about the timing, but he put his hand out and shook Captain Shultz's hand. They talked for a few minutes when Captain Shultz, who was in civilian clothes, asked, "What was James up to?" He said, "Just going to Tel Aviv to visit a friend." Shultz smiled and said "Good for you. They talked for a while then they shook hands and Shultz left. James took a deep breath, and his assigned partner had a concerned look on her face when James said, "We are good."

When it was time to board everyone boarded the El Al Boeing 787-9 with no issues. The plane had a flight range of 13,700 KM. So, they did not have to land unless it was an emergency. Some other people got on the plan which puzzled James. He leaned over to his assigned partner and asked, "Who are all these people?" She smiled and whispered to all her friends in Hebrew and they laughed. She said, "We figured as important as this mission is a full plane would look better when we land in Germany." She smiled and also, "Some of these men are your replacements when we land." James smiled and she added "They are not on the official flight manifest" and "Only Mossad knows who they are and what they are doing." Then the plane took off and leveled out over the Atlantic.

People walked around the plane stretching their legs and talking. A few of the men were talking to some of the women on board, while some of the other people on the plane including some of Captain Thomas's men closed their eyes and slept without interruption.

After napping for a good solid six hours Captain Thomas got everyone up and wanted an equipment check. All the equipment was Russian including the communication equipment. All the real high tec American equipment could not be used. Even clothing labels, shoes, socks, belts, hats, and watches would be made in the Middle East. All the men would wear cheap rings or necklaces made in a middle eastern country. This would help reinforce the storyline of a violent disagreement between Hezbollah and one of its factions. Arab groups were always splitting up from each other and creating different groups due to people disagreeing on what type of violence to commit against Israel or other countries.

Chapter 12

Safe House

When the plane crossed the French border everyone released their seatbelts and got up and went to the back of the plane. Once they gathered up in the back, they went over the mission including the regress again. Captain Thomas said, "Guys if we can't make it to Ramstein ,or any other American base we are to make our way to the American or Israeli Embassies over land." He looked around at his men and answered a couple of questions then said, "We will split up into twos and work your way to those two embassies if it goes bad." He paused and looked at his watch then continued, "If you need to leave the country head to either Switzerland or Italy, and again to those two embassies."

Captain Thomas said in a loud and firm tone of voice "Do not commit any crimes getting to a safe zone and do not hitchhike or take any buses or trains no matter what." Again he paused for questions but none came and he said, "Walking will be the only way and they were to remain in civilian clothes." Each one had a bag with their Russian weapons and Night /Heat vision equipment. Everyone understood what was expected of them and they all had the escape and evade plan in their heads.

He reached into his bag and pulled out a small gun from one of the bags he had and showed everyone. He said, "Each one of us will have a small pistol like this which shoots a dart that causes instant paralysis but only lasts for 22 minutes." James paused again and mentioned, "These are to be used against any friendlies including Polizei if needed and these were provided by the Israelis, any questions?" No one said anything. Captain Thomas then said, "Get some rest in a few hours we will start getting ready to jump."

Captain Thomas took his equipment and put it in the seat next to him. He noticed all interaction between his team and the Israelis had stopped. He leaned back and closed his eyes as he thought about Elizabeth and how their relationship is going before he fell asleep. Then, out of the blue, the plane hit an air pocket and he woke up and looked around. His men were all sleeping. The Israelis were walking around the plane, talking in Hebrew with each other. James closed his eyes and went back to sleep. He went over the mission in his head and thought about what General Allen talked about, checking things out himself before they hit the target.

Then his watch alarm went off. Captain Thomas turned the watch alarm off and he got up slowly and stretched while his team was starting to get up. Everyone double-checked their equipment to make sure it was ready to go. Captain Thomas went up front and talked over the game plan for the jump. Originally, they were going to jump from 35000 feet but that changed with the help of the Israelis.

While all the Israelis were preparing to get ready a man, who was in the front row the whole time talking on the phone on and off during the flight got up from his seat and walked right up to Captain Thomas and stuck his hand out, hand and in English said, "Good luck Captain." Captain Thomas looked surprised then smiled and shook this man's hand. This person also said, " I also want to tell you that our embassy and people are ready to assist you in any way on   the   ground" and he then gave Captain Thomas a radio frequency to be used if all else fails. They shook hands again and the man said. "Shalom."

James realized this was a very important person (VIP) in Mossad. Later, he found out he was the head of Mossad. This was so important James figured if he was in that guy's shoes, he would do the same thing to make sure nothing interfered with the plan. This mission and all involved countries could cause a major international incident.

One of the Plane staff went to the back of the plane and put on a parachute and he said for Captain Thomas to have him and his men follow him. Everyone followed this man through the center and a point at the bottom of the plane. Captain Thomas saw a door that looked like it was added after the original construction of the plane. The agent looked up and smiled and said, "We had this put in for missions like this." Captain Thomas smiled and said, "It was a good idea." He then turned to his men to line up. The Israel agent hooked himself to a hook on the plane and he hit a switch and he opened the door.

The Israeli yelled out in Hebrew and English "Get ready." Everyone lined up in a row in front of the door and prepared to drop through it. Captain Thomas went down the line of his twenty -four men. This was a large size of men if this was a normal mission. However, since this was so important all areas had to be covered to prevent failure and to keep the problem from turning into a big mess.

 Once Captain Thomas went down the line and checked everyone, he observed no one was having problems with their equipment which would be strapped tight on everyone to keep from breaking loose.

The last one he checked was Sargent David who in turn turned around and checked Captain Thomas. When he was done, he gave Captain Thomas the thumbs up. Captain Thomas gave the thumbs up to the unknown agent at the door. The unknown Israeli agent spoke Hebrew into his mike. The Pilot over the speakers stated, "Everyone stands by 60 seconds."

The unknown agent listened to his headset and initiated a countdown from 60. When it got down to ten seconds, He counted down with his fingers so everyone could see and be ready. When the time came the Israeli agent gave the go sign to Captain Thomas who yelled "go, go, go" as everyone pushed to get everyone to drop out the door. It was a different type of jump but still a jump.

When Captain Thomas was out the door, he looked at the El Al plan which kept on its normal course, and headed to Berlin Germany To refill and take on some Israeli citizens and tourists while returning to Israel.

They jumped out at 15,000 feet and headed for an open field a few miles West of Gaiberg to land. The jump was at 11:00 P.M on a Wednesday during a new moon night. This helped since there was little light except for the cities and towns the men could see while coming down. This helped, So, the odds were against anyone seeing them coming down.

The security risk when they hit the ground is hoping nobody decided to take a late walk in the countryside. James looked at his wrist monitoring watch and it showed everyone was on course to the drop zone and so far, there were no problems yet. He knew Murphy was always waiting for an opportunity to louse things up.

Everyone knew when they were to deploy their RA-1 Parachute and direct themselves to the ground. Once everyone made it to the ground they gathered and pulled out their dart guns in case they needed them.

They gathered up their chutes and piled them in a spot preselected by a scout team two days before. They pulled out their plastic M-4s with their 30-round banana clip. The Russian weapons were put in their rucks. This was to support their claim of a field exercise if they run into any Polizei or regular citizens. There would bother types of equipment at the safe house to be used.

Everyone began to walk east to the Gaiberger Eag road in a Ranger file like they were in a field exercise in case they were seen. After about 15 minutes of walking the point man observed the Gaiberger Eag road. Everyone was wearing night vision and the point man raised his open hand which meant stop and everyone stopped. He motioned for everyone to get down and all the men went down on one knee with everyone looking around.

Captain Thomas walked up to the point man with LT Deaton. The point man told the two officers "The road is about 100 yards ahead of them." Captain Thomas said, "Move out and keep it quiet."

After arriving near Gaiberger Eag Road, Captain Thomas had everyone break up into two groups. One-half of his men were on his left along the ditch of the road and the others on his right. Lieutenant Deaton stepped up to Captain Thomas and asked what are we doing? LT Deaton was a little puzzled about the change of plan. Captain Thomas told him "he received a change over the PRC-167 line right before we jumped." James said, "LT, I should have told you before we jumped." James smiled and said, "Unfortunately you were preparing to head out the door." LT Deaton smiled and said, "Good, and by the way, you owe me a beer." Captain Thomas smiled and said, "We will see."

Captain Thomas told LT Deaton, "There will be trucks coming from Ramstein AFB and each will be 5-10 minutes apart from the others." LT Deaton was told the drivers were told it is an infiltration exercise involving Air Force EOD and TAC-P. These drivers were told they will stop at a certain location and some men will get in the back and the driver and co-driver will take them to a drop-off point at Blumenthalstrabe and Werderp streets where they will stop, and we will disembark.

Captain Thomas said, "Once they hear three bangs near the back of the truck, they are to head back to base." Captain Thomas said with a smile, "What the drivers do not know is when they get back to the entrance they will be immediately detained and secured in a building and guarded by the Air Force Security Police until this is over." The drivers and co-drivers will still be told they are being detained as part of the exercise. They will also be interviewed to make sure they followed orders and both men smiled. James with a grin mentioned, "They will immediately get transferred to Osan, South Korea AFB so they are out of the way."

Chapter 13

Intel gathering

While driving to the drop-off location, everyone was quiet, and nobody said a word. The truck driver and the assistant driver were told before they left to not talk or ask any questions unless asked by the men they picked up. After about 20 minutes the first truck stopped and everyone in the back jumped out of the truck, ten minutes later another truck came to another location and the men in the back jumped out. The truck then headed back to Ramstein AFB to report they completed their mission. The drivers and the co-drivers were then escorted to a building where they were debriefed and questioned heavily. Once the four airmen were done being questioned, they were escorted to a plane and sent to Osan, South Korea. All their stuff was already packed and on the plane. They were all single but that is why they were selected. They were upset at the beginning but when they were told they were each promoted one grade they smiled, and their attitudes changed. They got on the plane and headed to South Korea.

Both groups worked their way down the blocks to the safe house with no problems or issues. When they were approximately 100 yards out, Captain Thomas stated on his mouthpiece the "dragon has arrived." The other person stated, "The dragon is clear." After arriving at the safe house with no interruption and both teams entered the building without being seen and especially not making noise to draw attention in case someone was looking out the window. Noise at night always travels farther than it does during the day.

Once everyone was inside the building, half the team went upstairs, and the other half stayed downstairs. Captain Thomas went to the

DIA agent in the house and they began talking and going over things. They shook hands and, Captain Thomas told the Lieutenants to "set up a guard duty rotation." The schedule was put together for one guard on each floor and to be rotated every two hours and the wake-up was at 0700A.M. Both levels of the small floor were covered with men sleeping. Captain Thomas also passed on orders if any Polizei gets close to the house to wake him immediately. He then radioed the Command Center "The chickens are in the nest." He received an immediate response, "Copy Out."

At 7:00 A.M, everyone was up and preparing to exit the building and start gathering information on the town. Single- and two-man teams would disperse to gather all information possible in the area and around town. Each team was assigned to gather intelligence on the town Polizei, emergency response crews, and what the town people do during the day, evening, and early in the morning. Information was needed on also where the Polizei live in the community. This could help or hurt if they can respond quickly. They were not worried about the townspeople due to the strict gun control the German nation has had since the Nazis outlawed personal weapons back in the 1930s. Shotguns and certain hunting rifles were authorized, and they were all registered with the local Polizei.

At 8:00 A.M., after everyone was briefed people started to head out through the front and back doors every 5 and 10 minutes. The back door lead into an ally and ran into streets on both sides. The front door opened into a small street and two individuals jumped on bicycles and headed in opposite directions north and south. Thirty minutes later two more came out on bicycles and headed north and south. After two hours of dispersion of 10 men, the rest stayed inside and waited until the evening when it would be their turn to head out.

Captain Thomas radioed a short message, quick and to the point to the Command Center. "Gathering information, No issues, Out."

There was no response due to making sure the signal does not get picked up by the German intelligence or anyone else who might have the proper monitoring equipment. This was a do not trust the host leadership in any way. Germany is overrun with many different countries' intelligence organizations that monitor NATO and each other.

When it was 3:00 P.M. teams began to return with intelligence to hand over to Captain Thomas. Later on, Captain Thomas and Lieutenant Deaton headed out and walked around the area bouncing around the clubs close to the target. They avoided the University grounds due to the cameras throughout the university grounds. There were cameras around town, and they were trying to locate them so they would be aware of where not to go when they leave the area. They want no cameras showing them getting on an American Air Force boss.

When evening came and it became dark, Captain Thomas and Lieutenant Deaton headed to the street where the targeted building was. They climbed a tower and made it to the top and began watching the building with night vision. They noted there were two men each walking on each side of the building and there were also two men on the roof. The men on the roof had AK-47s hanging on their shoulders. The men walking around the building seemed to have sidearms that were partially covered by their shirts. While looking around the buildings surrounding the target, Captain Thomas observed two men on the roof across the street watching the entire street. They too were carrying AK-47s. Captain Thomas took pictures of everything and everyone. They must do everything the old way in collecting intelligence.

Captain Thomas and Lieutenant Deaton stayed until 04:00 A.M. making notes on when the men were relieved and what everyone was doing. Around 04:30 A.M., they noticed the guards started to get tired even after they rotated over guarding their assigned post with other men at 0200 A.M. They began sitting on chairs and sitting against the staircase and napping out.

About 20 minutes went by when they heard someone come out of the building through the front door, making a loud noise, and everyone jumped up and started to patrol their assigned area. Captain Thomas noted their behavior and how they reacted to what happened, so, he and Lieutenant Deaton stayed longer and observed when the person who came out finally went back inside allowing the guards to relax and go sit down. Lieutenant Deaton took a picture of the person who stepped outside for fresh air. He had a hat on covering his face.

Captain Thomas and Lieutenant Deaton headed back through town and made it without being seen or noticed. Two guys walking down a street in a college town would not be a major issue with anyone. They looked like typical students.

They entered the safe house, once they were given the green light by the soldier on guard duty. When they both entered, they noticed most of the men were sleeping except some men who were getting ready to head out. Captain Thomas went to the radio and checked in with the command center and then signed off when he was done. Lieutenant Deaton and Captain Thomas went to their sleeping spots on the floor and went to sleep. Before James fell asleep, he went over everything in his head he saw with Lieutenant Deaton and everything he put his eyes on the whole area except the internal University grounds.

Around 11:00 A.M, Captain Thomas woke up. He stood up and stretched and looked around and went and grabbed a couple of food rations and ate. James went and used the bathroom and showered on the first floor. Once he was done, he went to the kitchen table and waited for both Lieutenants to wake up.

Once the Lieutenants woke up and cleaned up, they came over and sat down and ate, and began discussing a plan of action. They all agreed to do at least one more day or two of gathering information and putting together the intelligence already gathered. They did not document anything and relied on their memory which was the key to this, and they could not afford to leave any evidence around once they were gone. If they were discovered, they would have only Russian weapons and the State Department would have a big headache getting them out of prison.

Captain Thomas and Lieutenant Deaton and Lieutenant West's careers would be over, and this would be the worse international incident involving two major allies. This could also hurt NATO and cause mistrust between Europe and America. There have always been issues involving NATO. Enemies of NATO would love to see a split in this organization. NATO has already been weakened since the end of the cold war. This would turn it into a joke of an organization with no teeth if Captain Thomas and his team get caught or fail in completing their mission.

Everyone repeated their information gathering for the next two days. After 72 hours of the nonstop gathering of intelligence. Captain Thomas and Lieutenants Deaton and Lieutenant West went over all the intelligence gathered. They continued to send smaller teams out to make sure the townspeople and Polizei are doing their usual routines.

Captain Thomas also had team members go by and check on the targeted building to see if there are any information changes gathered. He kept sending out team members throughout the evening with new information gathered. He decided this was the night. He believed he had everything he needed, and all intelligence showed there were approximately 35 men involved. One photograph showed a person who appeared to be Gonzalez when he stepped onto the roof for five minutes. Gonzalez was never observed leaving the building at any time by himself or with anyone. Captain Thomas left that information out of any transmission he sent to the Command center in case someone picked up the communication.

Captain Thomas later radioed the Command Center and said "0:300 AM is the kickoff unless new information by you says otherwise." He then added, "person of interest appears to be in the building and has not been witnessed by anyone leaving the building." While the planning was going on, Scout teams continued to go out and scout the entire area before they would be going to hit the target. They continuously saw no changes or threats to them or the mission. Captain Thomas reviewed his plan from all steps and possibilities with his two Lieutenants. They would hit the building across the street which had guards on the roof. One sniper team would take them out while the other worked their way to the roof of that building. Their job would provide cover from their angle. Both sides of the main targeted building would be covered from up high.

All the scouts made it back by 01:00 A.M. Everything was the same as the other two nights. Captain Thomas gathered everyone around and said, "This is it." He turned to the communication Sargent "Send a signal game time confirmed 03:00 A.M." Captain Thomas gave the briefing, and everyone responded individually about what their job was and if everything goes well what they will do, and what they will do if it turns chaotic. There were questions asked by a few then everyone got up and checked their equipment.

Captain Thomas told both Lieutenants "It's show time" and he checked his men to make sure they had Arab Keffiyeh that look like the Hezbollah scarfs. Each Lieutenant took their team five minutes apart. Both sniper teams left 10 minutes before. Captain Thomas before everyone exited made sure everyone had a certain type of shirt on. He put on his special goggles and looked and turned them on. He could see where everyone was. This new technology will help American soldiers know who was friendly and who was a foe.

Captain Thomas and the soldiers assigned to his part of the mission moved out slowly through the alleyway and streets. This way the intelligence gathered showed there were no cameras on these streets or houses. They moved down the street quietly but quickly. Half of them on one side, and the other half, on the other. A few dogs barked but so far, they observed no one and everything was good so far. He checked with the other teams and they were almost at their assigned position. Captain Thomas looked up into the night sky and he thought he observed a drone. He hoped it was theirs just following them and monitoring things from the sky.

They kept going and worked their way in and out of the streets and alleys when suddenly, a drunk came walking out of a house and walked out to the middle of the sidewalk. He tried to light a cigarette but was having problems due to his intoxicated state. Captain Thomas and his group stopped where they were and looked for cover. The drunk staggard then stopped, and he looked up and saw Captain Thomas and squinted trying to focus on what he was looking at. Captain Thomas, under his breath, said, "Damn, this could go bad."

Captain Thomas immediately pulled his hat down and took off his Arab Keffiyeh and handed it off to the person behind him and staggard towards the drunk acting like he was drunk also. His men were looking at each other like what the hell is he doing?

When Captain Thomas got up to the drunk, he spoke to the drunk German and said evening, and then he asked the drunk if he had a smoke and a light. The unknown drunk said yes and reached into his pocket swaying back and forth and pulled out a cigarette pack. They both leaned and bumped against each other laughing while they lit each other's cigarettes, and he said thanks. He then walked away from the drunk and he said thanks and kept walking away. The unknown drunk staggard down the street took a left turn on the sidewalk and kept going until he was out of sight.

Captain Thomas put out his cigarette and put it in his pocket and ran back to his group and said let's go. They moved out until they reached their assigned position. He got on his radio and said, "They are in their position." It was 2:48 A.M., twelve minutes to show time.

He looked through his Russian night vision and watched the guards sitting down as they have the last couple of nights. James checked with the Command Center and stated ready when you are. The Command Center responded and said, "Eagle One you are green." Captain Thomas responded and said "Copy." He checked with the other teams, and everyone was ready. At 2:59 A.M, Captain Thomas said Robin Hood you have a go. Both Sniper Teams were using the Dragunov Russian sniper rifles with silencers to provide perimeter cover and remove any threats.

Sniper Team One then put the first target on his site and pulled the trigger. The guard was two buildings over on the roof. They missed him during the intel gathering and scouting. The 7.62x54mmR caliber round was sent and entered the terrorist's left temple and exited out the other side. Then the second terrorist who was on the opposite building stood up and looked to his left when suddenly, the second 7.62x54mmr caliber round entered through his left eye and went out the back of his skull and he fell dead on the ground. Robin Hood said two dead. Then he took out the one guard on the roof of the targeted building who could have sounded the alarm. The guard being asleep helped and Robin Hood came over his mic and said one dead.

The second sniper team was already heading up the outside stairs to the roof. Once they got to the roof, they dragged both bodies and moved them out of the way. They took their position and said Little John is on site. Their job was to take out all enemies that attempt to enter the building or try and leave. They were also to keep an eye on any Polizei who might be walking around or driving by, and they knew their job well but if the Polizei come and get involved in the incident they were all going to be in big trouble. One thing they would not allow is for their colleagues to get trapped inside or out. Both sniper teams without any approval came up with their own plan in case it all goes bad. Sometimes you must plan outside the box in case the ones the bosses want you to follow do not work out.

Chapter 14

Target

At 03:00 A.M., Captain Thomas (Thunder one) said, "Robin Hood and Little John, you have a green light." In seconds all four Guards in front of the building were shot and killed immediately. Robin Hood stated in his mic, "Four dead." Lieutenant West took his team and fired the two-silence rope launcher onto the roof, and it caught onto the ceiling. They then began climbing the three stories to the roof. The snipers provided all the cover they needed.

After two minutes, the team made it to the roof, and both ropes were pulled up. The team stepped up to the stairs door, which would take them down the stairs to the third floor, and lined up, ready to enter. Lieutenant Deaton notified Thunder One, "They were at the green line." Thunder One acknowledged "ten four." Thunder One took his team to the front door and lined up.

Lieutenant West took his team to the back door, and they lined up and stood by. Captain Thomas was preparing to give the green light when suddenly, the front door opened, and an unexpected terrorist stepped out smoking a cigarette. Immediately the point man stabbed the terrorist in the throat and brought him to the ground. Thunder one yelled to all teams, "Thunder and lightning, I repeat, Thunder and lightning." All three teams entered the building. It was approximately 3:04 A.M. The point man said into his mic, "One terrorist is dead."

All three teams flooded into the hallways slowly and worked their way through the corridors and hallways. While clearing rooms and hallways, a bad guy was shot, with the shooter announcing to the coms, one terrorist was down. They were taking no prisoners with all threats to be eliminated with extreme prejudice.

So far, eight suspected terrorists on the third floor have been killed with their AK-47s next to them. They made it three-fourths way down the hallway when two men exited one room, and they were shot down quickly, but unfortunately, one had his finger on the trigger of his weapon, and it went off. Captain Thomas said the word 'Damn it' in his mic and told everyone to "go-go-go and shift gears."

Immediately the whole building woke up, there was yelling and orders being given in Arabic, and men started coming out of rooms all over the place like rats. All three teams began shooting anyone who was not dressed like them. All three teams removed their opponents as quickly as possible and switched to their AK-47s from their handguns. The intelligence S-2 and civilian intelligence gathered were way off on how many people should be in the building. There was between 50-100 terrorist throughout the building, which was not even close to the 35 observed over the last few days.

The three teams ended up clearing their floors and went to the first floor, which was just cleared by Thunder One and his crew. Then men were placed to guard the main entry points. While searching for all intelligence information, they discovered a basement that was not on the blueprints they had. While looking at it, it looked new and was done most recently.

They went through the door, and immediately Sargent Holden was hit in the left upper chest. He fell down the stairs. Then Lieutenant West threw an M84 stun grenade down the stairs, and it went off. They headed down the stairs, and rounds were being exchanged while Sargent Holden was pulled out of the way, and the team medic, Sargent Thomas, no relation to the Captain, began conducting first aid on him. Sargent Holden was alive and conscious. The teams worked their way down the stairs and found a lab in the basement. It looked like it was dug out and expanded.

They then observed a door that suddenly closed, causing several members of the group to head for the door.

Sargent Larry yelled, "Hey LT, come here asap." LT Deaton stepped over to the tables and said, "Damn." On the big table was a bomb set during the assault by someone. The other tables had other types of explosives and pieces to build bombs. The big one was approximately three feet in length and two feet high. LT West called out for the team two demolition team members to step over.

Lieutenant West told them you have two minutes to disconnect the weapon before it goes off. The two Sargents went to work trying to disarm the IPC (Item of Primary Concern). However, they were unable due to their high-tech construction. Staff Sargent Austin, who was Air Force EOD and Nuclear weapons expert, stepped over, looked it over, and began working on it with the help of the two army demolition team members. Staff Sargent Austin finally found the wire to disconnect it, which shut it down. Lieutenant West smiled and said, "Staff Sargent Austin, I am glad we bought you along. The young EOD expert smiled and said, "Me too."

Captain Thomas told five of his men to "line up at the door," and they immediately complied. The door was opened with ease when a grenade fell to the floor. The point man yelled, "Grenade." Everyone dove as far away from the grenade to get out of the way of the explosion when it went off. Once the ringing from his ears was gone and the smoke cleared, Captain Thomas got up, looked around, and asked, "Is everyone alright?" Sargent Mays said, "I caught some fragments." The other team medic, Sargent David, went over and began treating Sargent Mays. Captain Thomas said, "Grab all the paperwork and let's get the hell out of here." Lieutenant West turned to the demolition's men and asked, "Are you sure they disarmed?" All three men looked at the Lieutenant and acknowledged the bomb was disarmed. Captain Thomas knew the Germans would discover the disarmed bomb, so he decided to leave it. Everyone went back up the stairs, and everyone exited the building, running. All three teams split up and headed to the safe house in the preassigned directions. They heard sirens in the background. People started to look out the windows to see what was going on. There were a lot of shots being fired and yelling coming from one building. Captain Thomas, in Arabic, said, "Get your asses moving."

Everyone knew the minute they exited; they were to speak only Arabic. Captain Thomas earlier briefed everyone when they got out of the building and got about 100 yards out to toss their weapons into garbage cans or ditches. This was to set up a false feud between Hezbollah and another Jihadi group that did not exist. With people looking out their windows, they heard what sounded like Arabic to them running out of the building; they observed those unknown men running down separate alleys as smoke poured out of the building, especially the windows and doors. Once the shooting stopped, people started coming out of their houses now that the shooting had stopped to see what was going on. Then four more Polizei vehicles drove up, and the officers jumped out with their weapons. They entered the building as more Polizei vehicles drove up.

A fire truck was called for, and more ambulances were requested as heavy smoke poured out of the building. More Polizei drove up, and a few went and began interviews of any witnesses. A couple of men told the officer he saw men come running out and go in different directions. Two of the men stated they sounded like they were Arabs. One officer headed in the direction where some suspects were witnessed to go. About 20 yards from the building, he found an AK-47 and Arab Keffiyeh, which was the color Hezbollah uses. He picked it up and noted where it was discovered. He ran back and told his supervisor, who showed up.

The Polizei Supervisor then stepped over to his car radio and ordered roadblocks 20 miles, 10 miles, and 5 miles out. He passed on a description of the men: they were tall, had black hair, and spoke Arabic. He was unaware that Captain Thomas's men were all wearing black headcovers. It was estimated the witness's description involved more than 15 men.

The Polizei supervisor observed a three-inch mark on the butt of the AK-47. It was a Hezbollah flag on it. The Supervisor ordered some of his men to go in two different directions, where the witnesses told him the unknown men went. He was unaware that one group split one block up. Before he headed back to the incident location, he told other Polizei to start checking down the streets and alleys for evidence.

Captain Thomas and his men attentionally dropped their weapons to be discovered on the side of the roads and dumpsters heading in the opposite direction of the safe house. They all scattered in pre-selected directions so no one would gather attention. They all slowly worked their way back to the safe house. When sirens headed down the street, they hid behind whatever they could. Then when the sirens went by, they headed quickly to the safe house.

The two wounded were assisted by two others who helped them walk down the streets and alleys. Everyone entered the safe house, and when everyone was accounted for, they gathered everything to identify who was there. Both wounded men were being treated and prepared for their trip. IV bags were hooked into both men, and were given blood. Time was important, and Captain Thomas knew it. He asked, "Were all weapons dropped?" Lieutenant West stated, "Yes, sir." All trash bags full of rations were tied up. Now the only thing they needed to do was wait for the transportation to get there. Captain Thomas stepped out into the night to see what was going on. There were sirens in the distance, far off, which was a good sign.

Now he was waiting on the communication which would tell them to prepare to get out of this part of Germany. He knew the Polizei would have roadblocks and patrols everywhere. The mission was successful in many ways but unsuccessful in others. He also had two wounded men, but they should be able to recover as soon as they get out of this mess. He was very proud of his man and how they performed their mission. It was ugly how it was done, but they got through it and gathered a lot of intelligence which will be turned over to the American intelligence community.

Chapter 15

After Math

After all, the men entered the safe house, and they immediately started to change clothes into U.S Air Force uniforms which were stacked under the floorboards as quickly as possible. They rotated guarding while everyone changed clothes. The Team Medics were treating the two wounded. They were in serious condition but stable. Very few words were being spoken by anyone. Once everyone was done changing, including the wounded, Captain Thomas got on his radio and asked, "When was the item going to be at his location?" The voice on the radio said, "Approximately two minutes to arrival."

Captain Thomas ensured everyone was prepared to gather all the civilian clothing in plastic bags to be loaded up on the bus and hidden. It was 3:30 A.M., so there should be very little traffic, except for the German Polizei running around town with their sirens going. Sargent Blanda came up to Captain Thomas and said, "The bus is here." Captain Thomas said, "Gentlemen get to the door." Everyone lined up and prepared to exit the building. Once an unknown person came over the radio and gave the signal, they headed out quickly to the bus. The two wounded were assisted onto the bus. Once everyone was on board, the bus headed to Ramstein AFB, looking like a tour bus with American soldiers.

The driver handed Captain Thomas an electric screwdriver and explained to him to unscrew the floor, put any weapons and equipment under the floor, then cover the floor again and put the screws back in tight. Captain Thomas handed it over to Sargent Blanda to unscrew the two separate floor covers. Once Sargent Blanda was done, the middle floor covers were removed, and the few remaining weapons and equipment were put in. The two wounded were placed under the front cover with their IV fluid and blood bags. The floor was resealed and secured. That section was altered to fit equipment or people to be smuggled. They were placed under the floor in case the Polizei pulled the bus over and checked it.

Once the floor was sealed, Sargent Blanda tuned to Captain Thomas and said, "Floor is secure, boss." Captain Thomas turned and faced everybody and said loudly, "Remember we are coming from Berlin on tour for three days R+R, and since everyone has been there before, it would be easy to answer any questions." He paused, looked around the boss, and stated, "Above one of you are two cases of cold beer, so grab one and at least sip some of it and don't drink the whole thing."

Captain Thomas watched everyone grab a beer and pass it around, cracking jokes as they passed the beer cans around. Captain Thomas walked over, grabbed a couple of beers, and took them to the restroom at the back of the bus. He opened them up and poured them into the toilet. Once he flushed the beer in the toilet, he walked around and handed the four cans to four different members of the team. Then someone raised their hand and asked, "Hey Boss, can we start hitting the latrine?" Caption Thomas Laughed and said, "Go for it."

The bus was heading west on Freeway 6 when they observed the Polizei heading in the opposite direction on the opposite side. When they were getting ready to cross the bridge over the Rhine River close to Sandhofen, the bus driver saw the bridge was blocked off by the Polizei on the far side. He slowed down and told Captain Thomas what was in front. Captain Thomas said, "I see them." He then turned around and loudly told everyone to play the part and, no matter what, not to resist in any way if arrested or detained. Everyone said, "Yes, sir." They started acting like airmen on leave with the radio blasting rock music.

Once the bus got close to the barricade, the bus driver stopped and opened the bus door, and two Polizei stepped up to the door. One walked up the stairs and said good morning to the bus driver in broken English. The bus driver smiled and returned a good morning to him. The Polizei looked at the bus and observed 22 United States Airmen in uniform; they looked like everyone was drinking. He smiled and asked the bus driver in English, "Where are you coming from?" The bus driver smiled and said in English, "Berlin." The Polizei officer then asked the bus driver in German, "Who are these people?" The bus driver had a puzzled look on his face and said, "Excuse me." The bus driver spoke and understood German but was not allowed to use it. The Polizei smiled and said, "Nothing," and then, in broken English, said, "I need to check everyone's IDs." The bus diver talked on the speaker IDs, gentlemen. So, everyone started to pull out their Ids and hold them out. One guy spilled his beer and said, "Shit."

The Polizei officer randomly checked the passenger's IDs, and he approached the airman who spilled his beer and said, "Nervous?" The Airmen said smiling, "No, it was a waste of a good German beer." The Polizei officer laughed and smiled and said, "I understand."

When the Polizei officer was done, he turned around and started to walk down the bus aisle to the entrance. He stopped and asked the bus driver if there "was anyone in the latrine?" The bus driver said, "I was driving. I don't know." The Polizei then turned around and walked to the back of the bus. He opened the restroom door and looked in. It was empty. He then headed back to the front of the bus, stopped, and asked to see the bus records. The bus driver handed over to the Polizei the bus papers, which showed the proper stamps and milage, gas refills, and total miles. He then said in German, "Thank You." The bus driver said, "Excuse me." The Polizei Office smiled and said in English, "Thank You." The Polizei Officer then stepped off the bus and waved them through. The bus driver waved, closed the bus door, and started heading down the road to the American base as quickly as possible.

When they were within six miles of Ramstein AFB on Highway 6, two vehicles began following them. Captain Thomas and others noticed them and told everyone to be ready to sprint to the base if needed. Captain Thomas pulled out his weapon with the darts that would put them, whoever they were, to sleep. The bus driver adjusted himself off his seat a little and pulled out a small radio and handed it to Captain Thomas, and said, "Call our location in and give us a straight shot into the base." Once Captain Thomas called in their location, a minute later, both vehicles following the bus drove around them and got in front. A message came back on the radio notifying me there were two vehicle escorts in front of you. Keep driving normally.

When the bus made it to the L369 turnoff, they followed the road to a side entrance when two more vehicles came out of no wear and followed the bus behind them. They followed the two leading cars to the East Gate. They drove through without stopping following the escort. They were escorted to the runway, where they observed a C-130 on the ground warming up. When the bus got next to the C-130, it stopped, the floor section was unscrewed, and the two wounded were removed and helped off the bus and placed on stretchers. They were carried onto the C-130 and secured on the part of the plane to be treated. There were two doctors and four nurses on the plane. They began treating both men without any interruption. The remaining weapons and all equipment were removed from the bus and placed on the C-130 as quickly as possible.

Once all items were removed from the bus, this included the beer bottles, and any other trash items were loaded in trash bags on the plane. Captain Thomas told one of his men to "get those bags on the plane." The bags were full of civilian clothes. He told his team to get out of those uniforms and put them in the bags. When they were done changing, they and all the clothes were put in bags; all the bags were taken back and placed inside the plane. Captain Thomas and the Bus driver went back to the bus and walked through the bus to make sure there was no evidence to identify who was on it. Then everyone loaded up on the C-130.

Captain Thomas and the bus driver then grabbed gas cans and poured gas inside the bus. Everyone was watching through the plane's back door. Then Captain Thomas threw a match, and the bus was on fire.

While the plane slowly moved away, they watched a fire truck come and put out the fire inside the bus. The firefighters were only told it was an exercise. The back door closed, and the plane took off, heading south to the AFB in Aviano, Italy. The C-130 was assigned to this base and flew to Ramstein AFB to drop off Military staff. The medical Doctors were from Fort Bragg, NC. The two Doctors were former SF members and understood secrecy. The four nurses were members of the Defense Intelligence Agency.

After a couple of hours in the air, the C-130 landed at Aviano NATO Base in Italy, where the Medical staff who worked on both soldiers exited the plane, and the flight crew was switched out with another one. Once the plane was checked and refueled, it took off for Cyprus and landed at the Larnaca International Airport after a long flight. No one could step off the plane, and once it was refueled, the plane took off and flew to Israel.

It landed approximately 24 hours after the mission at the Ramat David Airbase. When it landed, everyone stepped off the plane into the desert heat and stretched. Once Captain Thomas stepped off, he was surprised who he saw there waiting for them, non-other than Colonel Hazelwood. They shook hands, and Colonel Hazelwood patted Captain Thomas on the back and said, "You guys did a great job." Captain Thomas asked, "Can his two wounded men be taken to the base hospital for further treatment." Colonel Hazelwood turned around and yelled in Hebrew at someone about 10 feet away. A few minutes later, an ambulance appeared and took both men to the base hospital for further treatment. Captain Thomas smiled and said, "You speak Hebrew?" Colonel Hazelwood grinned and said, "Oh yea, long story."

Then a vehicle drove up, and out popped Lieutenant Colonel Roberts smiling. Captain Thomas and LTC Roberts shook hands. Captain Thomas asked, "What the hell are you doing here?" LTC Roberts said, "I am here for the debriefing," and with a serious look on his face, said, "Right now." Captain Thomas said, "Ok, boss, how about on the plane?" LTC Roberts responded and said, "Ok." Another vehicle with four other Americans drove up and exited their vehicle, and everyone loaded onto the plane. The flight crew was kicked off the plane, and LTC Roberts looked at Lieutenant Deaton and Lieutenant West and stated, "You two and the rest of the men are invited to sit in this also." Both smiled and said, "Yes sir," and everyone entered the back of the plane, and the door was closed. After 2 hours of everyone giving their information and what they did, the debriefing was completed. Colonel Hazelwood turned to Captain Thomas and LTC Roberts and said, "I am impressed." Captain Thomas looked at his bosses and said, "Unfortunately, that individual got away." Colonel Hazelwood said, "We will get him," and the back door of the plane was opened.

Once everyone got off the plane, they saw a bus with an escort vehicle in the front and back. Captain Thomas was puzzled and looked at his bosses and said, "What's up?" LTC Roberts responded, "You and your team are Germans heading to Eilat for two days on the Israelis' dime." LTC Roberts smiled and said, "Yep, and by the way, enjoy the beach." LTC Roberts said, "Guys, you are flying out in two days." Then LTC Roberts and those four intelligence officers boarded the C-130 back to the States. Colonel Hazelwood went and jumped in a vehicle with someone else sitting in the back seat, and the vehicle drove away.

Captain Thomas and his team sat on the bus heading south to Eilat. They were exhausted but relieved the mission was done. There was plenty of alcohol and a lot of joking and prodding each other after their mission. They knew they could not talk about the mission, so they discussed the fun times they would have in Eilat. Poker games broke out on the bus, and everyone was having a good time. The bus driver was a Shin Bet agent who joked with everyone. It was a good ride south. There were Shin Bet agents in front about half a mile ahead and the same in the back. There was also a Drone following them high up in the sky.

When the team made it to the Herod's Vitalis Hotel in Eilat, they all got off the bus and walked inside. Two men stepped up to Captain Thomas and identified themselves, and had a quiet discussion, and they then walked away. A big man in a suit with a name tag that said Manager stepped up to Captain Thomas with a small box and gave it to Captain Thomas and said, "Here are keys to everyone's room on the top floor suits Sir, the whole floor is only for your men and have fun and any questions please call me." He then handed Captain Thomas a card with a number to call and whatever they needed. Captain Thomas said, "Thank you," and shook his hand again, and he turned around and handed the keys off to everyone. He said two to a room gentleman.

They started loading up in an elevator when Captain Thomas looked around and saw several people spread out in the lobby. He smiled and knew they were their security assigned to watch over them. One stood up and stretched, and Captain Thomas saw a handgun holster on the right side. He then stepped into the elevator and went to the top floor. While the elevator was heading up to his floor, he started to relax, knowing the Israelis were watching them.

When the elevator got to the top floor, the elevator door opened, and Captain Thomas saw two men standing against the wall. He stepped out of the elevator and shook their hands. One talked and said, "There are two men on each end of the corridor for the whole time you guys are here. If you go anyplace, there will be people who will follow you." Captain Thomas looked left and right. He observed two men sitting in chairs on both ends. They stood and waved, and he waved back. He then walked to his suite feeling rather good with all the security around.

When he opened the door, he saw Lieutenant Deaton looking out the window over Eilat. Lieutenant Deaton turned around and said, "Well, we made it, boss." Captain Thomas said, "Yep, we did it, and look where we are." They smiled, and James said, "Gather everyone up and have them meet in this suite in 15 minutes." LT Deaton said, "Copy," and he exited the room.

In 10 minutes, the suite door opened, and everyone walked in. Captain Thomas smiled and told everyone to "go ahead and sit someplace." Once everyone sat down, Captain Thomas explained the rules while they were here in Israel. He told everyone the number one rule here is to do nothing to draw attention to yourselves. The second rule is nobody is to leave the hotel grounds. The third rule is, for now, you only speak German. The fourth rule does not embarrass our country and our Team. He stopped talking for a moment, looked around the room, and said, "Who does not understand what I said?" No one raised their hand. James said, "By the way, there are men here who are our security; they are our babysitters and will be following you guys." One last thing I want everyone to introduce each other by their full names in German. He then introduced himself to each person, and they did the same. Then everyone left. It was his way of making sure each person's German was good. People can forget things if they do not use it.

When everyone left the room, James, exhausted, went and laid on his bed. He set his watch for three hours. He was proud of his team, and he fell asleep. Two and a half hours later, a knock was on the door. He got up and groggily walked to the door. He opened it and was surprised at who was there. Other men were standing behind Lieutenant General Allen. They were all in civilian clothes. Captain

Thomas said, "Come on in, sir." Lieutenant General Allen stepped in and had his bodyguards stay outside.

After Lieutenant General Allen stepped into the suite and they both shook hands. Captain Thomas said, "How are you doing, sir?" The General smiled and said, "Fine, what about you?" Captain Thomas responded by saying, "Tired. I was taking a nap before I go and drink and sleep on the beach." They both sat at the table where General Allen discussed what would happen over the next few months. He explained when you get back to the States. We will go over the intelligence and items you guys gathered. For right now, just focus on relaxation.

With a look of concern on his face, the General said, "How are the two men that were wounded doing?" Captain Thomas said, "They are fine, sir. They are recovering at the local Military Hospital." General Allen said, "Good. By the way, you guys are leaving tomorrow instead of the day after." Captain Thomas did not need to ask why. He knew it was over security matters and possible attention falling on Israel. Captain Thomas said, "No problem, sir. By the way, what time do we check out?" General Allen smiled and said, "Noon."

They continued to talk about the men and how they were doing when General Allen asked, "Would you like to see Elizabeth?" James smiled and said, "It would be nice." General Allen said, "Those who have wives and kids are being flown to Kwajalein at this time with my daughter, who is also on the plane." The General smiled and added, "She wanted to see you, and she would not stop bothering me about you, so I gave in." Captain Thomas smiled but did not say anything. The General mentioned, "I believe she really cares for you." James responded, saying, "I care for her too, sir." General Allen smiled and said, "Well, young man, please don't hurt her." Captain Thomas looked at the General and stated, "I won't." General Allen laughed and said I hope not. I would hate to reassign you to the North Pole. Captain Thomas also laughed and said I would hate it also.

General Allen then discussed where he was going stating he was leaving for Germany tonight because the German Government believed we might have something to do with the incident inside their borders. He said, "The Germans are angry and demand to meet with me. I do not think they fell for the Hezbollah fringe group retaliating." General Allen paused and continued, "I will see what they have and stand by what we told them and nudge them into the Hezbollah storyline."

General Allen stood up, and then Captain Thomas stood up, and they shook hands. General Allen said, "James, I am proud of you and your team, and I would put you and your team in for awards, but unfortunately, the mission never happened." General Allen looked out the window and said, "Nice view." He looked at Captain Thomas and said, "By the way, The President is thrilled about the job you guys did. Take care," as he left the room. Captain Thomas looked down the corridor and saw some men in suits escorting the general to the elevator.

He went back into his room, looked out the big window over the water, and then went and crashed on the big brown couch in the living room. While lying on the couch, he closed his eyes and went over the last couple of days in his head on what went well and what went bad. He realized they were lucky only two of his men were wounded. The mission was tough, and they could not use the normal tools they would have used. This includes infrared to see everyone in the building and where the bad guys are. He also went over who set the booby trap at the door in the basement, which was dug out, and where the tunnel ended up. After going over everything in his head, he got up, poured himself a drink of bourbon, went outside on the veranda, and looked out over the water and the boats, far out on the blue water. He took a sip of his drink, smiled and realized this would be a good spot to bring Elizabeth. After napping for a little while, he got up, showered, and changed his clothes. All the rooms had a bag of civilian clothes for each man, including hygiene items.

After a couple of hours, James went downstairs and ate a good meal himself. He bought the Jerusalem Post and read it while eating his dinner. The interesting thing is newspapers outside America tend to report more things going on in America than American newspapers. Also, the television news report in more detail on things than the American news channels seen on television. You would never see a blown-up body or head on American television or in a newspaper compared to foreign news. They are also more likely to be more accurate than the American media.

Chapter 16
Kwajalein Missile Range

Kwajalein Missile Range is a U.S. Army Garrison in Micronesia in the south pacific. Its official title is called the Ronald Reagan Ballistic Missile Test Site. This base helps in conducting missile testing for the U.S. military. It's one of the most beautiful and largest lagoons on the planet. On the northern part is Roi Namur, which used to be two separate islands but combined into one island. They used rock, sand, and other materials to fill in to connect the two islands. Kwajalein is on the southern part of the lagoon with small islands all around—lots of suns, scuba diving, and fishing. On Kwajalein, most of the people who work on the island are civilian contractors working for the military. On one side of the island are housing and barracks; the other has a runway, a 9-hole golf course, and radar and other buildings. On the waterside by the golf course, you can see the former Japanese swimming holes which they used during WW2.

The people on the island use three main beaches on the lagoon side. There are two theatres, with one an inside building and one outside. There are year-round sports activities to keep people active: softball, basketball, tennis, and other activities like the two swimming pools. One is for families, and the others are for the unoccupied workers. The pools are saltwater, not freshwater. They usually have swimming events for the school on the base and competitive sports for both families and bachelors.

On the farthest point is what they call the Shark Point, where food garbage is dumped there. You can watch the Blacktip sharks, and turtles eat up the food. Some people fish off the point catching fish or even blacktip sharks. The funny thing is sometimes you can be ready to pull in a large fish when a shadow under the water heads towards the fish you caught, and when you pull the fish out, you get half, and the shark gets the other half. There are always things to keep you busy there.

Most workers' contracts are for one or two years, and some families whose parent works on the island could be there for years, heading on vacation once or twice a year off-island. Unless you are a slug, there are always things to do with plenty of sun, beach, and activities. The lagoon side has a port to unload ship items onto the base. It also has boats you can rent for skiing or fishing or check out some other islands. All base supplies must either be flown in or shipped in. The base has stood up to monsoons, hurricanes, and other disasters which come from mother nature.

At 9:45 P.M., a C-141 landed at Bucholz Army Airfield on Kwajalein Missile Range with the base Commander and his staff. Once the plane stopped, everyone grabbed their bags and walked off. Captain Thomas was in front. He stepped up and saluted Colonel Michaels, who returned the salute. Colonel Michaels smiled and put his hand out to Captain Thomas, and they shook each other's hand as everyone walked to the process area of the building without being checked in or searched. They were not officially there.

Colonel Michaels took everyone up to his conference room, where they sat down as he explained what the Army Chief of Staff told him. He repeated what he was told that they would be put up in one of the bachelor's barracks which was emptied two weeks ago. He added the envelopes on the table with your room keys and KMR false IDs with fake names. You have full access to all the amenities on the base. Your families are already here. They are at the visitor Hotel which is called the Kwaj Lodge. Please have fun, and do not cause me any headaches, gentlemen.

The Colonel also mentioned he was told not to mention you or discuss you with anyone, and if asked, he was to say VIPs and leave them alone. Captain Thomas stood up and said, "Sir, we will lay low as the best we can." Everyone stood up, and Colonel Michaels saluted them and walked out. Captain Thomas looked around the table and said, "Behave so we can go home." Then everyone exited the conference room and grabbed their bags. There was a bus that took them to their barracks. The married men went to the Kwaj lodge to be with their families. Captain Thomas went to the small officer's house he was assigned to. Lieutenant Deaton went to his.

Once he arrived at the house assigned to him, he got off the bus and went to the front door. When he unlocked it and entered the house, he felt around for the light because it was dark and turned it on when he heard hi James. He looked up and smiled, seeing Elizabeth sitting on the couch in a towel. She smiled and jumped up as the towel fell to the floor and ran and hugged James and kissed him passionately as she held him with no clothes on. James said to her, "I did not think you would come." Elizabeth said, "It's good to have a General as a father, and we will be here for a good while." James smiled and said, "Yes," as she reached over and turned off the light.

The next day Elizabeth got up and made breakfast while James was in a deep sleep. She knew he was exhausted and did not know what he did and was involved in, but she knew it was very important. Her dad told her whatever you do, do not ask any questions about anything he did or was involved in. Elizabeth promised her dad she would not and understood the seriousness of what they do. Elizabeth's dad said you will never be able to discuss where we are going and why.

James woke up, gradually got out of bed, and came downstairs around 09:30 A.M. Elizabeth said, "You still look tired." James smiled and said, "Thanks, but I need to set my clock since I will be here for a few months." Elizabeth smiled and said, "You mean us." James laughed and said, "Maybe." She smacked him playfully on the shoulders. He grabbed her and started to tickle her. She started to laugh and begged him to stop. James did and said, "What's for breakfast honey," and she said, "Pancakes and Ms. Piggy (Bacon)."

Once James was done eating, he got up, went upstairs, and showered. Elizabeth showered earlier in the morning when she got up. They agreed to hit the beach, and instead of riding the bus to the beach, they walked, holding hands and talking. When they thought they were lost, they asked a couple who were walking in the opposite direction which way to the beach. They introduced themselves to the other couple with the false names they were given to use. Then they went to the Emon beach, where Elizabeth and James looked at each other and went wow. It was beautiful. They threw their towels down, and James took his shirt off and flopped, ran, and jumped in the warm, clear water. He swam about 50 yards out, then swam back in the nice clear and warm water.

When he swam back to the beach, Elizabeth stood there watching him. She then walked into the water and swam to James. They enjoyed the beach, and James napped for a little while on his towel during the day. Elizabeth went in the water while James slept, and when he woke up, he went and jumped in the water, and they played in the water for a little while longer. Then about 2:30 P.M., they saw some of his crew coming to the beach, and everyone waved at each other. James and Elizabeth got out of the water, and James introduced everyone. They did talk in a low tone so the civilians on the far side of the beach could not hear. James then said remember, and nobody talked shop. Everyone laughed and said, "Yes, sir, one person laughing and was a little intoxicated said, 'Oh mighty one.'"

Around 4:30 P.M., everyone agreed to have a barbecue with plenty of booze, and money was put in the hat, with everyone agreeing on what was needed. They all agreed at about 7:30 P.M. to meet back here at the beach. James and Elizabeth got up and walked back to the house. They showered and then walked to the Surfway Grocery store, where they gathered food and other items. They paid for

128

everything and waited outside for the bus. Once the bus arrived, they got on and returned to the house, where they sat around the house, relaxing and talking. James worked into the discussion on how long will she be able to stay. Elizabeth said, "When my dad comes, I have to leave with him when he gets here." She smiled and said, "Not for a couple of weeks as she kissed him."

The barbecue during the evening went well, with lots of food and drink, with the men playing flag football for a while and the women sitting around talking with each other. They rarely have ever had a chance to get everyone together like this. The wives introduced themselves to Elizabeth, and they all sat around drinking and laughing and watching their men act foolishly on the beach playing flag football.

Suddenly three security cars drove up, and four men stepped out of their vehicles and walked up to the ladies, and one of them asked politely, "Who is in charge?" They pointed at Captain Thomas. Elizabeth pointed him out. The soldiers stopped and watched their leader approach the Base Security men. James gave them his false ID and asked in an intoxicated state, "What was up?" The lead security man said, "Sir, we got a complaint about loud noise," as he pointed towards some family quarters on the right and left sides of the beach.

James asked, "What time does the beach close" and he was told 9:00 P.M. James looked at his watch and said it was 8:15 P.M. The shift supervisor said, "Well, sir, please keep it down," and James said, "No problem we will tone it down." The security officers looked around at all the physically fit men and realized if they pushed them, they would come out on the short end of the stick. James could tell they felt intimidated by his men, and he patted the guy on the shoulder and said, "We will be done by 9:00 P.M., sir." James shook all their hands and went back to his men. He said, "Back to the game," but loudly said, "Let's bring it down a little," as the base security left.

At 9:00 P.M., they stopped, and everyone started to clean up. Security drove by and saw them cleaning up, and the security guy waved, and a couple of Captain Thomas's men waved back. Once the cleaning up was done, everyone headed out down the street to their quarters. When everyone had left, Elizabeth and James staggard back to their place. When they made it home, Elizabeth passed out on the couch. James, who was highly intoxicated, reached down and threw Elizabeth over his right shoulder and staggered up the stairs. When he made it to the bedroom, he put Elizabeth in bed and took off her flops, and covered her with the blanket. James staggard to his side of the bed and fell on the bed. He kicked off his flops and looked at the ceiling as it spun around in circles. He moaned and said to himself what an idiot drinking that much as he passed out.

As time went by, James and Elizabeth spent their time on the island almost always together. They even went to the gym together, where James did his two-hour workout, and Elizabeth did her own workout. He would run around the island, which is approximately 5 miles completely around. Then Elizabeth and James would swim laps in the salt pool. They would go to the family pool. They would see others throughout the days and weeks. James would go off and play golf at the 9-hole golf course with his men and play 18 holes. Sometimes James and Elizabeth would rent a boat and go fishing and water skiing. It was like a super vacation for everyone. The team got tighter, and Elizabeth and James got even closer.

Then one day, a C-130 Air Force plane landed unannounced at Bucholtz Airport on Kwajalein. This was not a normal scheduled air flight. Some people got nervous in the traffic control tower.

Chapter 17

The Visit

The C-130 had the proper code to land but left everyone confused in the Tower about who was on the plane and why they were there. The base Commander received a phone call from the tower who told them a C-130 landed unannounced, but they had the proper identification code. Colonel Michaels jumped up and knew that an unannounced C-130 coming from Hawaii via Johnston Island with unknown persons(s) on board had to be important. Only a VIP with a higher rank than him and a lot of military power was allowed to show up when they chose. He ran out of his office and grabbed the people who followed him, wondering what was happening. They watched the C-130 as it moved up and waited for it to stop. The plane engine was cut, and then the back section opened.

After a couple of the crew walked out, Three-star General Allen followed them, and Colonel Michaels saluted him, and they shook hands. Lieutenant General Allen said, "We need to go to your office, Colonel, and do not log us as being here." Colonel Michaels said, "Yes sir," as they walked through the processing area, and Colonel Michaels whispered to Major Fox, "Don't log them as being here." Major Fox went upstairs to the Tower and made sure nothing was recorded. Once Lieutenant General Allen reached Colonel Michaels's office, they walked in as the Colonel closed the door and said, "General, please take my seat." General Allen said, "Thank you," and he sat down. General Allen's people stood outside the door facing away and making sure no one entered the office.

Lieutenant General Allen, in his uniform, would intimidate most people with the Stars and medals. Colonel Michaels felt nervous about why he was a three-star General who was over some of the most elite units on the planet here on Kwajalein Missile Range. LTG General Allen sat in the chair and leaned back in his chair, and right off the bat said, "How are my boys doing?" Colonel Michaels sat down and said, "They are doing good and not causing any problems." LTG Allen smiled and said, "That's good to hear." He paused for a moment and said, "Just make sure no one messes with them." The General leaned forward on the desk and, with a firm tone of voice and a firm look, said, "I mean, no one messes with them." Colonel Michaels gulped and said, "They will be fine, sir, and my staff told me that they are enjoying the island and not causing any issues." LTG Allen smiled, leaned back, and said, "Well, that's good." The General said, "Colonel, I need you to find Captain Thomas and the woman he is with as soon as you can because I need to talk to them both." Colonel Michaels stepped out of his office and told his people to "go to house number 125 and bring the couple to my office asap."

Elizabeth and James were cleaning their fish catch when there was a knock at the door. James opened the door, and Major Ciccone said, "Captain, I need you and the young lady to come with me to Colonel Michael's office asap." James asked, "What's it all about, Major?" Major Ciccone responded, "I do not know." James smiled and said, "Give us a minute to clean up." Major Ciccone said, "No problem, Captain, I will be in the truck waiting."

James and Elizabeth cleaned up, went outside, and jumped into the truck with Major Ciccone driving. When they arrived at Colonel Michael's headquarters, all three got out and walked to Colonel Michael's office when. James saw a bunch of men and realized someone with a lot of ranks was there. Elizabeth was confused about what was going on and said, "James, what is going on?" James smiled at her, held her hand, and said, "I do not know, honey, but it will be ok."

When they got to Colonel Michael's door, one of the men guarding the door opened it. LTG Allen stood up, and Elizabeth saw her father and ran towards him and gave him a hug and kiss and said, "Dad, wow, this is a surprise." James following behind her stopped and saluted the General, and the LTG saluted back, and the LTG said: "At ease Captain." LTG Allen and James shook hands. Colonel Michaels immediately realized that Captain Thomas's companion was Lieutenant General Allen's daughter. There was no wonder the General did not want them to mess up because the Captain's girlfriend was his Daughter. This was one thing he did not see coming, and he was glad there had been no problems with them being here. Colonel Michaels understood this General had the power to help or finish his career with one phone call. A General overall Special Forces worldwide is not someone you want to piss off.

Once all the introductions and warm discussions were done, LTG Allen said, "I need to talk to Captain Thomas alone." Elizabeth smiled and said ok and went up to her dad and hugged and kissed him. Colonel Michaels led the General's daughter to the break room near his office, and he asked Elizabeth, "Is there anything she might want?" She smiled and said, "Just some coffee with cream, please." He got some coffee and handed it to her, and she smiled and said, "Thank you." She then sat down, and both Colonel Michaels and Elizabeth talked about the island and how it is a good place to live and work. She asked him, "Do you have any family" and he said, "Yes, they are here, and they are the rock of his life." She smiled and said, "I agree family is very important."

LTG Allen and Captain Thomas went for a walk on the runway away from everyone. LTG Allen took his jacket off due to the extreme heat and asked, "How are things going?" Captain Thomas smiled and said, "Great, sir." He looked around and mentioned, "Kwajalein is such a beautiful place and the military's best-kept secret." LTG Allen then asked, "How is Elizabeth doing?" Captain Thomas grinned and said, "She is doing great, and I believe she is having a great time here." He paused and then said, "You are lucky to have a great daughter like her, sir," and the General responded by saying, "Thanks, Captain."

General Allen changed the subject and asked, "How are the men doing?" Captain Thomas answered by saying, "They are doing good and enjoying themselves in this paradise." He then asked, "How are you doing, James?" James was surprised because General Allen used his first name. James said, "I am doing fine, sir," and asked, "When are we getting out of here, sir?" General Allen smiled and said, "The Germans were easily manipulated into believing it was an internal Hezbollah feud but realized they dodged an actual attempted terrorist act that reached into Germany and a couple of other countries."

General Allen explained what was going on in Washington and how the press had interpreted the incidents as a Hezbollah internal squabble ad printed stories of the terrorist plans of destruction. The other two targets were in France and one in England. The British handled the one site in London, and they reluctantly used the SAS, but after finding explosives there, the British Prime Minister apologized to the President for not taking it more seriously. The information gathered showed the target was 10 Downing Street, his own home. The Prime Minister told the President, "If he needs anything, he owes him big." The other target was in Paris, France. Before the French Special Operations Command could raid the terrorist hideout, it blew up before it could be raided. The rescuers found nobody alive but large amounts of documents showing what their target was. It was the President of Frances's home. They called our President to apologize and offer any assistance we needed because they realized how close they came to a catastrophe that could have initiated a civil war between the left and right over the Muslims living in France.

The only problem is the Germans, who still believe they were not a major target of any terrorist act or attempts. Even with all the explosive equipment found, bodies, and intelligence showing their Prime Minister was the target. They still just shrug their shoulders. The General shook his head and mentioned the team saved the idiot Prime Minister and her family's life. But as they say, you can't fix stupid. They are everywhere, including in Washington, D.C. The sad thing is that Washington is full of them, and they are everywhere, including in the military. James smiled and said," I agree, sir."

General Allen discussed how the President is thrilled about how successful his mission was and that all of you will receive medals, but the information is to remain Top Secret. He looked at his watch and said, "The answer to your question is when will you and your team be able to return home?" General Allen paused and said, "It will be a few more weeks." He leaned back in the chair and said, "The families will be coming back with me, including Elizabeth." Captain Thomas smiled and said, "I understand."

General Allen leaned forward and, with a serious look on his face, asked, "Are you two serious about each other?" James smiled and responded, "I hope so, I do really care for her, and I would never attentionally hurt her because she is one of a kind and very special to me." General Allen said, "Good, I won't have to send you to Antarctica or the North Pole." James laughed, then grinned and said, "If she were my daughter, I would probably do the same thing." General Allen said, "Well, at least we are on the same page."

James then changed the subject and asked, "When are my guy's families leaving?" General Allen said, "Tomorrow at 04:00 A.M, a C-141 is flying everyone to Hickam AFB in Hawaii, where they will spend three days in Hawaii at a military Base hotel and then fly to Travis A.F.B, refill, then straight to Pope AFB." Lieutenant General Allen then added, "You need to get your people ready to leave because your team is leaving tonight at approximately 2100 hours."

James was surprised and said, "Tonight, sir?" Lieutenant General Allen smiled and said, "You have had enough time of laying around and goofing off on the taxpayer's dime." General Allen went into detail about another C-141 coming and taking your team to Japan for two weeks of training with the Japanese Special Forces. He stood up, went to the window, and explained how they would fly to Diego Garcia and rest for a couple of days before they headed to Israel, where their team would train with their Commandos and you will learn what they can on Hezbollah for a month. General Allen turned around and said, "Your vacation is over, and be ready when you come back." He said, "James, this was the easy stuff," James smiled and said, "Yes, sir, it has been fun and one hell of an adventure."

They looked at each other, and they shook hands. General Allen looked Captain Thomas in his eyes and said, "I am glad you and Elizabeth are doing good. And James, I just want her to be happy." James again smiled and stated, "Me too." They stepped out of the Base Commander's office, and Elizabeth ran to her dad, hugged him again and whispered into his ear, "Daddy, I love James please watch out for him." Her dad grinned, whispered in her ear, and said, "I know honey, he is a good man, and you picked a winner." He knew he would try, but he knew Captain Thomas picked the job and its dangerous profession. Elizabeth asked, "How much time do we have left here?" He told Elizabeth, "We are leaving at 04:00 A.M. You need to get your stuff ready." She understood and kissed him on the cheek. Elizabeth looked at James, who told her, "I leave tonight at 2100." She was surprised and said, "Well, we better get back and get packed."

The General turned to Colonel Michaels and asked, "Is there a place I can rest and get cleaned up?" Colonel Michaels said, "You and your men have rooms at the Kwaj lodge under these names." Colonel Michaels handed them fake IDs and took them over in a couple of golf carts. James and Elizabeth took a vehicle, and they went and hunted down everyone on his team.

Once he found them, he told everyone their families were leaving at 04:00 A.M. The team is leaving tonight at 2100. Everyone seemed surprised, but they understood the time would come for them to leave. They went back to their quarters and got everything ready. They sheared the shower, made love in and out of the shower, then took a nap.

At 7:30 PM, Captain Thomas's guys started to gather at the airport. They all seemed a little disappointed, but they knew the vacation would end, and they would have to leave. A C-141 landed at approximately 4:10 P.M. The C-141 was refueled and prepared for its flight from the Marshal Islands. At 2000 hours, Captain Thomas and his men loaded their stuff on the plane with no difficulties. None of the families could be there. Lieutenant General Allen showed up in civilian clothes and approached Captain Thomas and his men, and they all saluted the General. Lieutenant General Allen said, "To carry on," and stepped up to Captain Thomas.

He shook Captain Thomas's hand and said, "Good evening." Captain Thomas responded and said, "Same to you, sir." They walked away from everyone, and Lieutenant General Allen said, "When they get to Israel, make sure your people pay extra attention to the training techniques and intelligence you guys gather and make sure your team listens to the Israelis and do not cause any problems."

Captain Thomas said, "There will be no problems, sir." Lieutenant General Allen changed the discussion and said, "James, how is Elizabeth?" James said, "She was asleep when I left. He then mentioned, "She fell asleep crying." General Allen smiled and said, "She will be fine." James responded by saying, "I know, sir." LTG Allen told Captain Thomas to "gather his team around, brief them, and I will answer any questions if possible."

Captain Thomas yelled out, "Gather around." Once the men surrounded him, he briefed them on what they would be doing.

Once he was done, he asked, "If there were any questions anyone might want to ask the General?" No one said anything. General Allen told the men, "We are proud of you; be safe, and I will see you soon." Captain Thomas yelled, "ATTENTION." Everyone stood at attention and saluted Lieutenant General Allen. The General saluted them back and turned and walked away.

Captain Thomas turned around and told his men to "go ahead and load up," which they did and found places to lay out for the long flight. He found a seat up front and waited for the plane to take off. Everyone talked about how much of a great time they had on the island, and it was well worth it. They all agreed it is a beautiful place and one of those places you would love to go for a vacation. They knew it was unfortunate that it's a closed base and not everyone can go there when they feel like it. They all agreed it was paradise and the military's best-kept secret when it came down to the best and worse military bases.

Chapter 18

Training and Recon

The C-141 took off at approximately 2100 hours, with the plane being recorded as dropping off supplies from Hawaii. Then it was sent to Japan to assist the Japanese in a field exercise. While flying west, Captain Thomas and his men made themselves as comfortable as possible for the long flight to Japan.

After about an hour in the air, Captain Thomas was brought up front due to a message from Washington on the secure line. James hooked up to the radio set and received a message telling him the game was changed. Their flight was changed to Australia for two weeks of training with the Australian Special Forces, and then they flew to Japan. Captain Thomas acknowledged the message, disconnected himself from the radio, and returned to his men. He told his men, "Things just changed. They are going to Australia for two weeks of training with their SAS." People started laughing. One person looked around and said, "It sounds like we are going a long way home."

After about six plus hours, they finally arrived in Australia around 03:22 A.M. at a military airfield in Australia. They unloaded their stuff and met some soldiers from the Australian Special Air Service Regiment. Captain Thomas approached a person in civilian clothes. They saluted each other and shook hands. Two Australian trucks drove up, and everyone loaded up. For the next two weeks, they would be in outback training with one of the best units in the world. They taught each other unique fighting styles and other things to help both groups of soldiers. After two weeks of training, Captain Thomas and his team loaded up in the C-141 and headed to Diego

Garcia for a few days' rest. The training in Japan was canceled for unknown reasons, with the entire team was puzzled about why.

After another long flight, they finally landed in Diego Garcia, and the plane moved up to the entrance and processing area, where everyone unloaded. They processed through with their fake IDs, which they are to always have on them while on the base. The base commander approached Captain Thomas, and they saluted each other and shook hands. They walked away from everyone, and the Base Commander told Captain Thomas, "They had free reign of the base per some people very high up in the Pentagon, and your guys have been assigned quarters for four days." Captain Thomas said, "Thank you, sir." The Colonel continued talking, saying, "In a couple of days, I will call you and let you know when your flight leaves and where you will be going." Both men saluted each other, and the Base Commander headed back into the building. Captain Thomas went up to his men and said gentlemen, we will be here for four days when Captain Johnson came up and introduced himself to Captain Thomas in a snotty way. He said, "You report to me every day, and you will need to let me know where you go and what you and your men do every day while you are here." Captain Thomas scoffed, and Captain Johnson said, "You guys need to shave and appropriately cut your hair. You guys look like bums." Captain Thomas grinned and rubbed his two-week-old growth on his face. He looked at his men, smiled, and said, "Guys, you look like bums." Captain Johnson said, "What's so funny, Captain." Captain Thomas said with a grin, "Who the hell are you?" Captain Johnson said, "You do what I tell you, or I will make things difficult for you, Captain." He then poked Captain Thomas in the chest.

Captain Thomas's men were watching the exchange when they saw the poke. Someone said, "Oh- Oh." Captain Thomas's smile faded, and he told Captain Johnson to "back off shit head." Captain Johnson said, "I run this base, and you are nothing." He stepped closer to Captain Thomas, and he was slammed into the ground in a blink of an eye. Before he knew what had happened, Captain

Thomas came down with his right knee into Captain Johnson's chest. Captain Johnson had a surprised and shocked look as he gasped for air. Then Captain Thomas yanked Captain Johnson up on his feet and told him, "Do Not Fuck with me, or you will be gumming your next meal." Captain Thomas whispered, "Do you understand me, Captain?" Captain Johnson shook his head up and down in an understanding manner. Captain Thomas let go of Captain Johnson and pushed him away, then staggered back into the building.

Captain Thomas turned to his men and said, "Loudly, I guess he does not know who we are." Everyone began laughing, with Captain Thomas smiling. He said, "Guys make sure you behave," and the men started laughing, and one said, "Captain Thomas if that clown complains, we are all witnesses on your behalf." Captain Thomas laughed and said, "Let's get our stuff, and the beer is on me," his men cheered.

Captain Thomas entered the building and asked the Security Officer, "Where the Base Commanders' office is?" The Base Security Officer escorted him straight to the Base Commander's office. He thanked the security officer, knocked on the Commander's door, and heard him come in. Captain Thomas opened the door and immediately saw Captain Johnson jump out of his chair and back up.

Captain Thomas stepped in and saluted the Base Commander, who returned the salute. The Base Commander said, "Gentlemen, how are we going to fix this and make it go away?" Captain Thomas looked at Captain Johnson and said, "Before anyone ever messes with another person, maybe he should find out who he is messing with first." The Base Commander looked at both men and said, "Captain, I agree" he looked at the other Captain standing against the wall and said, "Captain Johnson, let me introduce you to Captain Thomas of the 7Th Special Forces." He let that sink into

CaptainJohnsons' head, and he added, "He and his men are on their worldwide tour of death and destruction."

Captain Johnson then Gulped and apologized to Captain Thomas, who stuck his hand out, and Captain Johnson put his hand out, and they shook hands. Captain Thomas noticed Captain Johnson's handshake was a sweaty wimpy handshake. The Base Commander said, "Well, this never happened, right Captain Thomas?" Captain Thomas looked at the Base Commander and said, "Sounds good to me, sir." The Base Commander then opened a drawer and pulled out three small glasses, and poured everyone a shot of bourbon. They each took a glass and toasted the Army.

On the third day of Diego Garcia, Captain Thomas, who was on the beach with his men, was approached by Captain Johnson. Captain Thomas stood up, and they shook hands when Captain Thomas said, "Hey, Captain. Would you like a drink?" Captain Johnson smiled and said, "Working right now, maybe later." Captain Thomas smiled and said, "Sounds good. Come on by when you get off work."

Over the last few days, Captain Johnson and Captain Thomas spent some time together talking, drinking, and talking over things. Then on the last day, Captain Johnson came up to Captain Thomas, who asked, "What's up?" Captain Johnson said, "Your team leaves at midnight tonight on your C-141. You and your men are headed to the Middle East per the Pentagon." Captain Thomas said, "Thanks for the information, and he appreciated the positive treatment his men and he received here on this base." They shook hands, and "He said if you ever need anything, just call." Captain Johnson smiled and responded by saying, "Same here." Captain Johnson said, "You guys be safe and take care," and they shook hands again.

At Midnight Captain Thomas and his team were on a C-141 headed to the country of Israel. They had a great time relaxing on the beach and unwinding and unwinding in the middle of the Indian Ocean.

The plane ride to Israel was going to be a very long flight; everyone got comfortable and slept. One person from the back said, "One hell of a vacation," and everyone laughed, including Captain Thomas, who leaned back, closed his eyes, and went over the last several months in his head. Then Elizabeth popped into his head, and he smiled and fell asleep.

Once the long flight was finally over, they landed at the Hatzerim Israeli Air Force Base in the Negev desert, and once the plane stopped, they piled out and stretched and breathed the fresh hot desert air. They all walked around the plane, talking and cracking jokes about how they should be getting flight miles and how good it was to be back on the ground.

Captain Thomas started to walk to the building when two Israeli Army Officers approached him and identified themselves. One was Captain Aaron Yosef, and the other was Lieutenant Abraham Dayan. He identified himself, and they shook hands, and he said, "Lieutenant, any relation To Moshan?" Lieutenant Dayan smiled and said, "Distantly." Captain Yosef interrupted and said, "Hey, Captain, let's go for a walk." Captain Thomas said, "Sounds good. I need to stretch my legs some more," he turned to Lieutenant Deaton and said, "I will be back and get everything unloaded." Lieutenant Deaton saluted and said, "Yes, sir."

They walked down the runway while Captain Yosef explained the reason why they were in Israel. He told Captain Thomas, "You will train with us wearing our uniforms, and then a few of our people and yours will sneak into Beirut and scout out a possible site which is being watched because of information we received telling us something is going on at one of the docks with Hezbollah and a Cuban."

Captain Yosef said, "The Cubans' name is Gonzalez, and he is suspected of being a former Castro man doing his own thing of disrupting the West and possibly causing harm to us." He paused and then stated, "The sad thing is we do not know what he looks like, and there are some real nervous people right now in your government and ours." Captain Thomas looked at the Israeli Captain but did not say anything as the Captain discussed how they would go in and scout it out and see if we could find any reason to strike it if needed. Captain Thomas found out they would be training with Unit 269 or the Sayeret Matkal. Captain Yosef mentioned, "Our enemies call us the unit, and we are the group they fear most." Captain Thomas smiled and kept listening. He didn't tell them who this person was and was not authorized to tell them.

They started walking back to where Captain Thomas and his men were all gathered by the big building when two buses drove up with an escort of two vehicles. Captain Thomas yelled, "Load up," and said, "Lieutenant Deaton step over." LT Deaton came over and said, "What's up, boss?" They started walking, and he informed Lieutenant Deaton of what was going on and their agenda. Lieutenant Deaton smiled and said, "It was going to be an interesting time in the desert." Captain Thomas patted LT Deaton on the back and said, "More than you know."

All the men headed to the buses where Captain Thomas jumped on the first bus and LT Deaton jumped on the second bus, and they headed out following their escort to where they would be staying at. Someone in the back of the bus said, "What, no Eilat this time?" Everyone laughed, and Captain Thomas, without turning his head, said loudly, "Dickhead." People laughed, and Captain Yosef looked at Captain Thomas and whispered, "Your men are in good humor today." Captain Thomas grinned and said, "We will sweat it out of them that I promise."

The buses headed to the Tze'elim Army Base, the Israeli Urban Warfare Training Center. This base is used by soldiers in the IDF to train for Urban combat with Israel's enemies and to deal with the continuing internal conflict with Palestinians. While heading to the base, Captain Thomas looked out the window and observed a drone following them in the air.

Captain Thomas asked Captain Yosef, "What's with the drone?" Captain Yosef said, "That's our insurance card to make sure we have no disruptions with our travel." He looked at the American Captain and said, "By the way, did you know we were the first to use and arm UAV drones for modern combat to target our enemies." Captain Thomas grinned and said, "I know I read a book called Rise and Kill First, written by Ronen Bergman." Captain Yosef smiled and said, "I read it also; overall, it is an interesting book."

When they arrived at the base, they entered through the main gate after Captain Yosef showed his papers after he stepped out of the bus. The Army Security Officer saluted and looked at the orders he was given by the Captain, who also showed the Security Officer his ID. The Security Officer had met him before, so he knew who he was. Lieutenant Dayan also stepped out of the second bus and went up and showed security his ID. The Security Officer saluted and waved them through. The Security Officer had already been notified to run them through after being checked earlier by the Base Commanders' office.

They entered the base, and Captain Thomas asked, "How is the weather right now?" Captain Yosef smiled and said, "It's a cool 106 degrees," both men laughed. Someone in the back said, "Hey, boss, what did he say?" Captain Thomas laughed, saying, "It was a cool 106 degrees." Everyone laughed on the bus and knew there would be a lot of hot and sweaty days coming ahead.

Captain Thomas stood up and said, "This is why we went to the outback to train and try to adapt to dry heat." He sat back down, looked at Captain Yosef, and said, "What's the temperature at night?" Captain Yosef smiled and said, "It cools off some, and you guys will see." The buses drove up to the barracks they were to be assigned, and Captain Yosef stood up and said, gentleman. Every one of you will be sharing a room with one of our guys of the same approximate rank.

Lieutenant Dayan and LT Deaton stepped up the stairs, and Captain Yosef said in Hebrew to Lieutenant Dayan to "gather everyone up." Captain Thomas looked at LT Deaton and said, "Let's get everyone off the buses and form up." Lieutenant Deaton said, "Done." Master Sargent James stood up, saying, "Let's get off the bus and form up." Lieutenant Deaton looked at Master Sargent James with a smile and said, "Thanks." Master Sargent James winked and said, "We got it."

Once everyone was off the bus, they lined up in formation. They observed a bunch of men in civilian clothes come out of the building, and they were outnumbered by at least 4 to 1. They observed the Israelis form up, and both Captain Thomas and Captain Yosef stood next to each other in front of both groups. Lieutenant Deaton yelled, "Attention." The Americans stood at attention, and he turned around and stood at attention. Lieutenant Dayan yelled in Hebrew, "Attention," and his men snapped to attention.

Both Captain Yosef and Captain Thomas looked at each other, and Captain Yosef said quietly, "You are our guest." Captain Thomas smiled and said, "Your house, my friend, go ahead." Captain Yosef said, "Thank you, my friend," and yelled, "English Parade rest." Both groups immediately went to parade rest.

Captain Yosef looked around and said in English, "We will be training together and visiting some unfriendly types soon." He continued talking, saying, "The Americans are being assigned to share a room with us, and I encourage everyone to learn as much as they can about each other." He paused momentarily and continued, "What we do here over the next month could keep the peace or bring war worse than anything this country has seen." Captain Thomas shook his head in agreement. Captain Yosef said, "Captain Thomas is there anything you want to say?" Captain Thomas said, "Yes, just

146

one thing." He looked directly at his men and said, "Learn Hebrew quickly. You might need it." Then he yelled, "Attention," both groups snapped to attention, and Captain Thomas said, "Fall out."

Both groups went over to each other and introduced themselves, including all the officers. After about an hour of introductions, the Americans gathered up their stuff and went to their assigned rooms. Captain Thomas and Captain Yosef went to the room they were sharing, and they sat around and talked about themselves and other things.

They were about the same age, but Captain Yosef was married with two children. Yosef was also educated in America at Boston College, and after college, he entered the Israeli military academy. After one year in the Airborne Infantry Unit, he tried out and was selected for this unit. After training, he married and had one boy and one girl. Captain Thomas smiled and said, "You are a lucky man Captain Yosef," who then responded, "When it's you and I, let's use first names, ok?" Captain Thomas said, "Sounds good, Aaron," and they shook hands. Then Aaron said, "Let's get your guys IDF uniforms," they got up, gathered everyone, and walked them over to supply.

Once everyone was given their clothing and equipment, they went to the armory and received their weapons and rounds, then formed outside their barracks. Captain Thomas told his men, "They had the rest of the day off and tomorrow to rest up." He smiled and said, "Stay out of trouble, and make sure everyone is standing there ready to go at 5:00 A.M. in two days." He discussed how the days ahead will be very long, and they will be hot and exhausting days. So be ready and get some needed rest. You guys will need it. By the way, do not do anything to draw attention to yourselves if possible. Captain Thomas looked around and finished by saying, "No fighting with our guests, only among yourselves."

Chapter 19

Training in the Desert

After the two days off, everyone was formed at 4:50 A.M. The officers walked out of the building, observing everyone in one formation. Captain Thomas and Captain Yosef grinned at each other, and Lieutenant Dayan and Lieutenant Deaton looked at both Captains to see if they agreed or disagreed with what the men did. Captain Thomas said, "It looks good to me." Captain Yosef also agreed.

Captain Yosef told Lieutenant Dayan, "Let's get this going," so both Lieutenants went to the front of the formation, and Lieutenant Dayan said in English, "Let's do some running." They ran in formation for the next 5 miles before the sun came up. It was five miles out and five miles back. Once they got back, they did pushups and sit-ups, then ran one mile to the dining hall. After everyone ate, they ran back to the barracks. Everyone showered and got ready for the training day.

Over the next three weeks, the training became more physical, and both the Israelis and Americans were exhausted. The training continued through the weekends even though the Jewish Shabbat is the Israeli's weekend and holy time. Also, the Americans had to learn Hebrew quickly, and every day, the Israelis would work with the Americans during the training and for a couple of hours in the evening. As the days passed, certain words came out only in Hebrew from the trainers and Israeli soldiers. For example, attention, parade rest, at ease, breakfast, dinner, bed, rest, weapons, bullets, shoot, grenades, flashbangs, chopper, radio, men, women, showers, barracks, and run. Every day they had to learn new words and meanings because they knew there was a reason for all this training.

When the third week went by, everyone was surprised when they were given a day off which turned into two days during the Jewish Shabbat. The next week it was back to full training. After being in Israel for a month, Captain Thomas and Captain Yosef were called to the headquarters for a meeting. The Lieutenants were told to get everyone in the training center and stand by. Both Captains headed to the Headquarters and waited to be called into the Colonel's office. The Colonel's aide stepped out of the office and said, "Gentleman, will you please come in" Both men complied as they entered the room and saluted Colonel Cohen, who saluted back.

Captain Thomas was surprised at how many officers were in this big room. Then he turned his head to the right when he saw a familiar face. Lieutenant General Allen stood up, and Captain Thomas immediately saluted him. General Allen returned the salute. Captain Thomas observed some other Israel Generals mixed in with General Allen's staff. Both Lieutenant General Allen and Captain Thomas shook hands, and Captain Thomas shook hands with everyone in the room, and Captain Yosef did the same.

Colonel Cohen said, "Gentleman, if you can all follow me," as he walked through the crowd, and they headed into the secured part of the building. The Colonel hit the keypad with his private codes and opened the door. The security saluted the brass as they entered the large room, Captain Thomas and Captain Yosef bringing up the rear.

After everyone entered the room, everyone began taking a seat, and once everyone got comfortable, the room got quiet. Colonel Cohen stepped in front and began the briefing by discussing the information gathered by Mossad about a building on the dock in Beirut with a possible future terrorist attack on Israel. He went into more detail about watching this building for six weeks and observing men going in and out heavily armed, and it is confirmed they are members of Hezbollah, which has said many times they will destroy Israel and kill all the Jews. The screen turned on, and a live picture came over the screen from a drone of the building being watched. It showed four men guarding the building. Colonel Cohen turned it over to Military Intelligence or which is known as Aman.

Major Levi stepped forward, showed a face on the screen, and said, "Unfortunately, we do not know anything about this person." He looked around the room and continued by saying, "We know this guy is not Arab or from any Middle East country. He appears to be Spanish with a lot of connections." Major Levi handed out some photos of the unknown person and continued his briefing, saying, "He has been traced and followed from European countries, Lebanon to Venezuela; however, our agents lost him in Mexico City in a traffic jam, and he gave us the slip." He explained more about their agents tearing Mexico City up with negative results. They discovered he made it to the airport and flew out before our people could get to the airport. He added the plane he was on went to Cuba. He added, "This person is into something, and it's not good, and it is believed he was involved with your German trip Captain Thomas." Captain Thomas and General Allen looked at each other with a grin on their faces.

Lieutenant General Allen slowly stood up and said, "Gentlemen, I have most of the missing pieces of the puzzle," getting everyone's attention and started walking around the big, long desk. The General said, "The name of this person is Gonzalez, and he is a bad guy, and I mean, he is 100 % Pure evil." The Israelis looked around at each other as he continued talking. "He is Cuban, and he worked for Castro, and there is nothing he hasn't done, and he is cold-blooded as you can get and extremely calculated, and he is always a few moves ahead of everyone." Captain Thomas leaned forward with a surprised look when Lieutenant General Allen looked at Captain Thomas and said, "Sorry, son, it was a need to know, and you were flying around the world.

Captain Thomas leaned back but appeared to look irked when General Allen looked back at him. Colonel Cohen asked, "Is there any reason for his behavior General?" Lieutenant General Allen said, "Yes, Colonel, all our reports show he went off the deep end when his son was killed and became more violent, and even Castro had to tug his leash a little." Everyone looked puzzled, and someone asked the General, "Could it have been Castro?" Lieutenant General Allen said, "No, it was me because I shot and killed his son many years ago." Everyone looked around the table in puzzlement. He continued, saying, "this took him off the deep end, and he has been seeking his revenge for all these years."

General Allen let what he said to sink in their heads and has been working against the West and its allies for many years. He explained when he was a young Lieutenant doing a rescue mission, we killed some people, including Gonzalez's son. He added," I shot and killed his son, not knowing who he was and who he was related to because my only concern was the safety of my men and the people we rescued." Captain Thomas leaned back in his chair and smiled when he listened to the General tell his story on why he shot this guy's son.

After Lieutenant General Allen finished his story, he turned it back over to Colonel Cohen, who asked both Captains, "How has the training been going?" Both Captains looked at each other and laughed. Colonel Cohen grinned and said, "What's so funny, gentleman," with everyone looking at the two Captains. Captain Thomas said, "Sir, we went from a deadly serious discussion to training in a blink of an eye." Captain Yosef jumped in and said, "Well, sir, we start training at 05:00 A.M. and stop at 1700 hours." Then Captain Yosef looked at Captain Thomas, who jumped in and said, "Everyone is in the dining hall by 5:15 P.M., and everyone gets cleaned up and out cold by 7:30 P.M." Everyone chuckled, including LTG Allen. Colonel Cohen stated," Now let's get down to business," he signaled to a man in civilian clothes who stepped up to the front of the group.

A Mossad agent stepped up and requested to use a few of the men to sneak into Beirut and conduct a recon of this building in Beirut, Lebanon. Drones can only do so much, and we can't get our people close enough to see what's going on inside this building. We were going to push to use the Navy's Shayetet 13, but they are busy targeting the smuggling of weapons into Gaza from Iranian smugglers. We want a 12 men's team with six Americans and six Israelis to sneak in, watch, monitor, and report what they see over two or three days.

Lieutenant General Allen stepped in and said, "Captain Thomas, now you know why we wanted your guys to learn as much Hebrew as you can and why your unit was sent here." He paused and continued saying, "I want you plus five of your men who speak the best Hebrew to go with you no matter the ranks." Captain Thomas said, "No problem, sir, we will get it done."

After some questions were answered, the meeting continued and went over the game plan from getting in and getting out and the units who would be involved. It was agreed the team would be taken to a coastal area near Ashkelon, where a small site has been built just for them. The training site will also be similar to the small port in Jabalia, Gaza. This will make any Palestinians who monitor the area think we will be heading south and hitting them. This information will be passed on to Hamas and Iran, keeping them focused on Gaza and anything around Garza. Hopefully, this ruse will work.

Both Captains were told to practice for both places to make sure if anyone was watching that Gaza was the target. This will either remove anything in the area that they do not want us to hit, or they will reinforce what they are protecting. Once your team is training Captains, then within 24 hours, we will know what they have. This whole thing is serious, and it will help us find out what's going on at the Beirut dock and get the Palestinians to show their hand in Gaza.

Once Captain Thomas and Captain Yosef were dismissed, they headed to their barracks, where they saw all the men coming out of the barracks. Captain Thomas told Lieutenant Deaton, "Go ahead and form everyone up."

Both Israelis and the Americans formed up, and Captain Yosef said, "At ease." Captain Thomas explained something had come down from the higher-ups. Twelve of us will be on a mission and divided into two teams: Six Americans and six Israelis. The rest of you will continue to train, but down to 8 hours a day. You are still required to remain on base, and there is no leave. Both Captain Yosef and I will be leading these teams when Captain Yosef looks at his clipboard and calls out five Americans' and five Israelis' names.

The ones whose names were not called out had angry looks on their faces because they did not get called. Captain Thomas looked around and stepped forward, and said Gentlemen, these names were called because of our different skill sets for this type of mission. He then yelled out to Lieutenant Deaton, who responded loudly, "Yes, sir." Captain Thomas stated, "Get every one of our men and get them in the day room now." Lieutenant Deaton said, "Yes, sir." Lieutenant Deaton yelled attention to everyone and said, "Fall out." Lieutenant Deaton said, "Americans to the day room, and the Americans followed his orders and headed to the day room."

Captain Thomas looked at Aaron and asked, "When do you want to leave?" Aaron said, "How about in two hours." James responded and said, "Sounds good," and asked how? By car? Plane? Aaron said no. Choppers. We have two assigned to us. He pointed to the two on the runway about a couple of hundred yards away. James said copy and then headed to the day room to talk to his men.

When Captain Thomas walked into the dayroom LT Deaton said, "Attention." Captain Thomas said at ease and sat down. Everyone looked around for chairs, and they also sat down. Captain Thomas said, "Look, I know everyone wants to go, but this mission is for a small group, not a large one and gentlemen, those five were the best in speaking Hebrew. He paused and added, "Why do you think we tested you every day on your Hebrew and by the way, the two snipers were needed because of their special skills." Everyone in the room knew Captain Thomas was irked because he could tell some of his men were angry and seemed to blame him for their failure. They knew he cared about them and always looked out for them, and they knew he would run to hell and back for them.

Staff Sargent David stood up and said, "Sir, we understand, and the rest of us, while you are gone, will hold down the fort, sir," he looked around, and then he said, "It might seem that we are mad at you and Lieutenant Deaton, but we do understand it's us that failed in that area." David then sat down.

Captain Thomas looked around the room and said, "Anyone else?" Then Sargent Mays said, "Sir, I feel better already." Captain Thomas asked, "What do you mean?" Sargent Mays smiled and said, "Well, sir, my back feels better knowing that you will be gone, and I don't have to carry you for a while." Captain Thomas and everyone in the room laughed, and then he shot Sargent Mays, the bird and said, "Why am I not surprised the smart-ass comments coming from you." SGT Mays smiled and shrugged his shoulders.

When there were no more questions, Captain Thomas said, "You guys be careful and train smart." He looked at Lieutenant Deaton, who was still laughing and was wiping the tears from his eyes and said, "Lieutenant Deaton, it's all yours." He turned around and said, "Those five, grab your stuff and be outside at 2:15 PM."

Lieutenant Deaton yelled out, "Attention," and everyone stood. Captain Thomas smiled and said, "You guys be careful," and they responded, "You too," and Captain Thomas said, "Fall out." He looked at LT Deaton and told him, "Be careful," LT Deaton said, "You too, sir," and they shook hands. At 2:15 P.M., All twelve men were outside with their weapons and rucks. Captain Thomas and

Captain Yosef each had a six-man team. Their code names were Thunder and Lightning. Captain Thomas's team was Thunder, and Captain Yosef's team was Lightning. Each team had three Americans and three Israelis. They all casually walked to the Blackhawk choppers laughing and joking with each other like they had known each other all their lives.

Before they loaded up, Captain Thomas told the men that we speak Hebrew or Arabic once we got on the choppers. No English ever. Try and keep it in Hebrew, but if you can't speak Hebrew, use Arabic. Everyone here speaks Arabic. So, we will know what you mean. Again, no English. If you do get caught, whatever you do or say, do not speak English ever.

A vehicle drove up, Lieutenant General Allen got out, and Captain Thomas and everyone immediately stood at attention. Lieutenant General Allen responded, "Carry on," and said, "Captain Thomas, take a walk with me." They walked away from everyone, and LTG Allen said, "Are you ready, Captain?" Captain Thomas responded, "Yes, sir, we are." LTG Allen said, "Son be careful. Use your head and think things through and remember the big picture." Captain Thomas said, "We will be fine, sir. These are good men." Lieutenant General Allen smiled and responded and said, "Good and by the way, Elizabeth said hello, and she is worried about you and misses you." He paused and added, "She keeps asking me when will you be coming home?" Captain Thomas smiled but said nothing. The General said, "Once you guys are done with your mission here, you guys will be heading home for a good long break." They shook hands and saluted each other. Lieutenant General Allen turned around and went and got in the vehicle he came in. Captain Thomas jumped into his chopper, and both choppers took off and left the base.

Lieutenant General Allen watched the choppers take off and head west. He liked this young Captain who was seeing his daughter for many reasons and never used dating his daughter to get anything out of anything. The more he puts on this young man's plate, the more Captain Thomas says to keep it coming, and if his plate is overflowing, he just gets a bigger plate.

He knows his daughter loves this young man and hopes it works out between them. His daughter told him before he left, please bring him home, and she was told there was more going on than I can tell you. She started crying, wiped her eyes and said, "She understood." Then she said, "Please, Dad, don't let anything happen to him." He hugged her and said, "I will do what I can, but he decides on that part." Elizabeth hugged her dad and went inside the house at the farm. He then got in his vehicle and left.

The two Blackhawks headed west to the training site with his men, watching everything around them and below them. They noticed an armed drone following them as cover. Captain Thomas closed his eyes and relaxed hoping this mission would be it, and he could go home and see Elizabeth. He missed her. The sad thing is neither of them could write to each other or talk to each other.

 When they landed on the beach in the very southern part of Ashkelon, close to the Mediterranean Sea, they got out and looked at the beauty of where they will be training. They thought they saw a small village about a hundred yards away, but it was the mount site with a wooded-built dock. Captain Yosef said, "It can all be dismantled in 24 hours when we are done." Captain Yosef said, "We will live in the mount site, and the med is the bathtub, and the porta-potties are throughout the mount site." Everyone laughed, and someone said, "Yea, no one wants to step on a hot steamy landmine."

Chapter 20

Prepping for Beirut

The next day everyone was up at 5:00 A.M. and went for a light five-mile run on the sandy beach. Two and a half miles out and back, then the last 200 yards, they had to carry a person of their size on the run for a hundred yards, then switch to finish up. Captain Thomas added sprints of 50 yards in the sand, and they did those until everyone, including both Captains, was puking.

When the PT was done, they all went into the Mediterranean Sea and swam around for about 10 minutes to cool off, and after cooling off in the med, they walked over to eat breakfast, drying off in the warming sun. They ate their breakfast rations, still drying in their clothes. As time went by, they air-dried quickly due to the dry heat and went and changed their socks and got into their boots before they cleaned up their trash and started the full day of training.

They split up into their assigned teams, and both teams went off and sat in the sand and discussed what they needed to do to get the training over as quickly as possible and the usual taking care of each other and the usual teamwork stuff. Then both Captains went over how everyone was doing and how to improve for the final exercise to get the approval to get going in their assigned mission.

The four instructors showed up in a chopper with rucks and more weapons to be used during training. Also, four cases of blanks were unloaded. They did not bring a lot because they were doing a recon, not a hit-and-run.   Five minutes later, another chopper landed with six men armed. They were there to provide security during the day. The last thing they needed was a terrorist attack during training being so close to Gaza. There were also two armed drones, always flying around the area and one over the med to make sure nothing came in from the sea.

They walked through all the scenarios they could imagine and went through what they call a crawl, walk, and run phase of training. The first day was the crawl phase through each scenario. Once they went over each one in the morning, they ate lunch and then went through everything throughout the day. They finally stopped training at 4:00 PM and went for another five-mile run, repeating the same activity they did in the morning and then finished with pushups and sit-ups.

Once the PT was done, they all gathered around as a team and went over the day and everyone's views and opinions to either add to the training or remove some of it. Both Captains agreed to look over what was discussed and make any changes they seemed fit to do. Then about 5:15 P.M., two choppers flew in with twelve new security, and the day watch security was flown out. The twelve men had sleeping bags beside their rucks and weapons.

Six would guard the area during the evening and the other six from midnight to 8 A.M. Around 7:30 PM, everyone stripped down and went out in the med with to clean up from the day. After cleaning up, they went back to where everyone was sleeping and crashed into their sleeping bags. Two drones flew over quietly throughout the evening and night. The drone covering the med observed a boat several kilometers out, but they were fishing. They ran the number on the boat, and it came up belonging to an Israeli fishing family.

Some things were added to the training the next day, and others were removed to improve the training. They did their PT, ate, and jumped back into their training. Both teams went through the crawl faze for three days until everyone could do it without problems. After the crawl phase, they speeded up the exercises to the walk phase. At the end of the day, both Captains walked away from everyone and sat down by the entrance of the mount site and discussed the training which was going on. They both agreed they should move to the run faze from now on without holding back. Both men agreed on the training and hit the sack after getting cleaned up.

The next day there was no PT; after breakfast, they went straight into training. And nothing was held back. Captain Thomas said, "Before they started, if anyone screws up, it's 100 pushups once they are done." All the men looked around at each other, but they knew he was serious, then they went full board into the training. Both Americans and Israelis messed up throughout the morning, and once they were done, it was discovered everyone, including the Officers, had knocked them out. Nobody said a word as they did their pushups.

Captain Thomas and Captain Yosef went to their area, where they discussed things and ate their lunch, and went over what was going on and how things were working out. They both agreed things are getting better, but the training is too slow. Captain Yosef mentioned that it would be another month before we were ready to go at this rate. James said, "Aaron, Let's cut it down to the three most possible situations and go from there because the men are forgetting and mixing too many scenarios up." Aaron shook his head up and down in agreement. Aaron told Thomas since we are going in at night, how about we start running them this evening? Thomas agreed, smiled, and said, "Right after we eat." They both ate and then gathered everyone up to go over the new agenda.

Once everyone lined up, both Captain Thomas and Captain Yosef explained some changes to the training, and they went over the three top scenarios with the bigger odds of happening. They went over both plans step by step and what was expected from all of them. These plans had enough room to adapt to many different directions if needed. Captain Thomas started a question and an answer session for about an hour, and when the discussion ended, they split up into their assigned teams. Then for the next four hours, they walked through both scenarios, and everyone went over what each person

159

was required to do. They would each learn each other's job in case someone is killed and injured and are unable to do their job.

At 7:00 P: M. they started up again; this time, it was at the run phase. They trained until around 10:30 P.M that night without interruption. It had been a long day but more successful than the other days. Everyone was pulled out at one time or another to observe what it looked like, and if they saw anything, they could add or see something that needed changing.

Once everyone got cleaned up, they all crashed, except for Captain Thomas and Captain Yosef. They went off and went over the day and concluded that the training was more successful and better than before. Both men agreed to keep things heading in the same direction. They shook hands and went to where the teams were and crashed. James lay in his sleeping bag and closed his eyes. He went over the day in his head and finally fell asleep. Aaron did the same thing.

When the sun came up, everyone got up. They straightened the area up and went and ate breakfast, and once they were done eating, they held a meeting and went over the full day and that it will be another run/sprint day with nothing held back. Both Captains knew they were running out of time to get everyone ready, and they had everyone hitting it again and again.

They skipped lunch and pushed through all the attempts to get it right, and around 4:10 P.M., they got the three scenarios down pat. They kept going, and around 6:00 P.M., they stopped for dinner, sat around, ate, and talked about the long day. Captain Thomas said, "Everyone should get some sleep after we eat because we will start at 01:00 A.M. tonight and go for it." Captain Yusof smiled and said, "Why not." Once everyone finished eating, they got cleaned up in the Mediterranean Sea and crashed for the evening.

At midnight everyone woke up, got dressed and started to get ready. They checked their weapons and got ready for the exercises. When it was 01:00 A.M, they went full board throughout the morning with only water breaks. At about 10:15 A.M., the last practice was done with four straight practices without any screw-ups.

As Captain Thomas and Captain Yosef walked down the beach and went over the night and morning practices step by step. They were pleased and agreed it was time to call the bosses; they were ready. They headed back and told the men they had the rest of the day off. But they cannot go anywhere. You guys have a private beach. Enjoy it. They grabbed their radio and called the people on the other side and said we have a go.

Captain Yosef received a call about 20 minutes later, and he took down all the information in Hebrew and translated it to James. He looked at it and said, "Well, I guess you are doing the debriefing." Both looked at each other and laughed. James said, "Maybe we will work on the reading part next time." Aaron grinned and said, "Next time."

They went and gathered up everyone, including those who were napping, and Captain Yosef went over the plan. This evening a bunch of VIPs is coming to monitor the whole exercise and give us the thumbs up or thumbs down. They will be arriving around 1900 hours. Go ahead and crash and get some rest. This will be an all-night affair. Captain Yosef asked, "If there were any questions," and a few questions were asked about the VIPs, but nothing important. Captain Thomas said guys get some rest. Some of the men went and laid down, others jumped into the med, and a few laid out on the beach.

At 19:05 hours, four Blackhawks and two chinooks landed next to the Mount site. Captain Thomas and Captain Yosef approached the men getting out. The men in uniform were all IDF officers, and two men who were Americans were in civilian clothes. Both Captains saluted the IDF Brass, who returned their salute with the two unknown Americans identified themselves as they headed over to the area Captain Thomas and Captain Yosef used as their office.

Two other men brought video equipment and a map to the room. Everyone had to either stand or sit on the ground, including the High ranking IDF General. The Military Intelligence officers went over the up-to-date information gathered over the last 72 hours, and a Navy Officer who was in an IDF Uniform in disguise discussed the type of Lebanese Navy who may be in the area when they go in.

He discussed the seven ships which the Lebanese government purchased and what type they were. For example, they were four OPV frigates of 65 and 75 meters in length each, and three from the United States, three Protector-class OPVs. All have arrived in the last year and are being used by the Lebanese Government nonstop without any break time or repairs. They have other ships, but those new ones were the ones to worry about with the type of weapons, engine speed, radar above and high-tech underwater equipment. The Lebanese Government used them to stop weapons smuggling, illegal immigration, and other issues. But they can hinder us if we run into them. Captain Thomas and Captain Yosef looked at each other with concern. Then Captain Yosef raised his hand and said, "Well, how do we get in?"

Colonel Alon stood up and said, "Your teams will play Halo, and you will swim into the dock at night, monitor what goes in and out, and collect any intelligence you can gather." He paused, then continued talking and said, "It will be the entire weekend, and the dock is usually closed, so that helps not get seen." Colonel Alon mentioned they would Jump in at 2100 Friday evening and be there for 48 hours exactly, and if they get discovered, fight their way out to the ocean and swim out as far as they can and hit the signal button and keep swimming. The Americans will be in the area and will come to you as quickly as possible. He pointed to a building on the map showing it was across from the dock. It is an old building closed off due to being prepared to be torn down. They can see the building, the dock, and what is around it.

The teams will be split up and worked out of two separate buildings, with team one in this building and team two under construction. Again, they should not have to worry about any workers during this period due to it being a weekend, and nobody will be in the area. Captain Thomas asked, "Will we be able to deviate from this plan in case things are not what they seem?" Colonel Alon of the IDF said, "No," then Lieutenant General Allen, who walked in through the back door, surprising everyone said, "Yes," and mentioned sometimes pictures and videos are misleading. He then explained he wanted both Captains to know they do what they need to do on the ground to gather all intelligence they might be able to get. Colonel Alon apologized to Lieutenant General Allen and said, "Sound good, sir," LTG Allen looked at Colonel Alon, smiled and said, "I apologize for overriding you, Colonel, but since my men are going, I insist they have the latitude to adapt if needed." Colonel Alon said, "General, no need to apologize, sir, I understand, and we are on the same page." LTG Allen said, "Good."

Colonel Alon continued the briefing and discussed how their teams would swim out and hit this button on this round ball. It will send out a signal for 35 miles. A U.S. sub will be in the area and will come in and pick you guys up. However, they will not come up for you. They will be about 100 yards deep, and Navy Seals will come up from the sub and bring you guys down to the American sub, and you will board it, and it will bring you back to Israel.

He said, "By the way, when you are floating in the med and feel something nudging you under the water, it could be them or a shark. Just saying." Everyone laughed. Captain Thomas asked about the threat of the Lebanese frigates. Colonel Alon said, "We will set a ruse for them to chase down to Tripoli and Tyre, and this will dilute the area because they will be too busy dealing with other issues while we will drop you in."

Major Ariel stood up and said, "Tonight at 2100 hours, we are going to go over everything life. This includes regressing into the med for a good three-mile swim into the sea." Once the meeting was over, preparation was initiated by all parties involved. Captain Thomas knew that when you have time to practice, you practice for what could happen and might happen. It always helps all military units when it's for real. You always train as you would fight. This saves lives and usually helps the mission stay successful. Units that half-ass train ALWAYS SUFFER HIGHER CASUALTIES AND SHOWS POOR LEADERSHIP.

When the meeting ended, Lieutenant General Allen stepped over to Colonel Alon and said, "I apologize for embarrassing you, Colonel, in front of everyone. It was not my intent." Colonel Alon put his hand out, and they shook hands. Colonel Alon said, "Sir, we are glad you are here with us. That's all that matters. Colonel Alon also said, "As you Americans say, it's all good." Everyone in the room smiled after seeing them shaking hands.

Chapter 21

Beirut

They loaded up in the Chinooks used to substitute the C-130, flew out to a designated sight, and jumped airborne from the back of the Chinook. They swam into the mount site and went and staged themselves into two separate makeshift buildings each would go to. They worked their way through IDF volunteers who played dock security. They added more security men in the area, including the regular 8-9 men who normally guarded the dock. Once they started collecting information, they regressed the water and swam out to the designated site, where a Navy boat picked them up. The exercise went to 6:00 A.M when it was completed. Everyone went back to the mount site and went over the debriefing from the beginning to the end.

The observers went over what they saw as good and bad during the exercise. The men were dismissed, and both Captain Thomas and Captain Yosef stayed back, and everyone discussed their opinions of the mission. Both Captains were asked what they thought and did they believe they were ready. They shook their heads in agreement, and Captain Yosef said, "We are ready." General Azrail of the IDF stepped in and said, "Gentlemen, good luck to you both." He looked around at everyone else and said, "You have a go, and I will let Washington and the Prime Minister know it's a go for Friday." Captain Yosef said, "Thank you, sir." Everyone either shook hands or patted each other on the back as they left the area.

Everyone respected General Azrail in the IDF, where he had a big career in Special Operations, and all of Israel's enemies shook when his units went after any terrorist. It is even rumored he led a squad into Iran and sabotaged a nuclear site which caused great loss to the Iranian government, and his last name means the Angel of Death.

Captain Thomas pulled Captain Yosef over to the side and said, "Aaron, we need to get to a site where we can rest, and where do we fly out of?" Aaron said, "James, I will find out." Aaron went up to the Colonel, and they stepped aside and talked in Hebrew for a few moments, and then Aaron stepped over to James and said, "We leave in two hours for a base in the north." Captain Yosef explained why they needed to leave because the people come in to take down the mount site, they take everything apart, and I mean everything. They each grinned and went to talk to their men about what was going on.

Two hours later, two Blackhawks landed, both teams loaded up, and the choppers headed north. While heading north, they observed a bunch of trucks heading to the mount site to take it apart and clean it up. The beach area would look like nobody was ever there. Captain Thomas heard Captain Yosef say look down by the large hill and he pointed. James looked and saw three young Palestinians with binoculars watching them running south on a full sprint. He snickered and realized they would warn their contacts, who would notify Hamas or other groups they might be heading their way. Fish to a hook is a good thing; when we don't show up, they will wonder what is going on and where did we go.

They flew north to the Ramat David Israel Air Force Base, and after they landed, they went to a hangar where all their equipment was waiting for them. All their equipment was laid out for each team member. The teams would be using all Israeli equipment and weapons after checking out all their equipment. They cleaned their weapons and laid back, and napped.

After a few hours, the men woke up and ate the Lebanese food which was brought to them. They have been eating Lebanese food for a whole week to make sure their body odor does not come out as a Western European or American. It's not only a threat in a jungle but any place. They went over photos showing where the explosion was at the Beirut port and how close they would be to where the explosion was. The area is a good location to hide and monitor things.

At 20:55 hours, they loaded up a C-130 with their equipment. Captain Yosef and Captain Thomas saluted their superiors and shook their hands, and got on the plane. The C-130 took off and headed west out in the direction of the Mediterranean Sea. Once they made it over the med, the plane flew higher into the night. There was not much talking on the flight. Most of the men had their eyes closed and were resting. When the plane flew about 50 miles off the Israel coast, they turned north without any threats or the brass canceling the mission. There were two Israel F-16 Fighting Falcons following about a few miles behind them, providing cover. They were there just to make sure the Lebanon Air Force did not interrupt the mission in any way.

While flying higher, the pilot and copilot looked to the right, and they could see the lights of Sidon as they were about 20 miles south of Beirut. Captain Thomas put his earphones down and gave the signal. They are not going to Halo like they were originally going to do, but there was a change of plans. The C-130 suddenly began the plane dropping down to 300 feet, where everyone would jump into the Mediterranean. Captain Thomas went up to Captain Yosef, shook his hands, and said, "Be safe, Aaron in Hebrew," Aaron responded and said in Hebrew, "You to James."

Captain Thomas yelled, "Get ready, gentlemen," and everyone stood up and checked their equipment and each other. Once Captain Thomas was done checking everyone, they felt the plane drop some more. He grinned and said, "Get ready, men." Once the plane leveled out, Captain Yosef yelled, "Hook up," and both teams hooked up with the back of the C-130 opened. After the green light went on, Captain Thomas's team was first out the back, and Captain

Yosef's team followed next. After they all went out the back door into the night, the C-130 gained attitude quickly and headed back to Israel.

Once both teams landed, they split into two teams and began swimming toward the docks, estimated to be approximately 3 miles away. The Mediterranean was calm, which helped with the swimming toward the land, which they practiced many times. Usually, it was even farther out during training. While swimming in, they observed farther off some fishing boats, but none were a threat. They did not see any of those high-tech Frigates from France and kept swimming. There was no moon, so that was a good thing also. The bright lights of the city were a good thing for the men to swim for. It lights up the sky for them, and they finally make it to the docks.

They climbed out of the water and headed to their observation point. They worked their way to the damaged buildings remaining from the dock explosion's brunt on August 4, 2020. Hezbollah assigned leadership for the dock ignored all safety percussions and were just incompetent, causing a major hit to their followers and people's trust. Hundreds died, and thousands were wounded, with many homes destroyed.

The French came in and assisted in investigating what happened, who was at fault, and where the blame should go. The French Government helped financially also, but the big question is how much of that money ended up buying weapons for Hezbollah against Israel.

When both teams made it to their observation post, they assigned a rotation for everyone to watch for anyone who might trip over them. A sniper team also hid up in the middle Container crane on the dock. Since it was a weekend, they were not being used. Their job is to watch from high up and provide cover if needed.

Once everyone was set in place, Captain Yosef got on his radio and started 48 hours and counting. He was acknowledged by the words 48 hours and counting, meaning the clock has started the countdown to regress and get out. Everyone started watching the building and everything around it. It was 0415 A.M. when the signal was given. They noted security on the dock and how many men were guarding it. They noted four outside walking around it. They were carrying AK-47s and watched and noted everything.

When the morning sun came up, it was noted a new shift came on and relieved the morning security guards at approximately 7:30 A.M. Then four men came out of the building, and four relief went inside. Nobody else went in or out throughout the morning. The Lebanese army patrolled the dock, and they approached the men who were guarding the building. They talked for a few minutes, and the six-man Lebanese army patrol finished their patrol and exited the dock. Nobody came to the dock until 1500 hours when a vehicle entered the dock with an escort.

The vehicles stopped in front of the building, and ten men exited all three vehicles. They noticed one man got out of the middle vehicle last, and he was escorted to the building with the entrance door opened for him and entered with his security escort following this unknown man. The man looked familiar, and he was trying to figure out who he was. He didn't have time to grab his binoculars.

Captain Thomas made notes and recorded on the digital camera of the vehicles and all the men who got out of the vehicles and entered the building. The camera showed the time and date. Captain Yosef also filmed from his location about 100 yards away. The bay had very little traffic, with only a few small fishing boats going in and out but nothing major going on. It was a sunny day with clouds in the sky. About two hours later, the door opened, and the unknown person exited, and he looked very upset. They exited the building, and five men who were not accounted for also came out. Those men must be sleeping in there.

The five men were lined up, and this unknown person walked up and down, looking at them and talking with them. Captain Thomas could tell he was angry with them. Then this unknown person grabbed an AK-47 from one of his security, and they observed three men raise their hands. Then this person shot the two people who did not raise their hands. Then this person yelled at the other three, and they ran back inside the building. He tossed the AK-47 back to one of his bodyguards, walked back to his car, and jumped inside. The rest of his men loaded up, and all three vehicles left the dock. Captain Thomas could only tell that they drove west. He was puzzled about why those men were shot and what they failed to do to get themselves shot. He looked round to see if they could sneak into the building, but there were only two ways in, and they were both guarded. He had no problem going through the front door, but he knew his orders were not to be seen by anyone if possible. Collect all information possible and get out. The unknown man had a hat on he couldn't ID the man.

Chapter 22

Threat in Beirut

Captain Thomas and his men watched the security guards drag the two bodies to the edge of the dock and throw them into the bay like they were bags of potatoes. The security guards laughed, turned around, and returned to protect the building. Captain Thomas was recording everything nonstop and was amazed at the ease and calmness the shooter had of killing those two men without remorse or worry. The teams observed another shift rotation at 1600 hours. Nothing happened during the evening except the security sitting around smoking, playing cards, or sleeping. Sometimes they got up and made their rounds, but most of the time, they sat in chairs, smoked, and talked.

At 11:30 P.M., the morning shift arrived, for everyone who provided security inside and out during the evening left. The new security walked around, and it was noticed the three individuals who avoided getting shot did not leave and were not observed coming out of the building. It was figured out they must be sleeping in there. They had everyone's faces on video recordings, so maybe both the U.S. and Israeli intelligence can figure out who everyone is. Captain Thomas was racking his brain on what was happening in the building.

Captain Thomas started at 11:35 P.M because everyone did a two-hour guard duty. James took his men's first shift, and Captain Yosef did the last shift with his team. All videos were uploaded and forwarded to headquarters in Israel, where they downloaded them and immediately began analyzing them. Normally they would have carried equipment headquarters could see at the same time, but they needed to go in as light as possible. The night went quiet, and around 7:30 A.M., the new security men came in and rotated with the morning watch security protecting the building. Everyone was up at 0800 A.M. and watching.

Around 8:12 A.M, the same three-vehicle convoy from yesterday drove up, and the same men exited their vehicles, including the same person from the day before who shot those two men. He went into the building first, with his security entourage following him. Five minutes later, the three men from yesterday were dragged out of the building, and the man in charge pulled his gun out and shot all three of them. Captain Thomas and his men looked at each other and knew this man they couldn't identify was just cold-blooded and seemed not to care about life. After shooting the three men, he said something to one of his security, and he got on his cell phone and made a call. After he was finished, he hung up and put his cell phone in his jacket pocket.

The three bodies were being dragged to the bay when Lebanese soldiers drove up. The person in charge of the army soldiers approached the unknown person in charge, and they looked at each other, and suddenly they started laughing and hugged each other. This was not a good sign for Captain Thomas and Captain Yosef. The three bodies were on the ground when a truck drove up, and five people were dragged out of the back of the truck. The unknown person pointed to the three bodies and pointed to the building. The five men ran into the building. The Lebanese supervisor saluted this unknown person, and everyone got in their vehicle and left the dock area. All this was on the video, including all faces.

The million-dollar questions were who this guy was and why he could just shoot five people over two days, and the Lebanese did not care what this guy did. They even saluted him, and the million-dollar questions were, who was this scum bucket and what the hell was going on in the building? Why would this person shoot five people who looked like they were in lab coats? Captain Thomas then called Captain Yosef "Thunder to lightning," and Aaron acknowledged him. Captain Thomas told Captain Yosef to "meet me downstairs," they both climbed down and met behind a huge crane. Captain Thomas said, "Aaron, we need to get a closer look tonight." Aaron agreed and said," James, I will have two men try and get closer tonight around 2100 hours." James smiled and agreed. James said, "We will provide cover just in case, and remember to make no contact with these clowns" as they split up and climbed up to their positions.

Nothing went on except the shift rotations, and at 2100 hours, two of Captain Yosef's men worked their way down the crane and went into the water. They worked their way to different points to better observe what was going on in the building, but unfortunately, all the windows were covered up. They worked their way in the dark to different positions but could not see anything at all. They spent three hours working their way around with negative results. After failing to get close enough to see inside the building, the two men worked their way back to Captain Yosef's position. They briefed Captain Yosef, who called Captain Thomas and told him negative results. James was not happy and had to bite his tung not to say the wrong thing over the radio. He knew he had to keep his composure.

At 01:00 A.M., the command center came over both radios and said to regress with the signal given to both teams to leave in 5 minutes. Both teams gathered up their stuff and worked their way down the cranes. The sniper team met them by the water where they would enter. They made sure all their equipment was strapped on tight, and they worked their way into the Mediterranean Sea. After a few miles, the water was getting rougher and moving inward, making the swim harder this time compared to when they swam to Beirut. So, swimming out into the med was tougher. They worked their way out, and Captain Thomas reached into his cargo pocket and pulled out a bag with the ball, which would send out a signal to the submarine. He removed the cover, and as he trod water, he hit the button. Then they swam for a little longer and finally gathered up and waited in a circle, floating in the warm Mediterranean Sea.

About 25 minutes went by as they floated along with the current. The water was warm, so that was a good thing. They talked smack and cracked jokes about how they could all be fishbait, just waiting for sharks sooner or later. Suddenly, a head popped up in the middle of them, then a second and a third. The first one took his mask off and said Lt. Commander George at your service. Then six more Navy Seals popped up with scuba masks and oxygen tanks in the middle of the twelve men who were floating in a circle.

Everyone put their equipment on, and once everyone was ready, they turned and followed the Navy Seals down into the sea. They swam deep, and then everyone saw the submarine. It was a Dolphin Class 2 submarine just floating. When they arrived on the top of the submarine, one Navy seal reached down and opened the hatch, and everyone worked their way into the submarine and headed south to Israeli territory.

Once they entered Israeli territory, they came up 5 miles inside the territory of Israel and made their way to Haifa naval base, which is also Israel's main Submarine base for their navy. Israel spent a lot of money fixing up the base with help from their allies in Europe and America.

Once the submarine docked, Captain Thomas and Captain Yosef had their teams disembark and load up in trucks. Both Captains thanked the skipper and the Navy Seals for their help. They were then taken to a helipad, loaded up on two Blackhawks, and headed to Tel Aviv. Captain Thomas asked on his radio set, "Why are we going to Tel Aviv" and Captain Yosef smiled and said, "The big boys are there." Captain Thomas said, "Ok," looked at his men and told them, "The big brass is in town." His team smiled, and then some of them closed their eyes to rest.

Once they arrived in Tel Aviv, they flew straight to the main Headquarters and landed on the roof of the building. Both teams jumped off, and the Blackhawks took off. Colonel Alon and Colonel

Martin of the American army walked out of the building and approached Captain Thomas and Captain Yosef. Everyone saluted each other and shook hands. Colonel Alon of the Israeli army said, "Gentlemen follow me, please, as they entered the building." All the men were given IDs and went to the elevators. The two elevators took them to the center of military operations. The elevator doors opened, and they stepped out into something out of a high-tech Star Wars command center.

They all looked around in amazement at what they were looking at. Then a Lieutenant came up to Captain Yosef and saluted as Captain Yosef returned the salute, and the Lieutenant said, "Follow me, gentlemen." They followed him down the hallway into a large conference room. When they all walked in, there were about ten men at the large table. At the head of the table were Israel's Chief of Staff and Lieutenant General Allen sitting there holding some type of discussion. Colonel Alon went and sat next to Lieutenant General Allen, who stood up and said to Captain Thomas and his men, "Please, gentlemen take a seat. There is plenty of room," and everyone took a seat. General Levi looked at the Lieutenant and said, "Bring these men some cold water." The Lieutenant said, "Yes sir," and he left the room, and the door closed behind him. After introductions were done and cold water for the men was brought in, the room got quiet.

The screens were turned on around them, and General Levi stood up and started the briefing. General Azrail walked in, and he said before people could stand, he said, "Continue," and sat in the corner. When General Levi was done, Colonel Alon told Captain Yosef to "Go ahead and start with your debriefing, please." Captain Yosef went over his team's actions over the last couple of days with no interruptions from the higher-ups in the room. Then it was Captain Thomas's turn, and he went over what his team did and observed. When he was done, Colonel Martin, Lieutenant General Allen's new Chief of Staff, said, "The video was analyzed, and each person was identified, including the person in charge who shot those men." He identified the Cuban national as Gonzalez. The other men were Hezbollah soldiers. The Lebanese Officer has connections with Hezbollah.

Captain Thomas responded, "Damn, I couldn't identify him and said we should have hunted him down and eliminated him." LTG Allen looked over and, with a serious look on his face, said, "Yes, but that was not your mission, was it, Captain?" Captain Thomas looked at the General for a moment and answered back, "You are right, General. That's on me." The General continued talking, saying, "If you hunted him down at that time, there would have been a run-in with the Lebanese military or police, and it would have caused a major international nightmare." The General paused and looked around the room, and said, "Lebanon is on the verge of civil war between Hezbollah and everyone else. This might have helped Hezbollah and pushed the country 100% into the Iranian camp." Captain Thomas looked at the General and said, "Yes sir," with a disappointed tone of voice. He really wanted a shot at that guy, and he felt it slip through his fingers.

General Allen said, "If we chased him in Germany, it could have caused a run-in with the German Polizei, causing a big mess between allies and NATO members." He explained to everyone this could have even caused the closing down of all U.S Bases in Germany. The German people would have been screaming right into the Russian's hands at the top of their lungs. They are already a left-of-center country. A major protest would have broken out on all sides. During the code war, the Soviet Union funded through the KGB and GRU many of the leftist groups who were protesting missiles being placed in Western Germany. They failed, but this could have caused a complete collapse of NATO.

During the discussion, it was brought up that we still do not know what Gonzalez was planning and doing in that building. The Mossad agent who walked in a few minutes earlier interrupted the conversation and said, "We have flown over drones, but they have not picked up anything either, but we did follow the vehicle that had Gonzalez in it, and it went to the Beirut hotel, and he got out and went inside." He continued after pausing. He told everyone in the room the drone showed him taking a private jet to Iran, and we lost him 30 minutes after he entered Iran. Our drone could not reach that far, but our radar showed them landing in Urmia, Iran.

LTG Allen stood up and slowly walked the room and notified the men in the room we could have the building bombed, but that would cause too many headaches for some of us in this room. The mission was a disappointment, but some parts of the mission panned out on knowing Gonzalez being in Beirut means trouble and is now in Iran and before that in Germany. We need to find out where Gonzalez is hiding out and what he is up to. We need to send out a message to our allies to grab this guy for us if they get the opportunity. He then looked at the Americans and said, "Boys, you will head back to Fort Bragg with me in two hours, so go get cleaned up and get in some civilian clothes," the Americans said, "Hell yes." Captain Thomas stood up and asked, "If there was anything else, General?" LTG Allen said, "No, that's it." Captain Thomas and Captain Yosef stood up and saluted. The rest of the men stood and saluted with the generals, and they saluted back, and the Americans exited the room.

Lieutenant Friedman was outside and said, "Gentlemen follow me to where you guys can get cleaned up." LTG Allen and General Levi talked for a few minutes by themselves. LTG Allen asked General Levi, "If you see him again, do us a favor, eliminate him," General Levi said, "No problem." They shook hands and saluted each other. Then LTG Allen said, "He will head out with his men." General Levi responded and said, "Colonel Aron will take you to the choppers." General Levi said, "Be safe," and Lieutenant General Allen responded, "The same with you." General Levi told General Allen he needed to go and brief the Prime Minister, and he left with a few other Israeli IDF Officers following him.

Two hours later, Lieutenant General Allen, Captain Thomas, and his team, including the men left on the Israeli base, were on an American C-141 heading west over the Mediterranean Sea. LTG Allen and Captain Thomas went to the far side of the plane and discussed how the Israelis would keep an eye on the building with drones.

LTG Allen said, "Gonzalez getting away has been eating him up inside, and he feels like something big is going to happen, but what and where is the big question." He told Captain Thomas, "We will use all our resources to find him before he does whatever he is going to do."

He then asked, "James, how are you and your team doing" and James said, "We are doing fine, Sir." We are disappointed with the mission and how it went; however, this Cuban is a very interesting character, and hopefully, we can find out more about him and get another crack at him. LTG Allen smiled and agreed.

LTG Allen then said, "Enough about the shop. I want you to know Elizabeth is going to be happy to see you." James smiled and said, "Hope so, sir." LTG Allen discussed all the phone calls he gets from her. It's when, when, when. James smiled and laid his head back, and fell asleep. Lieutenant General Allen also laid his head back and slept.

After many hours of flying and a couple of stops in Italy, Iceland, and Fort Drum, New York, they landed at Pope AFB, North Carolina. Lieutenant General Allen was the first off the plane besides the crew and waited for everyone to step off the bird. Once all of Captain Thomas's men stepped off the plane, they lined up, knowing the General wanted to talk to them.

Lieutenant General Allen spoke to them about everything they have done and how it is Top Secret, and it never happened. They must not ever talk about what they have done-ever. Their records on the medals they will get will be very black and white, about two sentences long. Lieutenant General Allen continued and said he was proud of each of you men and to keep up the good work.

The General went down the line, shook each soldier's hand, and promoted the soldiers' Captain Thomas mentioned those who lost out on promotions because they were out of the country and could not get their paperwork in. Once he was done shaking hands, he turned to Captain Thomas and shook Captain Thomas's hand and said, "The men have 30 days leave, Captain, and this includes you." He winked, and Captain Thomas saluted Lieutenant General Allen, who turned around and headed to his vehicle, which driven up. His driver jumped out and opened the door, and Lieutenant General Allen tossed his bag into the car and got in. The driver closed the door and got in the vehicle, and they drove off.

Captain Thomas turned to his men and said congratulations to everyone and those who were promoted, and gentleman, we all have 30 days leave. They all clapped and said hell, yes. A bus drove up, loaded up their gear, got on, and headed back to the company area, where they unloaded their equipment when someone said, "I guess we are home." There was some laughter, but besides that, the bus was extremely quiet. They lined up, and Captain Thomas gave a speech about good work, being a solid team, and how lucky he was to have men like them serving with him. He shook his men's hands and said to turn your stuff in and get the hell out of here. They were dismissed, ran up, turned their stuff in, jumped in their cars, and took off.

When James was done doing some things in his office, he saw his dad first and spent some time with him and his girlfriend. His dad tried to pry a little information from James on where he has been and what he has been doing these many months, but James said Dad, I would love to tell you, but unfortunately, I can't. They both laughed, and James said, "Dad, the good thing is we did kill some bad guys." James then changed the subject and asked how they were doing. David and Ann said, "They were doing good, and they were concerned about him because you were gone without any way to get hold of you." James smiled and said, "It was for everyone's safety, and it's the business I chose." David said, "As long as you are ok, that's what's important." Once he was done visiting, he hugged his dad and whispered in his dad's ear, "I love you, Dad," David, with tears in his eyes, said, "I love you too, son, and I am so proud of you." James hugged Ann and whispered, "Please take care of my dad." She smiled and said, "She would." James said, "He had to go see Elizabeth," which they understood, and James left. Before James left, he hugged his dad again, and his dad said, "Be safe, son, and he loved him." James said, "I love you too, dad and he left."

James drove to Elizabeth's house, and when he pulled up, Elizabeth was already out the door running to him. He was smiling and got out of the vehicle, and she ran up to him and jumped into his arms. They kissed patiently for a minute, and then James let her down, and they walked to the house holding on to each other. They walked up the stairs, and Joseph and Mary came out and shook his hand. Mary Allen hugged him, and James hugged her back and said, "Thank you for the welcome." Everyone went inside, and James saw Lieutenant General Allen come out of the study with a grin on his face. LTG Allen shook James' hand and said, "Son, how are you?" James said, "Fine, sir. It's good to be home." LTG Allen wore civilian clothes and said, "James make yourself at home." James said, "Thank you, sir," and Elizabeth told James, "Let's go sit on the swing," with Elizabeth holding James' hand and taking him to the swing.

James and Elizabeth talked for a while, and then they had a nice barbecue, and everyone sat around and talked about the farm, army life, and things going on in the world and back to the farm. Elizabeth did not say much. She just sat close to James and held on to him. Her dad and his parents could see how much she cared for James. James, they knew he cared about Elizabeth, but how much was the million-dollar question? They just wanted her to be happy, and they could see the love blooming between them.

Around 9:30 P.M., James started feeling tired and stood up and said he had to go. It was a very long day, and he needed to sleep before falling over. LTG Allen looked at James and could see the exhaustion in James' eyes, so he said, "I insist, please stay in the extra room tonight." James said, "Thanks, sir, but I believe I better go." Elizabeth looked at her dad with a stern look, and LTG Allen said, "Son, I insist." James smiled and said, "Ok, sir, you win. Thank you." Elizabeth jumped up, smiled, and said, "Let me show you to your room."

James and Elizabeth walked to his car, and he pulled out a bag with clothing and hygiene items in it, and they went back to the backyard and told everyone good night. They all waved, and Elizabeth showed him his room, and They kissed patiently in the hallway, and after a couple of minutes, James said we better stop, and Elizabeth smiled and said your right. They kissed again, and they said their good nights to each other. James said good night as Elizabeth walked out the door. James closed the door to his room and kicked off his shoes and socks, and crashed. Elizabeth went back downstairs to spend time with her family, and her Grandma asked Elizabeth how James was. Elizabeth smiled and said he was out like a light.

Elizabeth switched chairs and sat down next to her dad and, with a smile, said, "Dad, thank you for bringing him home," as her dad just smiled. He said, "You know you picked a winner and that young man has a good chance for a great career in the Army." He kissed his daughter's forehead and said, "I see a great leader in him, and he has the respect of everyone around him and even me." She kissed his cheek, and he continued saying, "He is an amazing young man, and I hope he makes you happy." Elizabeth smiled and said, "He does, and as I told you before, there is something about him that makes him different and special." She also said, "I know he loves me, and I love him, but him saying those words will be tough to get out of him."

Elizabeth looked at her dad, who was looking at her, and she said, "We have all the time in the world." Her dad looked at his daughter and said, "It would be nice if that were always true." He remembers hearing his wife say the same thing many years ago. Life is not always fair, and things can change on a dime, and usually not for good.

Chapter 23

Fury

When James made it back, he spent almost every day with Elizabeth, and they spent a month just driving around the country. James still would get his daily workouts. Elizabeth would do her thing at the gym while he did his workout, keeping themselves in shape. James knows leave could always be canceled in a blink of an eye due to some emergency someplace in the world.

There were a few times he thought he was being followed, but he figured it was just his radar still being up due to his overseas missions, which can keep you wired up. So, he just shrugged his shoulders and had a good vacation. James did not tell Elizabeth what he felt because he did not want to worry her. They hit many of the beaches up and down the eastern coast and had a great time. Once James' leaves were up, he reported back to work and got back into the military routine.

For ten months since he returned, Elizabeth and James continued seeing each other whenever they could. They had no interest in anyone else and were taking their relationship extremely seriously. Elizabeth was back in school and was working on her master's degree, trying to get it done. They always talked on the phone and saw each other whenever they could. The only time they did not talk was when James was in the field. Time was flying by, and before they knew it, it was December, and the winter season was constantly full of ice and snow.

Christmas break was only a few days away, and Elizabeth was anxious to see James. One day some girlfriends in her class invited her to a Christmas party on Campus. Elizabeth called James to see if he would be able to come to the party at the school. James said yes, and he would pack and get on the road as quickly as possible and head her way.

James no longer had his Mustang because he had traded it for a new Jeep. He missed and liked his Mustang, but the car insurance was insane because it was a sports car. He told Elizabeth he had traded in his Mustang for a new jeep, and she asked, "Why," and he said, "The insurance was too high due to it being a sports car." Elizabeth understood and told James are you ready to copy the address? He said, "Yes," and wrote it down and then hung up his cell phone after she said, "Drive carefully."

When James was done packing his clothes, he jumped into his jeep and headed to the address she told him. James was looking for some downtime and planned on spending as much time with Elizabeth as he could during the Christmas holiday. Both have been driving back and forth, seeing each other whenever they could, between classes and field time.

Elizabeth arrived at the party around 7:30 pm at a house a couple of her girlfriends rented. There was a large mixture of college students, men and women, with some of the men being athletes for the University's football team. After a couple of hours, James didn't arrive, and Elizabeth decided to leave because she was tired of constantly telling one guy after another that she had a boyfriend and was not interested. She knew he was on his way and decided to leave.

The three Football players Elizabeth ticked off because she made them look bad were in the corner talking among themselves. Several of the observers walked by them and laughed and said woosh, strikeout. Some other people joined in and laughed, making the football players look foolish, and they felt humiliated. They were not used to that because they were used to women throwing themselves at them because they were big men on campus. The three football players looked at each other and said we would fix that bitch.

Elizabeth decided to walk back to her room which was about four blocks away. She told her friends she was leaving, and they tried to get Elizabeth to change her mind, but she decided to leave. They hugged each other, and she started to leave when three football players cornered her and tried to keep her from leaving. They again hit on her, and Elizabeth kept refusing, but they're like, 'Come on'. She finally was able to get by them and headed out the front door and outside, where she noticed the snow on the ground, and it was pouring down heavily. She bundled up and started walking down the street. She tried a couple of times to get hold of James. Unfortunately, the cell phone signal was weak, and she kept on walking to her apartment.

 While Elizabeth was walking, she didn't see three large males following her. Once she got halfway home by an open field, a large hand grabbed her, turned her around, and threw her down. They yelled at her and called her a whore, bitch, and cunt. They were mad because they felt she embarrassed them back at the house. The leader reached down and yanked her up, then slapped her, and she fell to the ground.

All three of them gave each high fives, and they noticed Elizabeth started to get up when one of the guys kicked her, causing her to fall back into the snow pile. She started to cry, and she remembered what her dad taught her don't be a victim, always fight back, and she did. As the leader reached down to pick her up, she side-kicked him in the groin. He bent over in pain, and she jumped up and started to run, but the other two grabbed her and tackled her hard, knocking the wind from her. She was smacked around for a minute.

While lying in the snow bleeding in pain, she looked up, and suddenly, she saw a glimpse of a large man come out of nowhere. It was James, and he struck their leader in the back of his head, causing the jock to collapse and blackout. The other two jumped up, turned at James, and attacked him, and both men pulled their knives out. Within seconds he came down hard on one's knee with his boot and broke the guy's knee and the other's right arm. They also received broken noses for good measures. James was red-faced with rage, yelled in extreme anger, and beat the other two with extreme violence, with each fist striking their faces. While they were rolling on the ground screaming in pain, Elizabeth saw James's eyes turn black, and his face looked ferocious as he stood over them with fire and rage in his eyes.

He then grabbed one by the throat, grabbed one of the knives on the snow, put it against the guy's throat, and said in a scary tone, "He should kill all of them if they ever did something like this again." He pushed it tight against the throat as the college football player's bladder opened. He pissed all over himself in fear.

He looked around and observed there were no cameras around and no witnesses, and it crossed his mind to kill them, but Elizabeth was the only reason he didn't. The second jock who stood up also pissed all over himself when he saw the knife being waved in his face. James threw the guy back down, tossed the knife, and yelled at them. If he ever hears them do something like this again, he will come back. As he pulled out a buck knife from his back and said, "He would hunt them down and cut their hearts out." He looked right at them and said, "Do you understand?" he continued to look at the two who were standing, and their eyes had a fear of seeing death looking at them. They were too scared to say anything. James yelled at them, "DO YOU UNDERSTAND ME?" as he held his buck knife in his right hand, tapping it against his right leg. They immediately responded back and said, "Yes," with panic in their voices.

James took a deep breath and said, "Remember what I said. Next time you will never open your eyes again. Now get your friend and your asses out of here." They helped their friend up and staggered away in the direction of the house that was having the party.

James turned to Elizabeth, stepped over to her, put his knife in his sheath, and lifted her in his arms. She was slightly dazed and teary-eyed, and he felt Elizabeth shaking. James held her in his arms and began walking down the street to the place she lived. The snow was coming down harder, and the wind had picked up, but James held on to her.

 While James was carrying her, Elizabeth was shaking and crying. James told her, "I am so sorry I am late, and I got you, honey." Elizabeth, teary-eyed, looked at him and asked him, "Why were you late, and what happened?" He said, "I slid off the road, and someone helped me get the vehicle out of the ditch." She looked into his eyes, kissed him, and said, "I love you, James." James wanted to tell her he loved her but didn't. He just grinned and smiled. Elizabeth, still sniffling, said, "I love you, James."

He carried her through the building door and into the elevator. Before the door closed, he heard one woman tell another woman, "I wished my boyfriend would do that." When they made it to her room, she handed him her key out of her pocket. James opened the door, and they went in, and he closed the door.

Once the door was closed, she stopped shaking and felt safe being with James. The room was warm, and she began kissing James, and they kissed passionately when she stopped and said again, "I love you." James looked down and looked up and said, "I love you too," and told her, "He has never said that to anyone before." They began wildly kissing each other, pulling each other's clothes off, and making love until they fell asleep in each other's arms. Before he fell asleep, he looked at her and made the decision he did love her, and he decided to propose to her. However, he did not know when he fell asleep.

The next morning, they woke up and showered, and he looked out the window and observed the snow had stopped falling. After getting dressed, they walked holding hands down to where his jeep was and got in his jeep. Elizabeth realized it was just down the street from the party she was at last night. She asked him how he knew she needed help. He told her he saw those guys following her, and he pulled over and followed just in case they were just walking down the street.

When he saw them attack her, he ran and did what he had to do. She smiled and said, "What was that?" He smiled and said, "Protecting the women I love." Elizabeth smiled, laughed, and said, "My knight in shining armor." He responded, "No knight, just a humble soldier." She looked at him and, with a serious look on her face, said, "Captain James Thomas, that's why I love you." He smiled and said as he was getting in his jeep, "Let's eat. I am hungry." She told James, "Let's go to IHOP." James grinned and told her, "He loved the breakfast meals they had there."

They started to drive down the street when they saw an IHOP, and they turned into the parking lot and parked. The couple looked at each other and jumped out and said, "Let's eat," and filled in on the great food that IHOP serves. James ordered the all-you-can-eat pancakes with eggs and bacon. He told Elizabeth, "I haven't had breakfast like this in a long time." She said, "Which is better, IHOP or my grandmother's cooking?" James smiled and said, "I am eating. No tough questions right now." She laughed as he was consuming his pancakes.

Chapter 24

Holiday and Marriage

During the Christmas holidays, they headed to Florida, and Elizabeth called her dad and told him she was with James and they were heading to Destin. Her dad asked her, "When will she be home for Christmas," and she said, "We will be back on the 24th of the month." He told her, "To be safe and have fun." Elizabeth told her dad, "She will."

They headed to Destin, Florida, for a week and rented a condo on the beach. After they arrived, they changed into swimming wear and headed out the door and onto the beach. The location was perfect; all they had to do was walk out of the condo's front door, and there was the beach. There was a big difference in the weather going from Fort Bragg, North Carolina, and Destin, Florida, in December.

While vacationing in Destin, they had a wonderful time doing what people do during vacations in Destin. James had decided to propose to Elizabeth but changed his mind and did not propose in Destin but back at Bragg. He bought a ring and kept it with him, and once he felt it was the right time, he would propose to Elizabeth. He loved her, but there were things he had concerns about. One was who her father was since he was a powerful man, and men like that are not tolerant of people who hurt their daughters. He knew he had to be sure about dealing with her dad, but he loved Elizabeth and loved being with her.

Once the new semester started, Elizabeth was back in college working on her Master's degree when James drove up to visit her. He finally made his decision and decided to propose to her during dinner at the restaurant he planned on taking her to. He thought it over and decided he would just have to deal with her dad no matter what, good or bad.

James picked her up for dinner in the evening, and both were very quiet while eating their dinner at a Chinese restaurant. He made the decision it was the right time, and he took a deep breath and looked at Elizabeth, who was quiet and not doing her usual talking. He said, "I am not perfect and have many faults, but I love you." Elizabeth was puzzled and was looking at James, wondering what he was doing and why he was acting strange.

She was worried about something and had something to tell James. Then it dawned on her, and she realized James was proposing to her. She started to smile and saw his face with a serious look when he said, "Elizabeth will you marry me?" James reached into his jacket and pulled the ring out, and she was smiling and said, "Yes, I will marry you." He smiled as he placed it on her finger, and they stood and hugged and kissed each other.

Everyone around clapped, and people said, "Congratulations." They sat down and continued eating their meal when Elizabeth put her fork down, looked at James, and said, "I have something to tell you too." He took a sip from his glass, looked at her, and said, "What's up?" Elizabeth looked down, then looked up and said, "I am pregnant." James got quiet for a second with a surprised look on his face. Elizabeth was quiet as she looked at James. He lifted his head and smiled as he leaned over the table, kissed her, and said, "I love you," and he smiled after, and she said, "I love you." He looked around and said loudly, "We are having a baby." People clapped, some said, "Congratulations again," and James sat back down.

Now that they were going to get married, they had to tell her dad and his dad, so they drove after dinner and went straight to the farm to tell her dad. Her dad was in the study reading some papers when James and Elizabeth walked in through the front door. They walked into his study, and he noticed Elizabeth was standing there with a big smile, and James looked nervous. He got up and hugged Elizabeth and shook James' hand. Then he asked, "How are they doing?" Both James and Elizabeth said, "Things are going great."

Elizabeth nudged James, who said nervously, "Sir, I have something to say to you." He looked very nervous and said, "Elizabeth and I are getting married." She smiled and stuck her hand out to show her dad the ring James gave her. Her dad smiled and said, "Congratulations," as he hugged Elizabeth and kissed her on the forehead. He then shook James' hand and patted him on the back, and said, "Congratulations, son."

He yelled out, "Mom and Dad come down here. There is some great news." They came downstairs, and Elizabeth ran to them and hugged them, and her grandparents asked, "What was going on?" she said, "James and I are getting married," and she showed them her ring. Her grandparents said, "Congratulation," and Joseph went and shook James' hand and said, "It's about time." James smiled but did not say anything. Mary came over and hugged James, saying, "Welcome to the family," and hugged him again. Elizabeth was smiling, watching everything. She knew everyone loved James because of the way he treated her, and he always showed concern for her. They all sat down and discussed when and where they would get married.

Elizabeth said, "We have one more good news," and her dad smiled and said, "Ok, what is it?" She stood up and said, "I am pregnant. We are having a baby." Everyone said, "Congratulations," but before it could be asked, she said, "I know what everyone is thinking, and the answer is no." Everyone got quiet, and she continued by saying, "We are not getting married because of that. James proposed to me before I told him I was pregnant."

Elizabeth's grandparents smiled again, and her dad stood up and said, "I had no doubt there is lots of love between you two." So, he asked, "When is the marriage, and how far along are you?" James stood up and said, "Sir, we are looking at it about a month from now," and Elizabeth said, "About four weeks." After a couple of hours of family talk, James stood up and said, "We must go so we can go tell my dad the good news." There were more hugs and handshakes as James and Elizabeth left the house and jumped into his jeep. Joseph Allen and his parents smiled, watching them enter the jeep and leave.

Joseph's dad looked at his son and said, "JR, well, son, you are in a tough position." Junior looked at his dad and said, "I know. God help me if I let anything bad happen to him, and God helps me if I babysat him where it could cause problems between those two." He understood Captain Thomas was a hard charger and wanted to do the right things, but he needed to understand his priorities just changed in his military career. He must be willing to make that change himself, not forced to.

Elizabeth and James drove to his dad's place and walked to the front door, and he knocked on the door a couple of times before the door opened. James' dad smiled, hugged his son, and asked, "How are you?" Then he saw Elizabeth and hugged her too. Elizabeth smiled, and he told them to come in. After they went in and sat down in the living room, David asked Elizabeth and James if they wanted anything. Elizabeth said, "Yes, please, just some water." James said, "None for him." David went and got Elizabeth some water. James asked, "Where is Ann?" David said, "She is at work." James and Elizabeth were sitting down, and James said, "Dad, I have something to tell you."

David smiled and said, "Let me guess, you two are getting married." Elizabeth smiled, said, "Yes," and kept smiling while showing him her ring. David leaned over and hugged Elizabeth, and James stood and hugged his dad. James said, "Well, since your ESP is working, we also have something else to tell you." David got quiet and said, "What?" Elizabeth smiled and said, "We are having a baby, and James proposed before I told him, just in case it crossed

192

your mind." David smiled and said, "James and Elizabeth, I am so happy for you two." Then he got quiet and looked down at the floor. James looked at his dad and said, "I know, Dad, she would be thrilled also, and I miss her too."

They stayed for an hour visiting, and then Elizabeth and James left, and they went to eat at a Texas Roadhouse Restaurant. He was craving a large T-Bone steak, and Elizabeth wanted a barbecue chicken. They had a nice time throwing peanuts around and at each other when Lieutenant Deaton walked in with his girlfriend, and James waved him over. Lieutenant Deaton introduced his girlfriend Barrie to James and Elizabeth, and James told Lieutenant Deaton to come and eat with them, but the lieutenant said, "No thanks, we do not want to intrude." James said, "Please, I insist," then Elizabeth moved over and sat next to James so Lieutenant Deaton and his girlfriend could have a seat.

They all talked and ate till they were full when Barrie noticed Elizabeth's engagement ring and said, "Wow, that's nice." Elizabeth smiled and said, "We are getting married next month." Lieutenant Deaton and his girlfriend both responded back, "Congratulations." Lieutenant Deaton asked, "If it will be a private affair or will people be invited." James answered, "Yes, we will send out the cards in a few days, and I hope you two will be coming." Lieutenant Deaton and his girlfriend smiled and said, "They would love to."

When it was time to go, James insisted and paid the whole bill. They got up, and James threw a 20-dollar bill on the table as a tip. The waitress smiled and said, "Thank you." James smiled and responded by saying, "You are welcome," as they were leaving. James shook hands with Lieutenant Deaton and Barrie, and James went to his jeep and opened the door for Elizabeth, and she got in. James closed the door, went to his side of the jeep, and jumped in, and they drove to his place for the night.

A month later, James and Elizabeth were married at the Fort Bragg Main Post Chapel and one of the original old-style churches built during the Depression, with many church items added over time. After the Christian wedding, there was a celebration at the Fort Bragg Stadium since the weather was perfect. As suspected, hundreds of soldiers, their wives, and girlfriends were there, with Alcohol flowing loosely. There were lots of taxis standing by, and around midnight the new couple exited with an escort out of the building. Elizabeth's dad left two hours earlier. James' dad and Ann left right after James and Elizabeth left the base for the hotel for the night. The next day they flew out of Fayetteville, North Carolina, to the Bahamas and beach time.

Once the plane landed at the International Airport in Nassau, Bahamas, they got a rented car and drove to the Ocean Club on Paradise Island. They stayed two weeks, enjoying the beaches and tours, and even went fishing. James played golf twice at the Paradise Island Golf Club with Elizabeth as the designated Golf Kart driver. Elizabeth said, "She liked the game," and James smiled and agreed to teach her after the baby was born. They then kissed each other, and she smacked him on the chest and said, "Get going." James turned around and went back and focused on his game.

They had a great time on the golf course, and once he completed his game, they went back to his room and changed into swimming suits. The weather was nice, and the skies were clear. When they made it to the beach, they laid out for a little while, and later they rented some Sea Doos, and they raced around the bay, with Elizabeth being more careful than James due to her being pregnant. They drove around and looked at the big houses next to the beaches belonging to the wealthy.

After about an hour of driving around on the Sea-Doos, Elizabeth told James she was tired, and they raced back to the beach in front of the Oceans Club, where they turned in the Sea-Doos, and headed back to their room, where she took a two-hour nap. James was not tired, but he just lay there looking at her sleep. James felt content for the first time in his life. He was with the woman he loved, and he was going to be a father.

While Elizabeth was in a deep sleep, James got up and grabbed a book off the kitchen counter he had been reading. He sat in the recliner in the room, read for about an hour, then opened the screen door and walked out on the deck. He looked around and was amazed at how beautiful the Bahamas were and how the beaches were so amazing.

He sat on a deck chair and put his feet up on the rail, and relaxed. He knew two weeks would go fast, but he wanted Elizabeth to have the time of her life. James began thinking about things she would like to do with a few things he might like. She told him she wanted to learn how to play poker, so he planned to teach her tonight at the gambling tables. He would coach her while she played, and he was also looking forward to playing some poker also. After she woke up, they went and ate at the Club Restaurant.

Once they were done eating a nice dinner at the club, they went to the poker tables at the Atlantis Casino. Elizabeth was sitting at the table with James behind her. They agreed that if she needed any advice, he would give it. If she did not ask, he promised he would not say anything. They both agreed to only gamble a set amount, with her going first. After an hour, she asked three times for advice, and James was right twice. She walked away with a three-hundred-dollar profit, and she was thrilled.

 When it was James' turn, he was a little more reserved and walked away with two hundred and sixty dollars. She started getting tired about forty-five minutes into his turn, and he noticed it and decided to step back. She asked, "Why," and James said, "I can see you are tied." When she said, "She is fine, and they can stay longer," he said, "It is time to go," and she responded by saying, "Ok, you win." James laughed and said, "No, you won, and you beat me by forty dollars." Elizabeth smiled and said, "I love you," as they left the building.

Chapter 25

Bad Guy

His name is Rafael Gonzalez, and he was born in Havana, Cuba. Once he became an adult, he served in the Cuban Revolutionary Armed Forces. As time went by, he made it into the Cuban Special Forces called the Black Wasp. He worked his way up and became a colonel over time in the Unit due to his aggressive skills and quick understanding of how to defeat the enemies of the revolution and future threats.

Rafael served throughout Africa, killing all enemies of communism with extreme National pride. He was always proud of his work and did not care who he killed for communism, men, women, and children. They were all the same in his eyes and were a threat at the time or in the future. What he did not understand at the time was when they entered a village, the children who survived would grow up angry and would challenge Marxism and be a threat to communism because of his violence against their families. He was right. This was always done for thousands of years by conquerors and their supporters to eliminate any future threats. Children would grow up and have pure hate for the soldiers who killed their family members.

 When he got older and became better trained, he realized the mistakes he made when he was younger. Revenge is a powerful tool, so he adapted. Instead of killing everyone, he picked and chose and got better results by manipulating people to his side.

As time passed, his superiors recognized his allegiance and loyalty to communism and the leadership of Fidel Castro. When Gonzalez was made General, he worked for Fidel Castro in pushing Castro's agenda at 100%. He was moved to the intelligence agencies and learned everything he could by being a sponge. As time went by in the intelligence agency, he targeted anyone who spoke ill of Castro and communism. He even successfully planted five spies in the United States, and their job was to pass on information on the anti-Cuban community in Miami. Through training at the Former Yuri Andropov Red Banner Institute, Gonzalez learned many more ways of doing things from the KGB. Gonzalez came back to Cuba before the fall of the Soviet Union and helped spread his knowledge in the Cuban Intelligence community.

When he came back to Cuba, he married another General's daughter, and they had one son and one daughter. He was happy being a husband and a father, and his career was going great, and he knew sooner or later he would be running the entire Cuban military. He believed communism and the fight for it had panned out and was spreading throughout the world.

Then like a car crash at full speed, the Soviet Union collapsed, and the oil and weapons and free cash ran out. Cuba had been running on credit and being the Soviet Union's lapdog for many years. They did whatever Moscow wanted or needed to be done, including helping to overthrow governments in Africa and South America.

When the Soviet Union collapsed due to heavy debt and a too-costly military budget, this caused Cuba to collapse economically—with money, oil, medications, and other supplies drying up, causing many people to question how things were running. Protests increased, and people were gathered up in the middle of the night and locked up. One was Garcia, who had a relative who was in American politics. This traitor sneaked into Cuba to help people get out and was betrayed for money. Castro did not care who this person was. He wanted all these traitors locked up as a threat to the revolution. This person was locked up in the El Pierre prison. General Gonzalez decided to put his best troops guarding him.

As years went by, General Gonzalez's son grew up and joined the Black Wasp unit, continuing a family tradition. General Gonzalez was now the second most powerful General in the Cuban Army, who always had Castro's ear. He made sure his son was assigned to the Pierre prison, which would be close to the family. The duty was safer there than any overseas duty. His son was close enough that he could watch over him and be close to his mother due to them being very close. General Gonzalez told the Warden of the Prison personally to watch out for his son, with the Warden promising to make sure General Gonzalez's son was taken care of and he would make sure nothing would ever happen to him.

General Gonzalez was sleeping one night when he received a telephone call from the El Pierre prison from the Warden himself. He was told there had been a major breakout at the prison by unknown forces. After listening, General Gonzalez asked, "How bad is it and how many escaped?" The information he received was some well-trained soldiers initiated the escape. However, four prisoners were caught and were immediately executed. General Gonzalez wanted to know how many were still missing, which the Warden told him. The Warden said, "Sir, I have some more bad news." General Gonzalez went quiet, got a chill up his spine, and asked, "What is it?" The Warden said, "Your son was shot and killed by the soldiers who caused the breakout." General Gonzalez got quiet and hung up the telephone when his wife looked at him and asked, "What's wrong?" He got teary-eyed and told her, "Roberto is dead." He paused and said, "He was shot and killed by some unknown soldiers who caused a breakout at the prison." Amanda screamed and cried and yelled in a hysterical voice, "No, no, not my baby," as Rafael hugged her tightly, and then he got out of bed and dressed. He picked up the telephone and called for his driver.

Before he left Amanda, who was still crying and hanging on to her pillow, whispering "no, no, no, no," and as he was getting ready to exit the bedroom, she lifted her head from her pillow, and with tears coming out she looked at her husband and said, "Kill them all." She said, "Rafael swear to me you will kill the men that killed our son." Rafael stepped back to the bed, lifted her chin gently, and said, "My sweet, I will revenge our son at all cost." Then he reached down, kissed her lips, stood up, and exited the room. She put her head on her pillow and continued to cry.

After 15 minutes, General Gonzalez's driver drove up, jumped into the vehicle, and said, "Take me to the El Pierre prison." He used his car phone and made several phone calls to have certain soldiers report to the prison. Rafael wanted revenge and for the whole world to suffer for not putting America in its place and denying the communist revolution. He knew it had to be the Americans, but he needed proof and planned to get it.

When General Gonzalez arrived at the prison, he got out, and everyone jumped to attention. They all knew who he was and how powerful this man was. The Warden came out and met the General with his staff, and he stuck his hand out to shake General Gonzalez's hand, but General Gonzalez ignored it and looked the Warden eye to eye and said, "Where is my son?" The Warden, with a serious look on his face, said, "Follow me, sir." General Gonzalez looked at a couple of men and said, "Follow me," and they complied. The Assistant warden and the Captain came running up, and they followed the crowd going inside the building. The group of men made their way to the medical department.

The Warden opened the door in the hallway, and General Gonzalez stepped into a small room where he saw his son on the table with three bullet holes in him. He clenched his fist and stepped up, and looked at his son's dead body. He leaned down and kissed his son's forehead, and he stepped back and said nothing for a couple of minutes. All the men were nervous and scared of what he might do.

While looking at his son General Gonzalez noticed his son's eyes were closed. He turned around and said in an angry tone of voice,

"Who the hell closed my son's eyes?" A young man named Sargent Lopez and about the same age as his son stepped up with tears in his eyes without any hesitation and said, "I did, sir." General Gonzalez said in an angry tone of voice, "Why?" The young Sargent looked down and, with tears still streaming down his cheek, said, "Because he was my friend, and he needed his peace, sir."

General Gonzalez stared at the young man for a moment, then stepped over to him, reached out, hugged him, and said, "Thank you, and thank you for being my son's friend." He got quiet for a moment and said, "Your tears tell me what I need to know is true." The young man hugged the General back tight and cried, and then he let go and said, "I am so sorry I was not there." He took a deep breath and continued, "We worked together, but we got split up." General Gonzalez let the young man go and turned to the Warden and asked, "Why were they split up?" The Warden said, "He felt those two men were too close as friends and could be a security risk. So, we broke them up."

The Captain immediately stepped forward and said, "Sir, we all concluded friendship is good, but they need to stay focused on their job instead of fishing and chasing girls." In an angry tone, General Gonzalez began yelling about how the friendship between two soldiers will always step up under fire. They always look out for each other and will risk death to save each other. That is true friendship. Because of you, gentlemen, my son is dead. Then he stepped away from everyone and looked at his son again.

Everyone in the room remained extremely nervous, watching General Gonzalez, who was still irate, take a deep breath and say, "Now my wife has no son thanks to you three men." Warden, what did you tell me you would do? The Warden hesitated and answered by saying, "He would look after the General's son." In a slow and scary tone, General Gonzalez stated, "You promised me face to face you would take care of my son." He looked around the room and mentioned, "You gave me your word of honor, Warden," and he turned his head and looked at the soldier who had just walked in and said, "Escort these men to the entrance -NOW."

Once everyone was back outside at the entrance, General Gonzalez had the Warden, the AW, and Captain lined up next to each other. He said, "Warden, you were told to look out for my son," as he paced back and forth in front of these men. The Warden AW and Captain were pleading for mercy, and they did what they could and were only doing their jobs.

There was a moment of silence with the Warden sniffled and said, "I am so sorry, sir. I tried to protect him." The angry General stepped up, got within inches of the Warden's face, and said, "You failed me, my family, and our nation" as he grabbed a soldier's 45 caliber weapon, turned around, and shot all three men in the forehead. They died instantly, falling to the ground. No soldiers dared to say a single word as the General handed the 45 handgun back to the soldier he took it from.

General Gonzalez turned to the other soldiers standing around and yelled out for them to get rid of this trash. Put them in a truck, drop them off at their family's doorstep, and tell their wives they were executed for treason. Six men immediately threw the bodies in the back of a truck, and they left.

Once the truck left, General Gonzalez yelled out to Sargent Lopez. Sargent Lopez ran up and saluted General Gonzalez and stood at attention. General Gonzalez looked around and said, "This young man is the new Warden as of now." He looked around and asked, "Are there any complaints or questions from anyone?" Nobody said a word or questioned the General. General Gonzalez looked around and stated in a firm tone of voice, "I thought so." He turned to the new Warden and said, "Get my son to the morgue right now." The Warden saluted and gave orders to make this happen. General Gonzalez said, "Warden Lopez," and the new Warden snapped to attention and said, "Yes sir," and General Gonzalez said, "Pick your own people as your assistants." The new Warden said, "Thank you, sir. I will not let you down." Four men went inside and carried General Gonzalez's son to a vehicle, put him inside, and drove off.

Colonel Jimenez and several vehicles drove up, and everyone jumped out, with Colonel Jimenez running up and saluting the General. General Gonzalez saluted back and said, "Colonel, my son is dead. He was shot by unknown assailants who freed some men from the prison." Colonel Jimenez was shocked by what he was told but continued to listen to the General, who told him, "I want you to hunt down every one of them and bring them to me, Colonel. You have 24 hours." The General stepped up to Colonel Jimenez, got close to him, and whispered, "Do not disappoint me, Colonel." Colonel Jimenez saluted and told his men to follow him. Before Colonel Jimenez got in his car General Gonzalez yelled out to the Colonel, and Colonel Jimenez said, "Sir?" General Gonzalez said, "Do whatever it takes. Do you understand me?" Colonel Jimenez said, "Yes sir," as he jumped in his vehicle.

When General Gonzalez arrived home, he found his wife asleep, so he let her sleep, showered, and changed his clothes. He went to his daughter's room and checked on her, and he saw she was also asleep. Camila was 16 and close to her brother, and he teared up about losing his son and went and sat down in the kitchen with a picture of his son. After a while, he became angry and swore to revenge for his son's death no matter how long it took and who was involved. Once his driver walked in, he told the General the car was ready, and he observed the General wipe his eyes and had his driver take him to Castro's mansion.

When General Gonzalez arrived at Fidel Castro's mansion, he got out of the vehicle, and Castro's Private security let him in. Castro was walking down the stairs in a bathrobe he got in France. After Castro made it down the stairs, General Gonzalez saluted Castro, and Castro saluted back. Fidel Castro hugged General Gonzalez and said, "What can I do for you, my old friend?" General Gonzalez looked down and raised his head, and Castro saw the sadness in General Gonzalez's eyes. Fidel said, "Let's go to my private study, old friend." Once they entered through the door, Castro closed the door behind them and said, "please take a seat." General Gonzalez sat down when Castro asked him, "Would you like a drink or a cigar?" General Gonzalez said, "No, thank you." Castro smiled, lit a cigar, and asked, "What can I do for you, my friend?"

General Gonzalez explained everything to Castro about what happened with the cigar falling out of Castro's mouth. General Gonzalez then mentioned the death of his son and how he died. Castro said, "What do you need from me, General?" General Gonzalez explained what he wanted to do and how it could take years to plan and strike back, but he was willing to bide his time. This included leaving the army and taking over the DGI (The Cuban Intelligence Agency) to put his plan together. Fidel Castro agreed and responded by saying, "We will announce his promotion at lunchtime." General Gonzalez responded and said, "Thank you." He told Castro his promotion would help him to seek revenge and let everyone know not to mess with Cuba and its leadership. Castro said, "No problem, but ensure the other duties are not ignored."

General Gonzalez stood up and shook Fidel Castro's hand when Castro asked, "Who is being punished for this catastrophe?" General Gonzalez said, "The Warden, AW, and Captain have been executed for treason." Castro smiled and stated, "We must never tolerate treason, but we must not allow the people to know another country entered our precious Cuba and conducted this incursion because it could cause the people to question my leadership." General Gonzalez agreed, and again they shook hands. Fidel Castro said, "General, you have my blessing to achieve what is needed to complete your objectives."

Once General Gonzalez left, he went back to be with his family and bury his son. His son was given a state funeral with everyone who was anyone was there. President Castro gave the eulogy to the young man who he claimed to be a hero of the revolution. General Gonzalez and his wife were very appreciative of Fidel Castro's words. This only confirmed his loyalty to this man and his agenda. After the ceremony, General Gonzalez kissed his wife and daughter, took them home, and went to his new office. All the escaped prisoners except for two have been caught or shot. Living on an island is an advantage because there are few places to hide.

When he returned to his headquarters, he walked in, and everyone who was there stood up. He told Lieutenant Perez, "Call the prison, and I will be there in two hours and have all those escaped prisoners lined up on the wall." The Lieutenant called the prison Warden and told him, "The General will be there in two hours and have those prisoners who were caught lined up to be questioned." The new Warden acknowledged the orders and hung the phone up.

General Gonzalez had a list in his hand, and old Lieutenant Perez, arrest these people and bring them to the prison alive, no killing; I want them all alive, Lieutenant, all of them. Lieutenant Perez took the list, saluted, and yelled for two men to follow him. LT Perez grabbed a few more outside, and they loaded up on the trucks and left to find and arrest the people on the General's list. Lieutenant Perez did not want to disappoint the General, especially with what he saw and heard. He knew the General could do anything he wanted and shoot anyone who disappointed him or failed him.

Chapter 26

No matter how long it takes.

General Gonzalez and Captain Hernandez headed for the prison and arrived with five vehicles of men in uniform when another truck drove up with five prisoners in the back of the truck. General Gonzalez stepped out of his vehicle and approached the new prison Warden standing in front of the prison waiting for the General. He saluted General Gonzalez, who saluted back and said, "Take me to your interview room." The Warden said, "Yes sir," as the General followed the Warden to the interview room.

Once they arrived in the interview room, there were three chairs in the room, with two on one side and one on the other. General Gonzalez and Captain Hernandez, besides the Warden, were the only ones in the room. General Gonzalez looked at the young new Warden and said firmly, "Do you have a problem with me trying to find out who initiated the escape and who is responsible?" Warden Lopez responded, "Whatever it takes, sir, your son was my best friend, and I want justice." General Gonzalez whispered, "Are you sure?" Warden Lopez said in a firm tone of voice, "Yes, sir." General Gonzalez smiled and said, "Good," and he reached out, and they shook hands. Captain Hernandez said, "Warden bring in the first prisoner." Warden Lopez responded, "Yes, sir," and stepped out of the room to get the first prisoner.

Two guards dragged in the first prisoner, and one of the guards stated out loud the prisoner's name was Fredrick, 46 years old, and he was found hiding with his family. He is known as Prisoner 110 and was locked up for attempting to flee with his family to America. In Cuban terms, the magic word is treason. Fredrick sat down in the chair, scared for his life. General Gonzalez said, "Prisoner 110, my

206

name is General Gonzalez, and I will only ask you once who were the men who attempted to rescue you and the others?" Prisoner 110 just shrugged his shoulders and said, "I do not know, General, but I would tell you if I knew." General Gonzalez said firmly, "What do you know, Prisoner 110?" Prisoner 110, who was shaking, said, "I do not know," when General Gonzalez stood up and shot him in the head. Prisoner 110 flew backward onto the floor, dead.

The guards brought in prisoner 132 with his wife and two sons, and General Gonzalez said loudly, "Now, prisoner 132, I will shoot you and your whole family if you do not tell me who freed you." Prisoner 132, in a scared tone of voice, answered, "I do not know." General Gonzalez pointed the gun at the prisoner's wife and shot her in the head. The two young boys started to cry when he said, "What information will save your family," raising his gun and pointing it at prisoner 132 sons. Prisoner 132 yelled out, "It was Americans. That's all I know." He looked at his wife dead on the floor and mentioned, "They spoke Spanish, then I heard one talk in English, and back to Spanish." General Gonzalez lowered his gun, smiled, and said, "See how easy that was. You are free to go home and bury your wife." The two young boys were crying as two soldiers came in and carried former prisoner 132 wives out of the room.

General Gonzalez turned to the Warden and said firmly, "I need all records on the two prisoners that were not found." The Warden responded, "Yes sir," and left to gather them up. General Gonzalez turned to Captain Hernandez and ordered him to shoot the remaining prisoners and have their families watch so they could spread the word not to side with our enemies and release the family members. The General paused, looked around, and smiled before saying, "I want them to tell everyone what not to do." The Captain saluted and said, "Yes, sir," and General Gonzalez went back to his headquarters and began laying down a game plan. He would get his revenge, but he just needed to know who they were. They would pay the price, and he would use every resource to find the answers he sought.

Due to the news reported to him of an underwater craft being chased by the Cuban military on the water north of Cuba and the near run-in with the United States military, General Gonzalez confirmed what he believed inside. The Americans were to blame. He knew more information would come in about the incident, with the American military providing a roadblock for the underwater craft that got away. One day he would locate those men responsible for his son's death and deal with them his way. He decided to wait to receive all the information from all the events which happened today before he went and reported to Castro about the military shooting match between the Americans and us. He knew he could not do anything to bring the Americans to their knees, but there were other ways of seeking revenge for the death of his son.

Later in the day, the Warden brought all the files he had on the two missing men to the General's office. Rafael read them several times, and he realized one of them had a nephew who was a Florida United States Senator, and he knew right there the Americans did it, and Someone in that Special Forces unit killed his son. He knew a mission like that could only be approved by the President.

General Gonzalez knew this would take years to piece together, so he began to work on a plan on how to hurt the Americans and some of their key allies even after his time serving his country of Cuba. Rafael was well aware he would have to increase his connections worldwide with all revolutionaries and anti-western groups. General Gonzalez would gather all loyal people to help him and make it into an organization. This goal could take years, but he had the patience and time.

As years went by, he gathered intel and put the puzzle and things together. He activated five spies that remained from Castro's special intelligence groups, and they were ordered to lay low and support any anti-Castro groups in America and get jobs and work around the Special Warfare bases. These spies will be his ears and eyes. General Gonzalez understood the Cuban American community was one of the most loyal American groups in America. He was aware of what could happen if they were discovered spying on the local communities. They would be killed and dumped into the Caribbean. General Gonzalez also reached out to groups in the Middle East and groups in Venezuela and other South American countries.

As more years went by, General Gonzalez traveled to Lebanon, South America, and Central America putting in pieces of his plan. He even traveled to Iran and became friendly with the leadership of that country. Whatever these groups and countries needed, he helped them out in all ways possible. He had Castro's full blessing even with the fall of the Soviet Union. Cuba needed friends in all areas possible. After many years of serving Fidel Castro, General Gonzalez was appointed to control the Cuban military fully. This appointment allowed him to have the military focus in all areas he needed, which allowed him full excess to all areas of the military and the intelligence community and the Government.

Twenty years went by, and General Gonzalez was retired by Raul Castro. However, Raul Castro allowed him to continue to use all resources needed to help him in his project to cause a mess with their enemies. General Gonzalez became vital with political pull throughout Cuba in the Government and Military. He was appointed to the Cuban embassy in New York City to help collect intelligence, and one day, while working in the embassy, he received a phone call from Fayetteville, NC. The agent on the other side said Green Berets were the ones who went into Cuba. The source was a retired soldier who was drunk in a bar talking about SF going in years ago and coming out with two Cubans. The Cuban spy said that was all and hung up.

Gonzalez sat down at his desk and let it sink in. He smiled because he knew it was the Americans, either American Special Forces or their Navy Seals. The information from the prisoner telling him years ago it was the Americans just supporting what he already knew. But he needed further proof with all the groundwork he has laid out over the years. This was just a piece of the pie, and he had a few more things to do before he pulled the trigger.

The next day he flew to Venezuela via Mexico City, and while there, he met with some contractors to build a fortress in the jungle in the northern part of Venezuela jungle. He paid what was required of his Venezuelan Army contact. Then he flew to Germany and purchased two buildings with false identification. Once he was done, he flew to France and did the same thing when he completed his agenda in Europe. He flew to Beirut, Lebanon. Rafael spent two weeks there meeting with his contacts and spreading money around to where it needed to go, and he purchased a building on the dock, which was always secured because of the security entry point.

Rafael spent some time on the beach and laid out the remaining parts of his plan in his head, and then after a couple of days, he took a flight to Tehran, Iran, to gather some items he would need and transport them to Beirut when he was ready. Once he was done in Iran, Rafael flew back to Cuba to finish putting things together in his homeland. After landing in Havana, Cuba, he drove to his office and gathered his men to see what they had done while he was away. He was briefed by his men, and he was satisfied with all the information he received, and he had his driver take him home. He looked out his vehicle's windows looking at his homeland and how beautiful it was, and he realized how time had flown by and how his country had changed for good and bad.

When he arrived home, his wife walked up to him and said any new information as she had been asking that for years. She wanted justice and those lives who were responsible for her son's death. Rafael said, "It was the Americans for sure and their Special Forces" as he looked into her eyes. He paused and then added, "His people are working on which soldiers entered our country and killed our son." She asked, "How soon?" Rafael answered her by saying, "We are almost ready to initiate our revenge," as he kissed her and whispered in her left ear, "Two to four years and we will get our revenge." She asked. "Why that long?" He kissed her forehead and said, "To get all the pieces in place to fit the time frame." She kissed him passionately and turned around, and walked back up the stairs as her dress slid off her body onto the stairs. Her head turned to him, and he followed her to their bedroom.

The years went by, and his plan was finally initiated thanks to loose-lip Americans filling in big pieces. They could piece who led the unit and where he was now. His last name was Allen, and he was a three-star General at Fort Bragg, North Carolina. One thing Americans cannot do is keep their mouths shut. As time goes by, people start talking and bragging about either themselves or someone else they know or were part of. No secrets in America ever remain secrets.

Chapter 27

Back to the Farm and another Tour

Elizabeth and James, after they returned to Fayetteville, N.C., officially moved into her grandparents' house with them and her dad. Her Grandparents insisted on it, so she was around family when James was gone. Lieutenant General Allen had no problem with it because he wanted to make sure his daughter was around people who loved and cared for her. He understood the stress she would have by herself when her husband was gone.

Things were going well for the Thomas family; they made all the examinations and follow-ups with her pregnancy. She was at the right weight, and the baby was growing inside without complications. After one visit, they found out the baby would be a boy. James was thrilled, and so was Elizabeth.

James had his usual training periods in the field with his company here and there to stay combat-ready. He could not take his private phone to the field, but he made sure Elizabeth and her Grandparents could reach him through the company headquarters if needed. When he was off work, he helped around the farm and learned a lot about farming from Elizabeth's grandpa. James even planted his own section of the garden and was proud of how his garden looked and how quickly his crops were growing. James also created a water source from the stream that went by the farm, using his engineering schooling to build it. The system worked without any problems, and Elizabeth was impressed. James said, "When it is all grown, we will have nice healthy food for the baby."

As time passed, James started to worry about getting an overseas assignment and being away from Elizabeth. Overseas assignments usually mean more TDYs making it tough on Elizabeth with a child.

One day Lieutenant General Allen and James went for a walk down the dirt road and had a long talk about work, family, and, most importantly, Elizabeth and the baby. Then Lieutenant General Allen said, "James, when it's you and me out here, please call me by my name, ok?" James smiled and said, "He would, but it will be hard due to who you are," Joseph smiled and laughed and said, "Fair enough."

Joseph turned to James and began discussing James' career. Joseph said, "I want to send you to Hawaii for a tour instead of Europe." James looked at him but said nothing. Joseph asked, "Do you have any issues with that, James?" He looked at James, who did not say anything. He continued and said, "I have no doubt you have been waiting on rotation orders coming out of the blue and with too much nonsense going on in Europe, and I do not want Elizabeth near any of that." He stopped, looked face to face with James, and said firmly, "Right or wrong, my daughter comes first in my life, and I also know yours." James agreed and said, "I absolutely understand, sir." James was curious about what his Father-in-law was saying, and then the words came out when he said, "I have blocked your transfer to Europe, and Your promotion to Major has been approved in 90 days, and you will move up to a Battalion XO position in Hawaii with the 25th Infantry Division." James was surprised and speechless.

Joseph continued talking and mentioned you need to look at your career and, most important, Elizabeth and the baby in your future jobs. James stopped and looked down, and he looked up and smiled and discussed how Joseph was right about how he loved doing what he does, but the minute Elizabeth and he got married, and with a kid coming, I understood things changed, and I agree with you, and I appreciate it more than you will ever know.

James stopped walking, looked straight at Joseph, and said, "You know I will never ask you or have Elizabeth ask you for anything, sir." Joseph smiled and said, "Sounds good, son. I understand."

James asked, "What do I tell Elizabeth about going to Hawaii?" Joseph smiled and responded by saying, "Tell her whatever you want to tell her, but you must be the one, not me." They shook hands and headed back to the farm. Joseph had no doubt his daughter made the right choice in marrying this man.

James, later in the evening, told Elizabeth the news that they were not going to Europe but were going to Hawaii. She said, "Beaches," and smiled, and she gave James a big hug, and he whispered in her ear, "When they go there, he is getting promoted to Major and will be a Battalion XO in the 25th Infantry Division." She said, "Why not SF?" He grinned and said, "He must look at his career and what is good for their family." James paused and looked into her eyes, and explained, "He can always go back down the road, but this will give us family time together with our child."

They hugged and went for a walk down the dirt road, talking about spending time in Hawaii and walking on the beach with the baby and maybe having another one after that. James smiled and said, "Wow, ok," and she said, "No more than three, with a laugh." He started laughing and said, "That's fine," as they kept on walking. They walked by the garden he had been working on, and he said, "Damn, we won't get to eat any of this." She smiled and responded by saying, "My grandparents and my dad will eat what it produces." He said, "Well, it won't go to waste, for that's sure." They held hands and went and sat on the deck swing. It was a nice day with only one cloud in the sky. It was a dark one, but it was only one. James laid out on the big swing. He had replaced the smaller one so he could lay it out. She laid down on him and moved around till she was comfortable due to the baby. They both fell asleep.

About two hours later, James, with his eyes closed, felt like someone was watching him, and he opened his eyes, and it was Joseph with a grin on his face. Joseph said, "Well, talking about goofing off." Elizabeth opened her eyes, smiled and said, "Hi, Dad." Her dad smiled and said, "Hey, honey." Both James and

Elizabeth got up and went inside with her dad. Joseph went up to change, and James grabbed a book and sat down in the reading room and read for a while.

Elizabeth knew when James sat down to read, he wanted to be left alone, and she knew this was his time to think and read, so she called it his quiet time. She started to go upstairs to see her dad when he came down the stairs. She hugged him and said, "Hawaii," smiling, and she said, "Thanks, Dad," and he laughed. She said, "Dad, it's not hard to figure out who did what." He smiled and added, "That's what I get for having a smart daughter." She responded by saying, "Thanks for promoting James' dad." Her dad said, "I didn't promote him. He earned it all by himself by his actions, and nobody can say otherwise," and he asked, "Where is James?" she told him, "He is in the study room reading a book that's what he does when he wants to be alone to think and have some time to himself." Joseph replied, "I definitely understand. Let you and me have a father-daughter walk and talk" as they went for a walk."

As time went by, she started to show her pregnancy, and everyone wanted to feel her stomach to feel the baby. They were all happy it was going to be a boy, and they agreed that, hopefully, the next one would be a girl. Elizabeth took classes online to try and finish her Master's Degree while James was doing his Army thing.

James was assigned to work with the Battalion XO part-time to learn his job. When he made it to Hawaii, he would understand the position and what the job curtailed. His days were long, and he was still responsible for his company. Lieutenant Deaton was holding down the fort and would be taking over the company as a newly promoted Captain.

James gave Lieutenant Deaton the best evaluation you can give someone because he was a damn good soldier, Officer, and friend. James also made sure all his men in his company were going to get promoted when they met their time frame. He was lucky to have those men in his command.

As Elizabeth got closer to her delivery, they both realized she could not make the long flight to Oahu, Hawaii. So, he put in an extension for sixty days till after childbirth to leave, and it was approved. Both Elizabeth and James didn't say anything, but they knew who had the final say. James was assigned temporarily as the acting Battalion XO since the regular Battalion XO was promoted to (LTC) Lieutenant Colonel and sent to Europe. He would not get his Major until he arrived in Hawaii.

James got to run around with the Battalion Commander, monitoring exercises and giving his recommendations due to his experience and knowledge. James also was learning he had to sit at a desk doing paperwork which he was not thrilled to do, but he understood it came with the job. He also still did his required Airborne jump to keep the jump pay he gets every month. James kept an eye on his old company and would drop in here and there and help the early promoted Captain Deaton when needed. James was happy that Captain Deaton was doing an excellent job with the company.

James enjoyed getting off work, being home for dinner, and spending time on the farm. He enjoyed farming and was getting to like working with the farm animals on the farm. James also got to spend extra time with his dad and new fiancé. Once a week, they would all meet at the farm and have a barbecue when James was not in the field. James was happy that both sides of the family enjoyed each other's company.

James' dad and Elizabeth's grandpa would go and look at the gardens and the crops that had been growing. Elizabeth's grandpa promised David he could have as much as he wanted from the garden, and David always thanked Joseph. David and Joseph were becoming good friends, and they would spend time on the porch talking about life and their children and the future baby that was coming.

Chapter 28

Vengeance and the Trigger

They approached the house silently, and two men popped the front door open and easily entered the house. The security system and electrical system were disconnected from the street without anyone knowing. Two others entered through the back door with no problem. The house was pitch black, but the moon gave enough light for them to walk through the house with no issue. Once the first floor was cleared and secured, Gonzalez entered the house with three more men through the front door. Six men on the outside had the perimeter around the house surrounded so no one could get out. Seven men went up the stairs quickly and quietly to the second floor with no issues.

The men split up and entered the bedrooms. The sleeping elderly couple woke up, and Joseph grabbed his gun while trying to get out of bed, but he was shot with silencers and died immediately. Mary started to yell for help but was killed by a shot to her head. The other team cleared the General's room, but it was empty. The third room was where Elizabeth was sleeping when she heard the noises and woke up. She knew something was wrong, and she grabbed her gun when they entered. She was already out of bed and had her Glock, model 19, from her dresser drawer. This was the one gun her dad taught her to use with 100% confidence. She pointed the Glock at the two men entering the room and squeezed the trigger five times, dropping both men.

A third man entered, and she shot him three times, aiming center mass as he fell back words and in his last words was a woman. Gonzalez, who had a tranquilizer gun, grabbed the least important man and pushed him in front of him as they entered the door.

Elizabeth shot the man in front twice, killing him, and Gonzalez shot Elizabeth three times with the tranquilizer gun. Watching her blackout, she looked Gonzalez in his eyes, seeing the hate in his eyes. Originally, he was going to have the General's daughter killed and take the General hostage. However, since the General was not there, she was the next best thing, and being the General's' daughter, it was the next best thing.

Elizabeth was picked up by one of Gonzalez's men, and he threw her over his shoulders, and they exited her room, headed down the stairs, and ran out of the house. They ran down the dirt driveway to their cars when Gonzalez told his men to leave all the bodies.

They did not know there were small cameras hidden throughout the house and outside that were hooked up to their own power souse. The cameras were about two inches in size. They were upset that General Allen was not there. This puzzled Gonzalez because all the intelligence they had gathered was perfect except for the missing General. They were unaware he went to a field exercise at the last minute at the Base. They taped Elizabeth's mouth, gave her a shot that would keep her unconscious for at least 12 hours, and placed the grey vehicle's trunk in it.

They took both cars and headed south to Highway 95, and once they got on Highway 95, they headed south. They did not convoy so it would not look suspicious to any Highway Patrol or any other Law Enforcement. The main vehicle stayed about a quarter-mile ahead but in view of the trailing vehicle. They also drove a tad over the speed limit, knowing people who drive the speed limit on a highway draw a little extra attention to themselves.

They made it to South Carolina with no problems, and they got off Highway 95, jumped on the 501, and headed to Conway, South Carolina. The Airport was about three (3) miles west of Conway. It was used by airlines to usually bring in tourists to Myrtle and North Myrtle beach resort towns in South Carolina.

Once they got there, they went to the Conway-Horry County Airport, where a private plane was waiting for them. It was now 4 am when they pulled up to the plain, and they took Elizabeth out of the trunk quickly and loaded her up on the plane. After the plane took off, they headed to Cuba. The plane was loaded with extra gas tanks and registered as a Dominican Republic private Plane with fake papers sponsored by Cuba through Venezuela's and Lebanon's allies.

Why he was missed.

Lieutenant General Allen received a telephone call from Fort Bragg, and he left the farm in the middle of the night and flew back to Washington. He was in a meeting on why Green Beret training standards have been being lowered over the last few years and the risk it does. He was upset because some of the soldiers who normally would not have made it were getting through due to political reasons. The Air Force started a few years ago by removing pull-ups and certain exercises from certain special types of training and then lying about it by saying it was outdated and unnecessary. This could affect the U.S. Military for years when poorer, physically fit soldiers hinder operations.

The next day during a meeting, Lieutenant General Allen received a phone call from his command office, and he was told his mom and dad were murdered, and his daughter was missing. He was also notified there were four dead Lebanese in the house. They all had what was to be a Hezbollah tattoo on their bodies, and the four bodies were in the room where they believed his daughter slept. The Police searched all over the farm, and they could not find her, and they believed his daughter was taken.

Lieutenant General Allen was also told there was a Glock Model 19 on the floor of his daughter's bedroom, and it is believed his daughter was the one who killed the four men. The General was told his dad didn't get shot off, and it is believed he was killed when he was getting out of bed. His dad had a 45 in his hand, but it looked like he did not have enough time to get a shot off, and then his mom was shot dead, also. He was told the FBI had sealed off the house and property from everyone.

Lieutenant General Allen sat down, got quiet for a moment and gathered his composure, and said, "He will be there in a few hours." He hung up the phone and looked around at the men in the room. Lieutenant General Allen looked pale, and he couldn't say anything. His aid jumped up and said, "General, are you ok?" The rest of the men jumped up and stepped over to his chair. He put his hand to his head, trying to think. He gathered himself and told them his parents were murdered by terrorists, and his daughter was missing.

Lieutenant General Allen realized he forgot to tell the Police there were hidden cameras around the outside and inside the house. He told his aid to call the FBI back and tell them to go to the basement and look in the upper closet. There is a DVR system recording everything. His aid immediately followed his orders. Lieutenant General Allen suspected someone, and he had no doubt who it could be.

He exited the building with bodyguards and headed to his car, which was fully inspected to make sure there were no explosives in the vehicle. He had a driver, and an armed military escort took him to Fort Meade Airport for an emergency flight back to Fort Bragg. While boarding the plane he turned to his aid and said call Captain Thomas at Fort Bragg and tell him to be in my office in three hours. It's an emergency. They both took their seats on the jet, and Major Johnson immediately called Captain Thomas and told him to bring his teams back and meet the General in his office in three hours.

Captain Thomas was at Fort Pope getting ready to fly to Fort Drum for a field exercise for a couple of weeks. He pulled his teams off the flight when he received the call to cancel the exercise and report to Lieutenant Generals Allen's office in three hours. Captain

Thomas notified everyone the exercise was scrubbed, and they were puzzled and a little irritated about getting the plug pulled on their trip, and they wanted to know what was going on. Captain Thomas was asked what was up, and he repeated what he was told and said just get all the gear and equipment unloaded.

 Once the Humvees arrived, they threw their gear and weapons in their vehicles and headed back to their company HQ. On the way over, they talked about all the possibilities of why they would be pulled off a flight and be returning to the Battalion Headquarters for a meeting with the higher-ups. Captain Thomas was wondering what the hell was going on. He called Elizabeth to tell her he was not going to Fort Drum, but she never answered, figuring she was asleep. They do not pull SF soldiers loading onto a plane for a training exercise unless something big is or will be happening. That is for sure, and he was hoping to find out soon why the big change.

Chapter 29

Target

Once Captain Thomas and his teams arrived back at the battalion headquarters, he told his company driver to take him to General Allen's Headquarters. Before leaving, he told his teams to crash in the day rooms but stay ready and not leave the company area as he was headed to the General's Headquarters. Lieutenant General Allen arrived two hours earlier at his office after going to the farm and showing the FBI the cameras and where the DVR was. The FBI was still gathering evidence when he arrived. The lead agent was shocked at how much evidence there was, and he told Lieutenant General Allen it was like they did not care about evidence being found.

Joseph's parents had already been removed by the FBI and taken for the autopsy. He had his driver and escort take him to his headquarters on base. Joseph was extremely angry about the murders of his parents and personally was going to seek vengeance on the people who did this. However, he was thankful his daughter was not killed during the raid on the farm. He swore he would do whatever it took to get his daughter back. Dam his career. When he arrived at his headquarters, he went straight to his office with his bodyguards staying outside his office. Four stood at the building entrance, four in his outer office, including his driver. All were carrying automatic weapons, including sidearms. More were arriving and helping secure the outside of the building, including roving Military Police patrolling the area.

When Captain Thomas arrived, he had a puzzled look on his face when he saw the soldiers fully armed at the building entrance. The soldiers saluted, and he returned their salute. They had him show his military ID and asked him who he was coming to see. Captain Thomas said, Lieutenant General Allen. One of the soldiers called by radio to announce Captain Thomas had arrived. Lieutenant General Allen heard and told the Lieutenant who oversaw escorting people to have him sent up.

Captain Thomas walked up the stairs and entered the building. He walked straight to the General's office and saw two more soldiers armed outside the door. They saluted him, and he saluted back, and they opened the door. He walked in and saw four more soldiers armed with one Lieutenant. They all saluted, and he returned their salute. He asked, "Where is the General." They pointed, and he stepped to the General's door.

James knocked on the door and heard the General say come in. James walked in and saluted, and he responded by saying, "Captain Thomas reports, sir." Lieutenant General Allen stood up, saluted back, stepped around the desk, stepped towards Captain Thomas and, in a low voice, said, "James, please sit down." James sat down and said what's going on? Elizabeth's dad looked like he had been crying. But James did not say anything then. He got a cold chill up his spine.

Once Joseph took a deep breath and gathered his composure said in a low tone, "James, my parents have been shot and killed." James was shocked and said, "I am so sorry what happened. Why and what happened?" Then Joseph said, "Son, they took Elizabeth." James started to shake and asked, "What happened, and who did this?" He closed his hands into clenched fists, shaking in anger and slowly asked again, "Who did this?" Joseph could see the anger on James' face. James looked up and looked at his father-in-law and said, "What are we going to do about this?" Joseph asked, "What do you want to do, son?" James responded in a straight, firm voice, looking at his father-in-law face to face, "We hunt them down, and we kill them all."

Joseph stood up, and then James stood up, and they shook hands, and James' father-in-law hugged him like a father does a son, and he stepped back and said, "I will call Washington to see how far we can go on this." James looked at his Father-in-law and said, "No rules, or I resign, and I go after them to save her and kill whoever is responsible myself." Joseph agreed but added, "We could have others who will allow us to push the envelope," and then stopped and looked at James and said, "I never had a son, but if I did, I would have wanted you to be him." He leaned on a chair, looked down, and said, "I know you love her and would do anything to save my daughter." Joseph told James to be here tomorrow at 6 am so we can get started. They both shook hands again, and James left the office.

Lieutenant General Allen looked at his son-in-law before he left and said, "Son, how far are you willing to go?" In a firm tone, James turned his head slowly, looked at Joseph, and said, "Whatever it takes to get her back." Joseph then told James, "Use people you trust with your life, be selective, and people who can shoot a fly-in midflight without blinking." James responded by saying, "Yes, Sir."

James told his driver to take me back to the company AO as quickly as possible, and after arriving, he walked in, got all the teams together, and told everyone what had happened. He then asked for volunteers when his favorite Sargent looked at everyone and said, "We are all in, right?" They all answered, "All in." Captain Allen explained all their cell phones needed to be handed over because their families needed to believe they were training at Fort Drum. He then told everyone to crash in the rooms not being used.

James went and laid down on his couch in his office with the light off and tried to sleep, but he was unable with his mind racing knowing his pregnant wife was kidnapped and he did not know if she was alive or dead. James swore he would kill whoever was responsible, no matter who it was and where they were. He just looked at the ceiling, and around 4:00 A.M., he finally dozed off for an hour of sleep.

At 5:00 A.M. James got up and took a shower in the company barracks, and at 5:30 A.M., He had everyone form up for his briefing. James notified Captain Deaton to prepare everyone for heavy combat and carry whatever they wanted. lieutenant West asked, "American weapons or Russian?" James said, "He prefers all Americans. I want them to know who was there and kicked their ass." Captain Thomas told Captain Deaton, "In five minutes, you and I are going to the General's Office."

Five minutes later, they drove away from the Company Headquarters in their Joint Light Tactical Vehicle (M1280). Once they arrived at General Allen's office, some men in Suits were around the building beside SF soldiers. They stepped out of their vehicle when two men in civilian clothes asked for IDs, and they showed them. Once both men were verified on the visiting list Captain Thomas and Captain Deaton walked up the stairs and entered the building.

After they entered the building, they observed more people walking around in armed military uniforms and men in suits. They signed in and headed to the General Command Center. The two men guarding the door typed in the code, and the door was opened. They saw a room full of military soldiers and civilians when they entered. They observed General Allen at the head of the table talking to a two-star General on his left and a Navy Admiral and an Air Force three-star General on his left. Captain Thomas and Captain Deaton stepped over to Lieutenant General Allen and saluted. Lieutenant General Allen stood and saluted back and told them where to sit. Two Colonels got up and let Captain Thomas and Captain Deaton sit where they were sitting. Lieutenant General Allen said loudly, "Let's start this meeting." Everyone stopped talking and prepared to give them the blame and pass on any information they may have.

Everyone in the room identified themselves as they went around the room, and once that was done, Lieutenant General Allen said, "Let's start with the FBI" he turned to the two agents and said, "Go ahead, gentlemen." The Lead FBI agent reviewed what they had discovered and the General's video. We traced the vehicle to a small Airport in South Carolina. The video cameras at the small airport show the suspects jumped into an Embraer Phenom 300 E plane and ended up heading south to the Dominican Republic and then Cuba and finished up at a small airstrip in northern Venezuela. The video we saw did show one man carrying what appeared to be a blonde woman over his right shoulder onto the plane. The plane took off at approximately 04:40 AM. We have notified the French Embassy in Venezuela to see what they can find out for us about the area and the people involved in the Venezuelan government. We all know we closed our embassy a few years ago due to political differences.

The CIA head agent stepped up and explained they believed this operation was controlled and initiated by Gonzalez and his followers. He is a former Cuban Intelligence officer close to the Castro brothers. His group was the one who was hit in Germany by an unknown group. He paused and then looked at Lieutenant General Allen and continued. He mentioned the Satellites show a base of approximately 50 kilometers inside the Venezuela jungle. We can't discuss this with the Venezuelans about it because they would probably warn them about us. It is believed there are approximately 100 to 150 bad guys there. He then hit the control switch, showed the base from different angles, and showed a picture of Gonzalez. He stated Rafael Gonzalez is pure evil. He will kill you, torture you in a blink of an eye, and his connection to Hezbollah has been verified by our agents. This man helps run Heroin throughout the world and splits his earnings with whoever will help him. His organization also does favors for Iran, Cuba, Hezbollah, and, we believe, Venezuela.

The head DIA agent stepped up and repeated the same information as the CIA, except for one big thing. The DIA believes the Gonzalez organization is the one who smuggled out plutonium with permission from the Iranian Revolutionary guard's assistance. The information shows they have used plutonium to make one or multiple dirty bombs. Everyone looked around the room with shock and surprise.

Lieutenant General Allen interrupted and asked, "Who is aware of this" and everyone in the room heard the DIA agent state, "The President, the Secretary of Defense, and the president's Chief Security advisor." The DIA agent mentioned the President does not even want the Vice President or anyone else to know because the more people who know this information, the more chance in Washington it leaks out. He then turned around and looked at everyone, then explained, "The President has deemed this Top Secret, and if it gets out, that person will be Court Martialed and you civilians, you will be sent to the Supermax in Florence, Colorado."

He pointed to the screen, "We believe this building is where the lab is, and the compound is about 150 yards in all four directions. Smack dab in the jungle with two roads." Everyone noticed there was one on the north side and one on the south side. He further added, "There are four towers with one by the main trance on the north road inside the wire, one on the south side with the other two on the east and westside." The photos showed two men in each tower, which is manned 24 hours a day. He continued, "We do not believe the men are Venezuelan more likely like Hezbollah soldiers since they are active in the drug trade in South America and the Middle East."

He changed the picture, showing men in the jungle patrolling in two five-man teams outside the wire 24 hours a day. The next photos showed four two men teams in F/O forward observer teams about 50 yards out of the fence line in the jungle. The next photo shows someone sending up a small drone to fly around the camp during the day. Captain Thomas said, "Sounds like someone knows what they are doing." Lieutenant General Allen then looked at Captain Thomas and said, "Start coming up with a game plan." Captain Thomas responded and said, "Yes, sir." One general said, "Sir, I can have my people do this instead of Captain Thomas and his teams." Lieutenant General Allen smiled and said, "Captain Thomas would you consider the General's help in this area?" Captain Thomas, with a serious look on his face, stood up and said, "I appreciate the help, General, but my men get the first bite of the apple." The Major General stood and said, "Captain, my team will do whatever is needed." Captain Thomas reached over the table and shook hands with the General. Then they sat down.

Once the briefing was done, Lieutenant General Allen said, "Gentlemen, I want a plan of operations within 24 hours, and all branches will be involved in this." He looked around and continued, "How no one is to be told what the other part is until all craft is in the air." Everyone was told to put it together, gentleman and be back here without delay. Everyone stood up and saluted Lieutenant General Allen, the Admiral, and the Air Force General. Lieutenant General Allen said, "Captain Thomas, go ahead and stay so we can talk," he went back to talking with the other brass. After they were done, they shook hands and saluted each other as they left.

Lieutenant General Allen said, "Son come and sit here, please." Captain Thomas stepped over to the chair next to the General. James sat down and said, "What do you want me to do?" Lieutenant General Allen told James, "I want you to get your people ready and be Loaded for hunting season." He added, "Please come up with a good plan to get her out. Remember, they want the Plutonium first, but my priority is Elizabeth first. He then paused and said, "She is my only child, James. Please don't let me down." James leaned in and said, "I would die for her and my child." Lieutenant General Allen said, "Son get everyone ready and sees you in 24 hours."

James could not go to the farm due to it being a crime scene, and he was furious for not being there and sad about the General's parents.

They were good people who did not deserve to die. He wanted his wife back and knew he would do anything to get her back. He went and crashed on the couch in his office and just laid there looking at the ceiling. He finally fell asleep around 3:00 am in the morning.

Chapter 30

Team Up

Captain Thomas sat in his office putting together a plan of operations to strike the base, rescue his wife, and capture the plutonium. He wanted one C-17 to use to take his people to Halo, about five miles out, and work their way in. James looked at the film and found a clearing in the jungle to jump into. The plane can fly 5200 kilometers distance before refueling in the sky. There would be three total birds. Two C-17s will drop in Seal teams seven miles out from the base. Their job is to protect parameter 2 5 kilometers out, to keep any response from the Venezuelan army or other allies to the bad guys from assisting the base personnel.

Captain Thomas put his plan together and called in Captain Deaton, and when he arrived, the door was closed behind him, and he took a seat. Captain Thomas went over the plan step by step. He told Captain Deaton, "I want you to critique it as a general would," as they went over the plan and made slight changes to it as they went through it. Once the plan for his team was completed, they went over which teams would do what, and he mentioned they were assigned the same Air force Staff Sargent Austin who assisted them in Germany to help with the Plutonium. Then he asked how everyone was doing with Captain Deaton, saying, "Everyone is pumped up and just waiting on you to give the briefing." Captain Thomas looked at his friend and said, "Let's get this show on the road."

It was 1:15 AM in the morning, and an AWAC flew twenty miles off the Venezuela coast. The plan to jump into the open part of the jungle was canceled after a foreign patrol was spotted crossing it. The six-man team swam in after being dropped by HALO 5 miles off the coast. They worked their way through the jungle with Captain Thomas in the middle as they walked in a Ranger file. The other teams were dropped south of the base and slowly worked their way closer to the base. Several Navy Seal teams were dropped to protect the perimeters and assist in the attack on the base if needed.

It was extremely hot and humid when it was not raining on and off as they headed south to the base of operations of the terrorist group. This is where they suspected a nuclear bomb or dirty bomb, was being made with the plutonium either purchased or stolen from the Iranian nuclear site where Iran was working on a Nuclear bomb.

Intelligence was discovered there enough was stolen to make a small bomb to be used to destroy everything within a mile of a downtown American city. The threat was made, and now the U.S Government is responding. The other separate SF reams were dispersed and made it in place with the five Navy Seal teams to encircle the base. Captain Thomas's team was overall in command of all ground forces involved. He was doing what he could to keep himself from losing his composure in this extremely dangerous situation. All he wanted to do was get his wife and the plutonium that could be used against millions of innocent people in a major city.

They were about an hour out when a seal team tripped over the scout team from the Terrorist group. A firefight happened, and another Seal team was ordered to assist by General Allen, who was overall in charge of flying just off the coast with a QRF team to assist in case needed and if the mission was successful in responding and evac everyone involved in the mission including the Plutonium and his daughter. His orders to his son-in-law were to do whatever was necessary to get the plutonium and his daughter.

Captain Thomas thought before he got on the chopper. Lieutenant General Allen walked up and whispered to Captain Thomas. "Son, please bring my daughter home." James told his father-in-law, "I will do whatever it takes." They shook hands, and James got on the plane with his team in snorkeling gear and had bags with their combat weapons.

Suddenly, Captain Thomas heard over the radio of the firefight occurring between the Seals and the terrorist group. He knew the success of the mission just dropped. However, he remembered some old history of tactics done in the jungles. He got on the radio and told General Allen to pull everyone out except his team. If they think we retreated and left, they might let their guard down. He continued telling him they would slowly work their way, and they would strike when the moment was right.

Captain Thomas also told Lieutenant General Allen to have those teams ready to redeploy when needed. The General told him, agreed, and said, "You have a green light." Lieutenant General Allen ordered all the other teams to withdraw and go and pick those teams up in their secondary pick-up locations.

Captain Thomas looked at his men, and they all shook their heads, not making any noise confirming to Captain Thomas that they all agreed to carry on. Everyone understood the importance of this mission and the repercussions of what would happen if they failed. Captain Thomas, using hand signals, pointed to his point man to move on as they slowly moved on in a Ranger file and worked their way to the mountain close to the base.

When they reached the base of the mountain, the point man observed three Venezuelan soldiers smoking cigarettes and joking around. Captain Thomas signaled his men, and they used silencers and took them out with ease. While patting them down and looking for any documents, Captain Thomas had two others change into the dead men's clothes. They grabbed their radios, took their weapons in case they were needed, and hid the bodies in a large pile of jungle plants. Once this was done, they headed to the top of the mountain, which stood over the base.

After the long climb, they reached the top of the mountain and looked down at the small group of buildings. There were eight towers, with two men in each tower. There were only two roads, one in the front and the other in the back, matching the photos they looked at back at Fort Bragg. So far, all the intelligence gathered was pretty accurate. There counted a total of seven buildings inside the perimeter. It looked like three were soldiers' barracks, and one looked like a dining building. Two others were small, like maybe they kept weapons and ammunition. However, there was one bigger than the rest and only one entrance into that building compared to the others. Some men in lab coats were going in and showing their IDs as they entered and when personnel exited the building. However, there was one small building with two guards in front with weapons. He looked through his binoculars and observed that it looked like small prison bars on the window, and he observed a hand come out of it. Those two soldiers laughed, reached to the ground, and threw dirt inside the bars. He felt Elizabeth was in there. They did a count of the armed men, and they came to an approximate number of 75. Captain Thomas spoke on his mouthpiece and notified the Operation center of what they had observed.

Captain Thomas sent back a live video to the Operations Center so everyone in the Command Center could see, and he requested an airstrike to take out all the towers and the barracks. However, the remaining ones must not be touched. He also requested to strike any remaining foes.

Captain Thomas stated, "We will work their way down the mountain, and once the strike is completed, they will work their way to both remaining buildings." General Allen immediately agreed and ordered the Admiral to get the choppers in the air five minutes after sending his aircraft to hit those targets. He also ordered more Planes in the air ready to enter Venezuelan air space in case needed. Four F-35 Lightning II were immediately put in the air, with another twenty to be sent up in case needed.

While the choppers were in route, Captain Thomas's team worked their way down the mountain and arrived close enough to strike right after the missiles hit their targets. Once they were spread out and locked and loaded, they waited for the airstrikes.

They kept watch and observed a small road along the fence line connected to the back gate. It was now 11 am, and the guards were looking outward when suddenly, all six towers evaporated in eight explosions. Once the explosion stopped and the remaining soldiers got up, shaking their heads, and walked around in shock. Captain Thomas and his team charged in with two team members dressed up as the rebels went first and began shooting anyone who was standing up or possessed a weapon. He yelled for his team to get to the laboratory and secure the bomb as he approached two enemy soldiers standing in front of the guardhouse. They were shaking their head and dealing with the ringing in their ears.

They only saw one of their uniforms walking up before Captain Thomas raised his head, pointed his weapon, and squeezed the trigger, killing both guards immediately. He approached the front and looked in and saw Elizabeth in ragged clothes, who was now close to delivery. Captain Thomas grabbed the keys from one of the dead guards and opened them up, yelling out to Elizabeth, who was on the ground. She looked up and saw James as he reached down and untied her. They kissed each other, and she said, "I knew you would come." James answered her by saying, "I would run through hell and back for you." He hit his com and notified the Command center he had the General's daughter. The General, who was in a chopper, heard the radio traffic while they were heading to the target pick-up point. Then the General received bad news from the AWACs that approximately 200 Venezuelan soldiers were heading toward what remained of the base. They were about three miles away.

Captain Thomas, while carrying his wife, ran out of the small cell onto the compound and observed a couple of his men come running

235

up and say, "There is an issue with the bomb." The EOD Staff Sargent Austin, who was on loan from the Air Force 21ST Ordnance Company due to his expertise in Nuclear weapons, explained The IPC (Item of Primary Concern) could not be disconnected due to the collapsing circuits to the miniature warhead they made would take too long to defuse and they can't blow it up due to the way it is set up. Staff Sargent Austin further added, "No matter what we do, it will explode and send radiation in all directions for about 4-5 clicks."

Captain Thomas put his wife down and said, "Staff Sargent, what is your name again?" The Staff Sargent responded by saying, "Austin." Captain Thomas asked, "Is this all the missing plutonium?" Austin shook his head and stated, "It's too small, and he believes most of it has been removed and taken someplace else, and the million-dollar question was, where did it go?"

Captain Thomas stated on the Coms to the Command Center EOD believes the bomb here is only half of the missing IPC. The Command Center asked, "If it was possible to move it from the area?" Captain Thomas responded, "No, it's too big to remove, and we need to get the person of interest out of here now." Staff Sargent Austin removed part of the cover over the timer and saw the clock showing that time was running out. As he looked up at Captain Thomas and, with a concerned look on his face, said, "Captain, we have 20 minutes to get the hell out of here and counting." The General, who was in the air with six other choppers, heard that and told them to prepare to extract all troops in the area. Suddenly there were explosions around them, throwing everyone to the ground, and gunfire was coming from the main entrance area.

A scout team from the Venezuelan army had arrived near the front entrance. Captain Thomas told Sargent Jamison to "Get his wife out of the way" and yelled at the Staff Sargent to "Set an explosive to the bomb for 5 minutes and head out with the team." He grabbed his wife as a firefight began between both sides. Captain Thomas and his wife were separated from his men due to more explosions and rounds from both sides being fired. Captain Thomas, on the coms, told his men to get out and head to the secondary evac location as fast as they could before the detonation.

He knew there was no way anyone could make it to the primary evac location as his team headed in the opposite direction through the jungle. James and Elizabeth headed east through the jungle. James knew Elizabeth was in bad shape, and being approximately nine months pregnant, she could not move up the trail fast when he looked and saw Venezuelan troops enter the remains of the base.

James tried to find cover for them due to the radioactive blast getting ready to happen, and he knew he only had a few seconds left before the explosion. James put Elizabeth in a ditch just enough for her to get in, covering her with leaves and brush, and he covered her with his body. As he lay on top of her, the Venezuelan scouts entered the camp right when the explosion happened. This explosion spread the radiation around for approximately four clicks. The wind would scatter it even farther. James felt the blast, and he held Elizabeth tight and close to his body, trying to protect Elizabeth and the son in her womb. The entire base was completely wiped off the map.

Once the dust cleared, James got up, helped Elizabeth, and dusted her off. He then helped her up the remaining few feet to the top of the mountain. Once they were able to get over the mountain, they headed down the other side of the mountain when suddenly Elizabeth fell to the ground and screamed as the extreme pain in her womb began. She said, "It's the baby, and I think it's time. My water just broke." With concern in his eyes, James started looking for a place to deliver the baby. He lifted her and carried her down the mountain, and when Elizabeth said its time, he found a small cave out of the weather to deliver the baby. James finally got his communication device working, and he contacted the command center and notified them of what had happened and where they were.

Lieutenant General jumped on, and he wanted to know how Elizabeth was doing. James responded and said, "She is in bad shape and getting ready to deliver the baby." The General told him the homing device was still working and they had their location, but the problem was it was too heavy with tree cover. The General told Captain Thomas his team had been picked up with two wounded but doing ok. They are stable, and they got out of the blast area.

The General told the Admiral on the radio to get a doctor to help Captain Thomas deliver his daughter's baby. Admiral Coleman got on the ship's radio and requested the ship doctor to the Command Center asap. Elizabeth was helped to lie down by James and made comfortable as possible. He used leaves and the rain jacket he had in his pouch to help make her comfortable. She leaned up, put her hand on James' cheek, and said, "I love you, and it's going to be alright." James looked worn out and felt a little strange from the blast but did not say anything. Elizabeth, with concern on her face, told him, "I have never seen you with a worried look on your face." James looked at her and said, "I am sorry I am just worried about you." She smiled and told him, "It was going to be ok, I promise." He smiled, stepped out of the small cave, looked around to see if they were followed, and went in back in.

Thirty minutes later, Elizabeth held their son, and James relayed to General Allen that he had a grandson. Everyone in the command center who was listening cheered, and the soldiers on the bird with the General shook hands with General Allen, who was smiling.

Elizabeth, while holding the baby, looked at James and asked, "What should we name him?" James, smiling, answered, "I don't know." She said, "How about James JR?" James smiled and answered back, "OK." James leaned down and kissed her and then called General Allen on the coms and said Elizabeth and our son are doing fine.

James looked at his newborn son, and reality kicked in. He had to get Elizabeth and JR out of harm's way as quickly as possible. James jumped up and said, "We need to go now." So, he helped his wife up, and she held on to their baby wrapped in James' jacket. James grabbed his weapon, talked into his mic, and told the General to meet him at the third retraction site.

While they were heading to the extraction location, James felt like someone was following them, and he kept looking around, turned on his heat sensor device, and saw only animals. However, he couldn't get over the feeling he was being followed. His training and experience told him to be alert. He wanted to speed up, but Elizabeth was worn out and couldn't go any faster. James kept telling her it was alright when he would stop to look around. He grabbed and kissed her with a fake smile, saying, "We need a vacation." Elizabeth smiled and responded, "Sounds good, honey. Let's go to a beach." James shook his head yes.

They slowly started to head up the hill when James heard what sounded like a chopper. James hit his mic and said, "Hey, general, who's in route? and where are they?" The General responded and said on the radio, "Captain, we are close to the pickup spot." Captain Thomas responded and said, "We hear you."

Elizabeth looked up and asked, "Is that my dad?" James responded, saying, "Yes, honey, your dad is coming." She weakly smiled and asked, "Can I talk to my dad?" James handed Elizabeth his mic, and she said, "Dad?" In a calm voice, the General said, "I am coming, just hang on," when Elizabeth said, "You are a grandpa, and It's a boy." The General smiled and told her, "I know" he was grinning, and everyone on the chopper smiled and yelled congratulations again. The General responded and said, "I love you, Elizabeth. It won't be long, I promise." She said, "I love you, Dad, please hurry" as she handed the mic back to James, who re-hooked it up to himself, leaned over, kissed Elizabeth, and told her, "We are going to make it" as he looked at his brand-new son.

James stopped one more time and looked around because of that feeling he had in the back of his neck. He felt like they were being followed, but he could not see anything out of place in the jungle. They finally reached the top of the hill to be picked up, so James called on his mic and said they were at the pickup point. The General's chopper headed down to the extraction point and ordered the six other choppers to provide cover.

James held on to Elizabeth as they saw the choppers heading toward them due to her weakness. The General's crew in the chopper were smiling and pointing when they saw the couple kissing. General Allen smiled and told the pilot, "Let's get this bird down now." The pilot lowered the bird to get close to the couple on the top of the hill so they could get in the chopper without any problems.

Then suddenly, a shot was fired from the edge of the jungle. Elizabeth went limp in James' arms, and he felt a sharp pain in his left shoulder as he fell to the ground with Elizabeth and the baby falling on top of him. Everyone on the choppers stopped smiling, and someone yelled out the word sniper. The men leaped into action, looking for enemy forces, and all the Blackhawks immediately began spraying all areas with machine-gun fire and Vulcan rounds coming from the choppers. They sprayed in all possible directions of where the shot possibly came from.

James forced himself up, and he knew he had been shot in the left shoulder, but his concern was for Elizabeth and his son. James lifted his wife, who had gone limp, and he heard the baby crying. James looked at the baby, who had blood all over him but was fine. No wounds on the baby, just him crying. James looked at Elizabeth as she was trying to talk. He wiped the blood from her face as he was checking to see if she was ok when he saw an exit hole in her chest bleeding out. He held the baby with one hand, and with the other, he held Elizabeth up in his arm and yelled out to Elizabeth as she kept trying to talk. She finally was able to put the words together and said, "I love you, James, and take care of our son" As tears flowed from her eyes, She died in his arms.

James was yelling, "Elizabeth, No, don't leave me," and James fell to his knees holding Elizabeth with one hand and the baby in the other, yelling, "NO" as he was looking up at the sky and again, he yelled out "Nooooo" and began crying.

General Allen saw what happened and felt a chill go up his spine when James fell to his knees holding Elizabeth and the baby. He looked down at the chopper floor, and he knew what had just happened, covering his mouth to keep himself from yelling. The chopper went quiet for a few seconds as the chopper landed with the other Blackhawks providing cover, still spraying the jungle with everything they had nonstop with rounds and cannon fire. Medics jumped off and grabbed Elizabeth and the baby. They also helped James onto the chopper.

While being helped on the chopper, James looked towards the area the shot came from, and he thought he saw Gonzalez with a rifle running down a trail with tracer rounds heading in his direction. Gonzalez stopped for a second, turned his head, produced a smile, and ran deep into the jungle, where he disappeared.

Once the chopper took off, James watched the medics attempt to save Elizabeth, but they could not. James grabbed Elizabeth's body and cried while holding her, while Lieutenant General Allen held his Grandson teary-eyed. James was rocking while holding Elizabeth as the chopper flew to the aircraft carrier, with only James crying and repeatedly saying, "No."

Once James stopped rocking after a while, he became angry, looked at his father-in-law, and said in a tone that even scared the General.

"Gonzalez is a dead man no matter where he goes, and wherever he hides, he is a Deadman. I swear I am going after him with or without you."

General Allen tried to hold back his emotions but could no longer. He had tears flowing down his cheek, and he wiped them off and said James, we will get him no matter what. The chopper finally landed on the deck, and several medics came running with stretchers. Elizabeth was put in one, and they attempted to put James in the other, but he refused and walked behind the stretcher carrying his wife. General Allen carried the baby and refused to hand it off until they made it down to the medical department to examine the child. Everyone on the flight deck watched what was happening. When Captain Thomas's men came running up and saw what was happening, they stopped and walked behind their Captain. Nobody said a word.

All his men were shocked to see Elizabeth being carried on the stretcher dead. They could not figure out what had happened and what had gone wrong. The last time they saw her, she was alive but worn out. Then they saw the blood from her chest and understood what had happened.

After their debriefing with the military intelligence, the men gathered in a break room, and all agreed on whatever Captain Thomas and the General wanted to do. They were all in, no matter what the consequences were. Captain Thomas was one of them, and they knew he would seek full revenge on the person and group who were responsible for his wife's death. No matter where he went, they would go with him.

Once they were done with their secret meeting, they went to Captain Thomas, who was talking in the General's room, when they heard a knock on the door. General Allen said to enter, the door opened, and Captain Thomas Men stepped in, and Sargent Ramos saluted and said, "General, Captain, whatever you guys are planning to do is fine with us. Both officers looked at each other, and the Sargent continued talking by saying. "We are all in no matter where it is, what the risk is, and who they must go against." They all stood at attention and saluted, and both the General and Captain stood and saluted back. In a low tone, Captain Thomas said, "Thanks, guys go get some rest."

Chapter 31

Three months later.

Captain Thomas and his team were 5000 feet in a C130, flying above Tyre, Lebanon. It has been three months, and Captain Thomas is fully recovered and ready to seek revenge on the man who killed his wife. James buried his wife and did not have to worry about his son because his dad was taking care of his son while he was away. His dad, with help from his fiancé, helped out.

All U.S Intelligence came up with the same results as well as other Western intelligence that the nuclear blast was not as big as it should have been. The CIA and the DIA believe 50% of the Uranium was missing and believe it is in Beirut. After three months of digging and hunting where Gonzalez was by all Western and Israeli intelligence agencies, he was located at a dock building in the Tyre Port Beirut. His hiding spot was less than two miles from the Islamic University of Lebanon.

The team prepared to HALO Jump in, secure the remaining Plutonium, and be ready to liquidate anyone or thing in their way. The Israeli Navy would help extract the team and return them to Israel. General Allen was in the AWAC flying off the coast with American and Israeli jets flying nearby if any Lebanese planes or Syrians attempted to interfere. This mission was Top Secret, and the order was coming straight from the President of the United States.

The operation was planned and put together in the Whitehouse with only essential personnel involved. The biggest mouths in Washington are the elected officials and their aids. If an elected official did not release it, it would no doubt be their staff who would blab it all over Washington D.C, with the press releasing it to the entire world. Then the mission would have to be scrubbed, and the persons targeted would disappear with the IPC (Item of Primary Concern).

The unit trained using the intel on the building and the docks and how breaching the building was to be second nature. A quick briefing on recent ISR footage revealed a large Hezbollah soldiers' presence in the area. James was told by General Allen, who was promoted to four stars the higher-ups did not want them involved, but the President, who owed a Senator a big favor, overruled the brass. So, we must do this right with a wink. James said, "Absolutely," with a grin on his face when they talked about it back at the Farm.

General Allen was going to be the new Army Chief of Staff, but he needed to tie off all loose ends with this serious international problem. Captain Thomas's men knew this was personnel for Captain Thomas and the General, and both men wanted revenge, and everyone could see it. They were told by the intel officer some Generals did not want Captain Thomas and General Allen involved, but the President overruled that brass because he understood how revenge could keep a man focused on achieving the goals which were important to him. The President and General Allen in the Whitehouse two months ago both agreed to do it right, but Captain Thomas will be allowed to do what he needs to do to remove ALL THREATS.

Once they landed about a hundred yards off the beach, about a mile from their target, they swam in and arrived at the beach at approximately 2:20 am, and when everyone was ready, they moved up to Senegal Road. After waiting for approximately 20 minutes, a Television truck they were waiting for arrived with two Shiite anti-government members. The truck stopped, and the driver got out of the truck and began smoking a cigarette and looking around nervously.

He had a baseball cap on, and after a few minutes, he turned it around backward, which was the sign it was all clear. Captain Thomas walked out and approached them, and code words were exchanged, and they introduced each other, and the rest of James' men jumped in the back of the truck. Hiding behind some of the televisions so they are not discovered in case someone looks in the back of the truck.

Captain Thomas, who spoke Arabic, sat in the front with the two anti-Government Shiites. They revealed Hezbollah was responsible for their families being killed while protesting Hezbollah policies when Hezbollah opened fire on innocent protesters, killing their wives and children. This incident changed their views on Hezbollah or the 'Party of God'. They said they would be aligned with anyone who would help change things for the better and help them get back at Hezbollah and their allies.

The driver identified himself as Ali Abdul and looked at the Captain, and asked, "Why are you here?" Captain Thomas slowly turned his head and, with no expression on his face, responded, "To kill the man that killed my wife." Quietly Ali murmured, "We are both seeking revenge and are willing to do what is needed." Captain Thomas looked out the window and said, "I will make the grass grow." The two Lebanese looked at each other, puzzled.

When they arrived at the dock entrance, the security guards at the entrance checked their IDs, and Captain Thomas acted like he was asleep with his beany covering his hair and most of his face. He acted like he was groggy, and he had his ID in his shirt and pulled it out. The security guard glancing at Thomas, asked a question and Captain Thomas, in Arabic, said, "Can I go back to sleep?" The security guard nodded, asking the others, "I bet he is the boss?" Yes, we must do the work while he sleeps.

The other security guard checked the back and moved a couple of the boxes around, then closed the back. If he had decided to move a few more TV boxes, he probably would have tripped over the team. They were sweating in the back. However, they were ready to shoot with their sidearms with silencers. Captain Thomas had pulled his suppressed Glock 19 out under his jacket and was ready to use it if necessary. Once the truck door closed, the men in the back took a deep breath, and Captain Thomas smiled. The two Lebanese rebels were sweating and nervous, but the security guards waved them through, and they felt relieved.

The truck entered the dock area and moved slowly toward the targeted building, where a few guards armed with AK-47s stood guard. The building was only a few years old and built with Iranian money.

They drove the truck slowly and finally stopped about 15 yards away from the building when Ali got out of the truck and said Assalam-o-Alaikum, which meant "Peace be upon you." Ali told them they would be unloading a bunch of televisions from Japan, and he stepped to them and said with a smile, "I would leave two over there for a trade if anyone is interested." The three guards looked at each other, and one said, "How about three TVs?" Ali smiled and said, "Ok, but it's got to be close to equal trade," when one of them said it sounded fair. One guard went inside the building and came out with a dozen boxes of American cigarettes. With Ali stated, "It's a good deal." They shook hands, and Ali returned to his truck and put the boxes of cigarettes in the truck's cab.

Ali went back and talked to Captain Thomas, who was still in the truck, providing a sitrep. Captain Thomas answered back, "Once the truck is unloaded, call them to the side where the televisions are so they can get them all at once." He got quiet for a moment and added, "It was going to get ugly very soon." The two Lebanese went to the building next door and told the outside security guard monitoring everything they were dropping off the TVs.

The security guard unlocked the large door and opened it up, allowing them to unload. While the televisions were being unloaded, Captain Thomas stepped out of his side of the truck with his Arab gear covering his head and part of his face. The men in the back of the truck prepared to exit when they heard Captain Thomas's signal. The armed guards were focused on the televisions being unloaded, and Ali called the armed guards over so they could get their televisions. When the three men stepped over to where the three boxes of televisions were, Captain Thomas, who worked his way around the back of the truck, stood there with his weapon with a silencer behind his back, waiting for the right moment.

When the three-armed guards finally stepped over to pick up the boxes, Captain Thomas executed all three men with shots to the head. The security guard came out, and Captain Thomas shot him with two shots to the chest as his men exited the truck.

Captain Thomas told Ali to "get his friend and get out of here before all hell breaks loose." Ali and Abdul jumped in the truck and headed out of the dock through the front gate, where the security guard at the dock entrance smiled and waved them through.

It was pitch black, with hardly any moon out that night. The team engineer exited the truck and went to locate the power source to the building. Once he found it, he notified the coms he found it and was ready to cut it. Captain Thomas told him to "stand by." Captain Thomas waited for everyone to get into place before the power was turned off.

The remaining team members stood prepared to enter when ready but far away from the building cameras. The sniper who split up earlier located a high spot to provide cover. Once the sniper reached the top of the crane, he whispered into his mic, "Cloud cover is in place."

Captain Thomas had an idea and told Captain Deaton to get Lieutenant West to prepare to run the truck through the front door. Lieutenant West smiled and said, "Hell, yes." The teams had activated their cameras so the Command Center could see everything and hear everything going on. Captain Thomas called the Command Center and asked, "Do we have a green light" when General Allen came over coms and responded, "You are green." James stated, "20 seconds."

When 20 seconds were counted down, Captain Thomas told Master Sargent Ellison to cut it. Master Sargent Ellison cut the building light, and all the lights went off in the building. However, the dock lights stayed on. Then Captain Thomas notified Lieutenant West to drive the truck show time. The truck did a big circle and drove through the front door at about 45 miles per hour, with the team coming in the right behind the truck as it crashed through the building and kept going about 25 yards into the building and stopped when it crashed into a column. Lieutenant West had jumped out after it crashed through the door and followed his colleagues into the building.

When they entered, there was yelling in Arabic, and some were shooting toward the truck. They thought someone was inside it. Captain Thomas gave the signal to head down the corridor staying out of the fatal funnel. The corridor opened into a large open area when they were fired on by several AK 47s, which were hidden behind some boxes and machines. They did not fire back, and you don't waste rounds on targets you can't see—in most cases, not all, but most.

Captain Thomas yelled out in Arabic, "All we want is the Plutonium and Gonzalez." Then he heard some laughter coming from down the corridor. Gonzalez yelled, "Well, is that Captain Thomas?" James yelled back, "Yes, mother fucker, and payback is going to be a bitch." Gonzalez yelled out, "How's the wife?" Thomas gritted his teeth and yelled back, "I am going to kill you no matter what." Gonzalez laughed and answered back, "How's the baby?" Thomas yelled out, "He is good." Gonzalez responded, "Damn, I thought I had a one-shot three dead, but oh well, it was a tough shot." He thought for a moment and responded to Captain Thomas and said, "We both have lost loved ones, I get my revenge, and you seek yours."

Gonzalez continued talking and said, "Hey, we are both dead men walking." James yelled out, "Some will live longer than others." Gonzalez laughed and yelled out, "The radiation will get us one day, and I win no matter what happens here." Some more shootings happened, and Gonzalez said, "Your General Allen killed my son, and I killed his daughter, your wife." He snickered and added, "By the way, that was a nice trick changing the timer and setting it up to explode sooner than I had it." Captain Thomas asked, "Where was your first target?" Gonzalez stated, "I was planning on smuggling it into your Miami, Florida, and killing all those Cuban traitors and exploding the other half right here in Beirut." He then explained how this would or could start a major war between everyone in the middle east and ruin an American city. James yelled out, "They are not traitors, dumbass. They just want freedom, something your dumb communist do not understand."

James wanted to push Gonzalez to make a mistake and yelled out, "I heard your son beg like a coward before he was shot, and he was crying for his mommy. Is that true?" Gonzalez got irritated and lost his composure, and started shooting in the area where Captain Thomas was. The Hezbollah soldiers did the same thing trying to shoot Captain Thomas. Captain Thomas's men worked their way around and saw the other men at their location. When the shooting stopped, Captain Thomas yelled, "Wow, was it something I said?"

James could see the bomb through the window and realized the wind would spread the radiation for miles killing tens of thousands of Lebanese and going into Syria and even Iran. Gonzalez gathered his composure and said, "Mmmm, maybe I will set this smaller bomb right now, causing a war of wars. He paused and laughed and said, "Captain, I will get my satisfaction, not like a Miami but enough satisfaction."

Gonzalez explained how setting it off here would cause the Iranians and Hezbollah to think it was Israel. True or False, they will always blame the Israelis and all the Lebanese, and all the separate groups will align and put their anger in the direction of Israel. Lebanon with help Iran declare war, and thousands will die on both sides. He then told Captain Thomas, "I win and get Chaos and revenge." Gonzalez smiled and laughed, paused, and finally said, "By the way, Captain, the timer is counting off."

Captain Thomas knew Gonzalez meant everything he was saying. He did not doubt that Gonzalez prepared a demolition explosion with radiation that would cause havoc in Beirut. With Gonzalez working with Hezbollah, they would both get revenge on their enemies, causing chaos and Hezbollah having a united front against the country of Israel.

The explosion and radiation would cause chaos and push the radicals to seek revenge in all directions, not just with Israel. Their hate for Israel and Jews, and Christians could cause a domino effect on the whole entire world. It would also cause an economic catastrophe, driving fuel prices through the roof and destroying Western countries' economies.

While Captain Thomas thought about what needed to be done, Gonzalez yelled, "Well, Captain, what's next?" Captain Thomas called his men on their comms to ensure they were all ready, and he said, "Let's do it." Thomas pulled a pin and threw it down the corridor when he heard someone yell in Arabic, "Oh shit," and a grenade in Arabic with a loud explosion.

Once the explosion occurred, Captain Thomas's team moved forward when they observed three dead Lebanese on the floor. Two more were able to find cover before the explosion and popped up and fired at the Americans. Lieutenant West and the other men immediately took them out. As they kept moving forward, they observed what looked like a huge room with a smaller room inside.

 When James and his team arrived at the steel door, he looked in and observed Gonzalez inside setting a timer explosive to a square steel box container. James looked at his team and told them to get out when his men started to argue, but James cut them off and told them to get to the end of the dock by the bay and call in for a pickup NOW. They looked at each other, with Captain Thomas yelling guys, that's an order, move.

General Allen told them over the comms to get to the pickup point now because the chopper was coming. They looked at Captain Thomas as they headed to the big opening of the building, where they ran the truck through. They exited the building and worked their way toward the pickup site.

Cloud cover notified the team there were two bad guys with weapons hiding 40 yards in front of them when Shots were fired at the team by the two unknowns wearing Hezbollah clothing. The team hit the ground and started to shoot toward the bad guys. Cloud cover said, "I got this," and took both out with two shots killing both men.

The team members got up and ran to the Blackhawk, which was coming down to pick them up. Once inside the bird, they called Cloud cover and told him to "shift gears." Cloud cover repelled from the crane and headed to the chopper. His team and the chopper crew provided cover until they jumped into the chopper.

They called for Captain Thomas, who responded and told them to "Get out of there," but they refused. Captain Thomas called the General, who agreed and told the chopper pilot to get out of there now. The chopper pilot said, "Yes, sir," and took off from the docks.

General Allen knew this was what Captain Thomas wanted for whatever reason.

Captain Thomas blew the door open with a hand grenade, entered the room, and observed Gonzalez get off the floor and turn around and say, "Well, well, well, the one and only Captain Thomas." James stopped and looked at Gonzalez with hate and anger. Gonzalez asked, "By the way, how's the family?" James gritted his teeth and said, "FUCK YOU." Gonzalez shook his head and said, "Oh, so sorry about the wife. I tried to hit the wife and baby, and of course, you, but one-shot three dead is a rarity, but she moved the wrong way right when I squeezed the trigger." Gonzalez then laughed and said, "Guess what, Captain?" James answered with a What now? Gonzalez started laughing and mentioned, "The funny thing is these bombs can't be turned off. So I still win."

Gonzalez gave an evil smile and said, "I win, even if I lose, Captain, I win," and discussed how, since we are both dead men walking, "Radiation is a dam bitch." Gonzalez explained since his plan with the other bomb failed in some ways, but not this time. He told James, "Even if you kill me, which bomb will you attempt to stop, the one with radiation or the regular explosive that will destroy this area anyway." Hezbollah even helped me with both. Gonzalez then said, "Jimmy boy, you're a dead man. Just face it." James gritted his teeth and said, "You first bitch." Gonzalez answered back, laughing, "Wow, such an angry young man, so how about I just kill you and solve all my problems." Captain Thomas yelled out, "Not today, shithead. The only one dying today is you with my hands around your throat."

Gonzalez smiled and asked, "By the way is General Allen listening?" Captain Thomas responded by saying, "he can see you and hear your sorry ass." Gonzalez waved and said, "Hey, General, how was your little girl's funeral?" General Allen, who was watching, said nothing. Gonzalez then added, "As you Americans

253

like to say, payback is a bitch." General Allen was quiet and then said into his mic to James finish it now.

James lunged at Gonzalez, and they fought by exchanging punches, kicks, throwing elbows, and head butts: no knives or guns, just straight hand-to-hand fighting. After a few minutes of fighting, James was knocked to the ground with Gonzalez on top of him, and he thought of his wife and, with both hands, popped Gonzalez's ears, causing extreme pain to Gonzalez, who fell off him as he grabbed his ears.

Both staggered up, and Gonzalez got behind James and tried to choke James when James said, "Fuck you," and struck Gonzalez with an elbow shot to his head, knocking him to the ground. Then James jumped on Gonzalez and began punching him in the face breaking Gonzalez's nose as blood poured out. Gonzalez flipped James off him, and they stood up when James pulled out his knife and told Gonzalez in a strong voice, ITS TIME TO DIE. Gonzalez slowly pulled a small gun from his left boot and said, "Not if I can help it."

While Gonzalez was raising his hand to shoot James with a gun, James charged Gonzalez and stabbed him in the throat. Gonzalez pulled the trigger and hit James in his left side. James fell to the ground, and he looked over and watched Gonzalez, who had a shocked look on his face, fall to his knees, bleeding out all over the floor. Gonzalez dropped the gun and fell backward on the floor.

James lay there for a few minutes in pain and thinking of Elizabeth and his son when he heard a voice in his head that sounded like Elizabeth telling him to get up. He then heard over his mic General Allen yelling, "Captain Thomas can you hear me" several times. Everyone on the AWAC, the Command Center, the Whitehouse and Israel's war room could hear what was said and only see some of the altercations with Gonzalez. They did observe everything else before the fight when Captain Thomas's mic and camera were knocked to the ground. They also heard the gunshot, and the camera showed Gonzalez covered in blood, falling to the floor with a knife in his throat.

James forced himself up and slowly walked up and pulled the knife out and looked at Gonzalez, and wiped his blade on Gonzalez's body. He then stood up and spit on Gonzalez as he stepped over to where his mic was and put it back on, and he grabbed the camera and stated, "Gonzalez is dead and rotting in hell."

Captain Thomas stated over the mic, "We now have three problems to worry about, General." General Allen responded and answered back, "What are they, Captain?" James said, "I have a bullet in my left side, and there are two separate bombs that are set to go off." The General asked, "What type are the bombs." James responded back and said, "One is the Plutonium bomb, and the other is a large explosive made from fertilizer, and both clocks are running at the same time." Everyone listening knew that radiation is more dangerous over a larger area of land, and the wind blowing inland can cause a war. The bigger explosion will wipe out everything around the dock.

Captain Thomas said, "I will remove the radiation bomb, and I need a clear air and sea space because of the bomb." James gave the direction he was going, checked the bomb out, and saw the timer with 35 minutes left and counting down. He checked the other bomb, concluded he could not disarm them both, and said in his mic that they go off in less than 35 minutes. General Allen said, "Get the plutonium bomb out of there."

James dragged the heavy box with the bomb in it towards the entrance in extreme pain and was to drag it out of the building when he saw a small boat on the dock. James forced it onto the boat and jumped into the boat, and since there was no key, he hotwired it, and the boat started up. James confirmed to the Command Center that he would take this out into the Mediterranean Sea.

The AWAC set a message out that worked its way to all the airlines to avoid the area at all costs and all boat operators. With planes in the air and all types of boats, the Airlines turned around and headed back to the original location they started at, except to Beirut. Israel Mossad used a spy to make a phone call to the Lebanese Army Chief of Staff and said an explosive was going off in 33 minutes and to get their EOD to disarm it. The dead bodies were one Hezbollah and one Cuban.

James had 32 minutes left when suddenly, he got weak and nauseous for a moment, and he realized he was sick because of what happened three months earlier and this contraption was leaking radiation also. James had to get it out of there fast and stirred the 2004 Cranchi Endurance in a western direction. The boat could go 36 knots or approximately 53 miles per hour. His goal was to get as far out in the Mediterranean as fast and far as he could and jump overboard before it exploded. While heading west and a couple of miles out, James asked on his radio, "Where was his team at?" Suddenly there was a chopper sound behind him, and someone said, "Hey, boss right behind you," as he turned his head and saw the Israeli Blackhawk providing cover in case needed. The chopper was about 20 feet from the boat on his right side. James' wound was throbbing, and he reached over and grabbed a towel he saw on the floor to cover his gunshot wound. He ripped it up and used it to wrap his wound.

When James got out as far as he could, he tied off the boat steering wheel to continue heading west since time was running out. As he watched the steering wheel keep heading west without help from him, he got lightheaded again and almost blacked out. James then slid out of the boat and into the water, blacked out as he sank. Two of his men jumped out of the chopper, dove down, and pulled him up. The chopper lowered its skids into the water, and all three men were pulled into the chopper as it flew as high as it could and in the opposite direction from the boat.

The men in the Blackhawk watched as they headed east when the small bomb exploded, spreading radiation around the air and water. The wind and water would help dilute the radiation as it went into the atmosphere. Captain Thomas never saw the explosion. He was unconscious and was being treated by the flight medic and his team medic. The Command Center told the pilot to head to Israel asap, and once they arrived in Tel Aviv, Israel. Captain Thomas was taken off the chopper, and his clothes were cut off and placed in bags. James and his men, including the chopper crew, were decontaminated while Captain Thomas lay on a stretcher unconscious at the time. After he was decontaminated, he was taken straight into surgery. The Blackhawk was decontaminated from one end to the other.

James was taken to the Tel Aviv hospital for radiation poisoning and further decontamination while his team and chopper crew came up negative. However, he was shown definite signs of radiation poisoning. Israel's radiation teams treated Captain Thomas and his men over the next week for all injuries and his radiation sickness. After Captain Thomas and his men were released after a week in the hospital, they were taken to the Negev base and debriefed as American intelligence came in.

General Allen arrived and checked in on Captain Thomas and his team. Everyone was debriefed by American and Israeli intelligence, and after the debriefing, General Allen presented Captain Thomas with his Major's leaf to him. The Israeli intelligence officers shook Major Thomas's hand and said, "Thanks, we owe you, Major Thomas. You saved what would have been a god-awful war and the death of tens of thousands on all sides."

The Israeli General then looked at the General and told him, "If you don't take care of him the right way, we will." He then turned to Major Thomas and awarded him the rank of Colonel in the IDF due to his courage and the risk of his life to prevent what would or could have caused a major war. Then he looked at General Allen and said,

"If he ever leaves your military, he is always welcome here." General Allen smiled, took the hint, and said, "He will be taken care of." The IDF General told Major Thomas, "If he ever needs anything, all he needs to do is call." Major Thomas acknowledged him by shaking his head up and down, and everyone except General Allen left the room.

Major Thomas looked at his father-in-law, and with the last three months coming to a head, tears came to his eyes and said, "I am so sorry I failed you, and I failed to save her." The General looked at his son-in-law and hesitated before speaking, and quietly, he said, "You did everything a man could do and more." General Allen looked at his son-in-law and paused before saying, "Most men would have cowered and taken their loss, son, you risked your life for her, and that's all a father can ask from his son-in-law." General Allen stopped for a moment and added, "Elizabeth loved you, and I am proud of you as if you were my own son." Then there was quiet in the room. General Allen continued talking, saying, "It's time to take care of your son and my grandson." They shook hands in agreement.

Major Thomas began asking questions about what happened after he blacked out. He asked whether the other bomb detonated. General Allen responded by saying, "No." He smiled and told how a phone call went out to the Lebanese Army, who sent their EOD in, and they were able to disarm it. Once they disarmed it, the Lebanese Army Chief of Staff received a phone call saying you are welcome from their southern neighbors who removed the more dangerous explosion. Their Chief of Staff told the unknown person that there might be peace between our countries one day. The unknown person said hopefully, then hung up.

General Allen told Major Allen, "You will be here for a while and just relax and enjoy yourself here, and your men will stay here for two weeks of sick leave?"

James knew his parents and the General would take care of the baby. Before General Allen left the room, he pulled out a picture of Elizabeth from his wallet and gave it to James, and then he left the room, which was under guard. Once the door closed, James looked at the picture of Elizabeth and broke down and cried, not for himself but because he failed and could not save the women he loved. James was being protected just in case there was any retaliation from some terrorist sympathizers who might have worked their way into Israel over the last few days. The news out of Beirut was coming out, and the worldwide press was focusing on the United States for preventing the incident.

The medical results came in a few days later, and the Doctors told Major Thomas the results. They were not good. He got quiet and told the Doc thanks for everything he had done. He realized he would not live a long life. However, he would do what he could during that time frame. James would stay in the Army until he couldn't handle the job. Radiation is strange. Some people live for a long time, and some shorter. He knew his field days were over, and he would be nothing but a desk jockey. James always made fun of them and how things came around and smiled for the first time in many months.

One day James looked up and saw a cross on the desk next to him and looked at the photo of Elizabeth in his hand, and he always considered himself to be a Christian, but he never practiced it. He promised Elizabeth when they got married, he would go to church with her, but he went with her here and there, but she did not force him. He remembers her saying one day, the moment would come when you realize the importance of faith, and he made himself a promise he would raise their child the way she wanted, including going to church and learning about God and faith. His work schedule would also allow him to be home at the farm with both sides of the family, helping out raising his son. James' new dads matter, and how they influence their sons in many ways. As he looked at Elizabeth's picture, he promised himself he would be a good father.

Chapter 32

Tradition

Twenty-three years passed, and it was 8 am, and three Blackhawk choppers landed in front of the new Walter Reed Hospital in Washington, DC. A bunch of soldiers (Green Berets) jumped out with the Army Chief of Staff, who walked quickly to the entrance of the building. The one man in civilian clothes was the Secretary of Defense. The Hospital brass was in front waiting for the VIPs as these men walked through the front lobby, and they stepped out of the way as these soldiers walked straight through the hallway to the elevator. The Army Chief of Staff, the Secretary of Defense, and the VA Hospital stepped into the elevator and went to the fifth floor. The other soldiers took the other elevators. Once both parties arrived on the fifth floor, they walked down the hallway and to a single room, room 510. The Hospital colonel told the Chief of staff this was the room.

One of the medical staff opened the door, and the Army Chief of Staff and the Secretary of Defense walked in with several other soldiers and hospital staff. The Secretary of Defense approached a man in his late 40's. He was sitting in a wheelchair and had hair down to his shoulders. He had about two-week growth of a beard. He was extremely pale and underweight for a once-powerful strong man. He was looking out the window, remembering the past, when he realized other people were in the room. The Secretary of Defense Allen approached him, whispered in his left ear, and told him it was time, son. The man turned his head and quietly said, "OK." The SOD snapped his fingers, and a soldier brought a uniform into the room. The SOD told the soldiers and nursed help him get cleaned up and dressed.

After Colonel Thomas was showered and dressed and escorted from the room in his wheelchair, they all stepped into the elevators with Colonel Thomas, and no one said a word. Once the elevator reached the first floor, the door opened, and everyone stepped out, and a soldier was pushing Colonel Thomas in his wheelchair through the crowd.

While being pushed into the front lobby, everyone was watching them. Two veterans sitting in the main lobby looked up to see the crowd coming out of the elevators and returned to their discussions when someone said loudly coming through. They attempted to see who was coming, and when they realized who was in the wheelchair and who else was escorting him, they immediately stood up and saluted with everyone else in the lobby who realized who was coming through.

Nobody in the lobby said anything, and it was as quiet as a church when the former soldiers proudly saluted this sickly-looking man. Once the escort was out of the building, everyone sat down and began talking about how great of a soldier Colonel Allen Thomas was. Colonel Thomas was wheeled to the nearest Blackhawk and was helped by the soldiers into a seat. The wheelchair was folded up, placed in the chopper's back, and headed to Fort Bragg, North Carolina.

The parade field at Fort Bragg was packed, and on the far side, there was a large open area for the choppers' landing. The ceremony was almost completed when it was stopped when A bunch of Green Berets in full uniform jumped out, and everyone was called to attention by the Commandant as the Army Chief of Staff got out with the SOD. Even the civilians stood up. The remaining soldiers getting out of the chopper, helped Colonel Thomas get placed in his wheelchair. Colonel Thomas was extremely weak and was just trying to hang on. His father-in-law leaned down and asked Colonel Thomas if he was ok, and James looked up and said, "I am good with a weak smile."

Colonel Thomas was pushed to where the graduating class of Green Berets was lined up, shoulder to shoulder. Colonel Thomas was wheeled up to a Second Lieutenant with the name tag which said Thomas. His full name was James Austin Thomas JR. The SOD looked at his grandson with a smile, and he was full of pride for his grandson. Colonel Thomas tried to lift himself out of the wheelchair to tab his son, but he slipped and fell back. People in the crowd showed concern for this man in the wheelchair when the soldiers around him started to help him when the SOD yelled in a hard firm tone. "STOP, LET HIM DO IT HIMSELF." The soldiers stopped and stepped back.

Someone in the stands asked, "why do they not help him?" Colonel Thomas looked up at his father-in-law and gave him a look of thanks. His Father-in-law understood James had to do it himself and would not want help. Everyone in the stands was watching, but no one said a word as they watched. Colonel Thomas straining with all his remaining strength, finally got himself up from the wheelchair and using all the strength he had left to keep himself up, he placed his son's Green Beret on Lieutenant Thomas's head.

while looking into his son's blue eyes, he whispered to him and said, "JR, your mom would be extremely proud of you, and I am proud of you, son, and I will be seeing her soon, son" As JR bit his lip to keep himself from losing his composure, he shook his dad's hand and surprised everyone he let go of his father's hand and reached out and hugged his dad tightly as tears flowed from his eyes whispering, "Dad I love you." Colonel Thomas held onto his son and held him and said, "I am so proud of you, son."

When Lieutenant Thomas felt his dad's legs buckle and lose strength, he held him up when the Commandant told the Lieutenant, "That's enough." General Deaton, the Army Chief of Staff, turned his head and looked at the Commandant with a pissed-off expression and whispered, "Shut the hell up, do you understand?" The Commandant, who was shocked, acknowledged what the COS said. Lieutenant Thomas whispered again in his dad's left ear. "Dad, I love you and am proud to be your son." Lieutenant Thomas then helped his dad get in his wheelchair. Some people were crying in the crowd. When Colonel Thomas was back in his wheelchair, Lieutenant Thomas wiped his eyes and stepped back in formation.

General Deaton looked at the commandant and, in a firm tone of voice, stated Lieutenant Thomas will be flying back with me when the commandant looked at the Chief of Staff and stepped up and, in an alone tone, apologized to the General and said I would take care of the Lieutenant's paperwork myself as they shook hands. The SOD stepped up and said to the commandant, "I appreciate it and Thank you." The Commandant realized the rumors he heard were true about Lieutenant Thomas. He knew General Deaton served under Colonel Thomas but just realized the rumors were not rumors but fact that the SOD was Lieutenant Thomas Grand Father, and the General was the Lieutenant's Godfather. The Commandant understood they were some extremely powerful men not to be messed with in any way, and he would make sure all Lieutenants Thomas' paperwork was in order.

Colonel Thomas was wheeled back to the chopper by his son, and before Colonel Thomas was lifted into the chopper by his son, Colonel Thomas looked up to his friend, the Chief of Staff General Deaton and said very quietly, "Thank you." General Deaton whispered to James, saying, "You are my friend, and I will make sure your son will be taken care of." James smiled and said, "You were always a good friend and thank you as they shook hands."

General Deaton could tell his friend hardly had any strength in his once powerful handshake, and General Deaton stood at attention and saluted his friend for the last time. He knew his friend and comrade in arms was short on time. James returned the salute, and everyone loaded into the choppers and flew back to Walter Reed Hospital. General Deaton watched the Blackhawks fly away, knowing he would never see his friend alive. As he teared up, his aid saw the general wipe his eyes and say, "General was he your friend?" General Deaton turned to his aid and said, "He was my best friend who was always there when I needed him, and vice versa, and No better man wore this uniform," General Deaton paused and said, "Let's go and get back to work." His aid said, "Absolutely, sir," and they left the parade grounds.

When the Blackhawks arrived at Walter Reed Hospital, Colonel Thomas was taken back to his room, where he was changed back into his pajamas and helped to his bed. Colonel Thomas had little strength left. The medical staff hooked him up with an IV and injected pain meds and a urine bag.

Colonel Thomas's pulse was getting lower, and his heartbeat wasn't normal and dropping. His Urine in the bag they hooked up was beginning to turn black as his kidneys were shutting down. The SOD ordered the soldiers and non-essential staff to step out. Colonel Thomas was moving around the bed like he was struggling with someone. They call it Terminal Restlessness.

Lieutenant Thomas whispered to his dad, and he again said, "I am proud to be your son, and I hope I can be half the man you are." James opened his eyes, lifted his head, and said, "I am proud of you, son, and his head fell back onto the pillow." Things were getting blurry, and he was losing focus with his eyes.

Colonel Thomas knew who was in the room, but they were becoming blurry when his dad arrived with James' stepmother. His dad had tears in his eyes, leaned in and whispered, "Son, I am here, son" James, with his eyes closed, smiled and squeezed his dad's hand and whispered dad, "I love you, glad you are here, and I am so proud to be your son." James' dad responded and said, "I am proud to have been your dad. I am so proud of you." James' hand slipped out of his dad's hand as his dad stepped back, holding his wife's hand.

James then heard a voice, soft and sweet, and he opened his eyes and saw Elizabeth as real as he remembered her. She reached out her hand and said, "It's going to be ok," and she said, "I love you, James." He smiled and reached his hand out to hers and said, "I love you," some tears streamed down his cheeks, and in a strong, firm voice said, "Elizabeth, I miss you." Colonel Thomas was looking straight ahead at something or someone. Everyone in the room got quiet.

James JR. asked his dad, "Are you alright?" His dad did not hear his son. He was looking at Elizabeth and said, "I am ready, please I want to go with you." She stepped forward and kissed his lips. The SOD grabbed his grandson and said, "Hang on." Lieutenant Thomas stopped and looked at his father, who had a strange look on his face. All everyone can see is Colonel Thomas reaching out to something in front of him and hearing what he is saying. Elizabeth smiled and said to James, "It's time," as he began to lift himself up when he closed his eyes with a smile, and his head and body fell back into his bed. His pulse and heartbeat slowly declined until they flat-lined. His body became relaxed, and he had a grin on his face. Lieutenant Thomas reached and grabbed his father's hand and held it until the warmth left his body. He leaned down, kissed his father on his head, and said, "I love you."

The Chaplin entered the room a few minutes earlier and began his prayers. Everyone in the room looked at Colonel Thomas and noticed the grin on his face. The SOD stepped up to his grandson and looked at each other. The SOD then smiled and said, "Your Dad is with your mom, and that's what he wanted." Young James smiled and said, "I know Grandpa," as he wiped the tears from his eyes.

Lieutenant Thomas knew his dad missed his mom and always felt guilty for her death and how he would have traded his life for hers in a heartbeat. Colonel Thomas never did remarry after Elizabeth died. Other women could have been good stepmoms, but James would never ask these women to be his wife. He never would take the next step. Then when the radiation started affecting him, he no longer dated. Lieutenant Thomas said his dad told him years ago, in Junior High School, that he missed his mom and had no interest in remarrying anyone, and she had his heart and soul. She was his soul mate for eternity. His dad dated many women but would not even think of getting serious again. Colonel Thomas was at peace with the women he loved.

EPILOGUE

Security of Defense Allen was back on the farm during the holiday season, sitting on the porch swing with a jacket on by himself, watching the sun go down. He was thinking about all the fun he had during his life on the farm and how he lost his parents, his wife, and his daughter. All he had in his life was his grandson and work; nothing else mattered to him. It has been four years since his daughter's husband, James, died of leukemia and 27 years since he lost his only child at the hands of Gonzalez.

Joseph was getting old and thinking of resigning from his political position, but the President talked him out of it. The President pulled the usual Your country needs you, and I need you and your experience. The President promised to allow SOD Allen to transfer his Grandson to the Pentagon no matter the political ramifications. Young James would be his aide and go wherever his grandfather went, and he was given more control over the Defense community.

The President and his Secretary of Defense went back many years, and the President, who was in his second term, never forgot what the SOD did for him and his family. The SOD could not do any wrong in the eyes of the President, and he knew he could trust him compared to most people in Washington who would sell their firstborn to get what they want.

While sitting on the swing and looking out at the farm, he observed an older woman of Hispanic origins driving a car with another female passenger, and they pulled up to the house. The elderly lady turned off the car and got out of the car and walked up to the porch, and smiled. Joseph said, "Can I help you" as he stood up. The lady, still smiling, asked, "I am looking for Mr. Joseph Allen?" Joseph smiled and said, "That's me. How could I help you?" Her smile went away as she pulled a gun from her purse and said, "Do you know who I am, Mr. Allen?" He responded "No" with a straight face and realized he was getting ready to face his doom. She said, "Loudly, you killed my son and my husband."

Joseph immediately knew who she was and responded, "I know I did, Mrs. Gonzalez, and I shot your son three times in the chest, and I have never forgotten it." He looked into her eyes, and he could see the hate. He also told her, "By the way, I did not kill your husband, my dead son-in-law. I killed your husband, who was preparing to kill or has killed hundreds of thousands of people."

She yelled at him to "Shut up" and screamed, "They were everything to me, and you destroyed my life and took them away from me." Joseph said, "I am sorry, but it was business, not personnel." She again yelled, "Damn you," as he leaned against the house. She cried and said, "It took me many years to find out what happened to my husband and who was responsible."

Joseph smiled and said, "I have lived a long life, and I have also lost loved ones along the way." She wiped her tears and said, "It all started with you and will end here." Then the other woman in her 40s in the car got out, walked up to the porch, and said in Spanish, "Is this the pig who killed my brother and father?" Mrs. Gonzalez said, "Yes, it is." The daughter said, "Mother give me the gun because I want to kill him." The old woman smiling, handed her daughter the gun and pulled another smaller gun out of her purse as her daughter Samantha said, "It's my turn," as she pointed the gun at Joseph's head and said, "Me Vengare."

Joseph looked directly at her and said, "Loudly, don't miss." Samantha said, "What?" And she said, "I won't miss shooting you, General, this is easy," and as she was getting ready to squeeze the trigger, suddenly there were two shots fired from inside the house, and when Joseph looked down, both women were on the ground with bullet holes center mass in their chest dead.

Joseph looked at his grandson, who pushed the screen door open and looked at his grandpa with the same grin his father had and said, "Grandpa, are you ok?" Joseph smiled and responded by saying, "Now I am," as he pulled his cell phone from his jacket and called the President about the shooting and what had happened. The President asked, "If everyone was ok," and Joseph said, "Yes, except the two dead women." The President told him, "He would call the Attorney General to get the FBI over there asap." Then Joseph hung up and dialed 911 and reported a shooting. They tried to keep him on the phone, but he hung up. He knew the more he said on the tape could be taken the wrong way, and the less said, the better on a recorded line.

When Joseph finished calling 911, James asked, "By the way, Gramps, who the hell was they, and why did they want to kill you so bad, Grandpa?" Joseph slowly and calmly reached down, took the guns out of the dead women's hands, and put them in his coat pocket to turn them over to the F.B.I when they arrived. The video cameras on the outside of the house he had hidden will show what happened.

Joseph smiled, put his arm around his grandson, and said, "James, I think it's time I tell you everything about your parents and me," as they walked inside the house. James smiled and said, "Sounds good, gramps he turned his head slightly, looked down at the bodies, and asked, "What about them, gramps?" Joseph looked at James and said with a smile," I don't believe they are going anywhere." James smiled, agreed, and said, "I doubt it," and then asked, "By the way, Gramps, how did you like those shots? Pretty good, weren't they?" Joseph smiled and replied, "Yep, good shots," as they walked inside the house.

And it Continues

Three weeks later, in Havana, there was a large crowd standing at a large funeral on a hot and muggy day, burying two women. A 22-

year-old Cuban woman with her cousin in his Cuban Uniform standing over two coffins at the Colon cemetery in Havana, Cuba, was mourning the loss of their relatives. The bodies had been sent back from the United States to Cuba with little explanation, except they were involved in a crime and tried to kill an important American. The coffins were sent via the Dominican Republic.

The Cuban government conducted an autopsy and told the family each was shot center mass in the chest, and the person conducting the autopsy believed the two women died instantly. Before the coffins were placed in the ground, the young woman went and put her right hand on her mother's coffin and said in a revengeful tone, "Me vengare."

GLOSSARY

A.F.B	*Air Force Base*
AK-47	*Kalashnikov's Assault Rifle*
AW	*Associate Warden*
AWACS	*Airborne Warning and Control System*
BC	*Battalion Commander*
BS	*Bullshit*
CHAPPY	*CHAPLIN*
CIA	*Central Intelligence Agency*
DIA	*Defense Intelligence Agency*
E&E	*Escape and Evade*
EL AL	*Israel Airlines*
EOD	*Explosive Ordnance Disposal*
EVAC	*Evacuation*
HALO	High altitude, low opening
ID	*Identification*
IDF	*Israel Defense Forces*
KWAJ	*Short for Kwajalein*
LT	*Lieutenant*
LTC	*Lieutenant Colonel*
LTG	*Lieutenant General*
M-4	*5.56x45mm NATO gas-operated weapon*
ME VENGARE	*My Revenge*
MOSSAD	Central Institute for Intelligence and Special Operations
MP	*Military Police*

NATO	*North Atlantic Treaty Organization*
NAZI	*National Socialist German Workers Party*
NVG	*Night Vision Goggles*
OP	*Observation Post*
PT	*Physical Training*
R&R	*Rest and Relation*
SOD	*Secretary of Defense*
SF	*Special Forces*
TAC-P	*Tactical Air Control Party*
XO	*Executive Officer*